Jue 2006

INGRID

AN

IMMIGRANT'S

TALE

BY ERIC J. BROWN

ISBN 0-9684384-1-5

Pioneers-Canada-fiction 1 title

PS8553.R68497153 2000   C813'.54
                          C00-900382-7

PR9199.3B6977153 2000

Printed and Published by
Magnolia Press
Box 499
Entwistle Alberta
T0E 0S0

Special Note: No character in this novel is, in any way, meant to represent any person living or dead. Nor Are the communities of Morning Glory and River Bend meant to represent specific locations or communities in Alberta.

DEDICATION

This novel is dedicated to all those brave pioneers who left familiar and comfortable surroundings to forge a new life in Canada.

These are the people to who we owe so much in building the great nation that Canada has become.

ACKNOWLEDGMENTS

Firstly : I would like to thank Edith Ferrier for her time and effort in proofreading this work. Her helpful suggestions and constructive criticism have contributed greatly to the success of this work.

Secondly: I would like to thank Jim Hagan for freely volunteering his time and energy in editing this work. His skills and helpful advice have both been vital in bringing this work to fruition.

Finally: A special thanks goes out to my wife Isabella, and sons John and Colin for their patience and understanding of my time spent on this work, and their constructive suggestions.

Author's Special Note.

Since most of the characters are Swedish immigrants, normal unaccented conversations between them are assumed to be in Swedish The two Finns, Kangas and Esa, also speak Swedish fluently without accents as Swedish is a second language for most Finnish people. The two Finns, however, speak English with accents which in many ways sound similar to the Swedish accents except for the absence of articles. The author has however, as far as possible, indicate to the reader which language, in any given conversation, is being used to help avoid possible confusion.

Preface.

You would have met Ingrid if you have read *Ginny - A Canadian Story of Love & Friendship.* In it you would have shared the lifelong friendship between these two women and their families. Since that story focussed on the life of Ginny, little is known of Ingrid's life before she met Ginny.

Ingrid - An Immigrant's Tale, is a story of a girl in her youth who is taken from all that is familiar to her when her family chooses to emigrate to Canada in 1910. Ingrid's story is probably reminiscent of that of many brave pioneers who left familiar surroundings for the rugged new land of Canada. In particular it recognizes the Swedish community, as there was a large-scale emigration from Sweden to Canada during this time period.

Since her father is a lumberman by trade, *Ingrid - An Immigrant's Tale,* focusses on another aspect of frontier living that went along with the homesteaders, the loggers and sawyers. As the homesteaders tackled the vast forest land of north central Alberta, an important relationship was forged between them and the lumbermen. The sawmills provided much-needed off-season employment for the cash-strapped homesteaders as well as access to finished lumber and its by-products such as slabs and shavings. The homesteaders supplied a ready labour pool for the logging and sawing operations especially during the winter months when there was little to do on the homestead. The homesteaders would often also allow loggers to take the timber from their land as both a means of gaining extra income and to help clear it for agricultural purposes.

Ingrid also gives an incidental recognition of another ethnic group long associated with the lumbering industry - the Finnish community. This is shown through the personalities of two colourful Finnish loggers hired by Ingrid's father.

Above all, *Ingrid* is a human story of loneliness and disappointment, and of hope and love. It reflects many of the hardship our brave pioneer ancestors had to face in settling this great land.

Chapter One

"Goodbye Sigrud," Ingrid sniffed as she clutched the handrail of the ship. A few wisps of her blonde hair, that escaped from the braids that were wrapped around her head, curled in the gentle breeze coming in off the Baltic Sea. She watched the harbour of Stockholm slowly recede as the ship moved through the archipelago that made up the Swedish capital. Even from this distance she thought she could still see Sigrud waving frantically. As the ship moved further away, she swallowed with the thought that she might never see Sigrud again. All that she knew was being left behind forever.

Ingrid's parents, Alfred and Agnes, also watched gravely as their familiar world was slipping away. Alfred absentmindedly twirled his thick, greying, beard with his fingers, his mind lost in thought. Agnes clutched the hand of her nine-year-old daughter Astrid, fearful that the child might fall overboard, though they were well-protected by a mesh attached to the railing. Ingrid's brother, Clarence, his mop of wavy golden hair nearly covered by his cap, held the handrail firmly with both hands wearing a satisfied look. Clarence, a curious and self-assured twelve-year-old, saw their voyage to this strange new land called Canada as a great adventure. The foghorn blew a deep note as the ship also bade its farewell to Sweden. Ingrid glanced instinctively up at the blue flag with the horizontal yellow cross, that fluttered on the masthead, glad that at least this little piece of Sweden was coming with her. The family watched until the last vestiges of Stockholm vanished over the horizon, then turned and went to their cabin. Ingrid watched a while longer as the ship skirted along the Kalmar coast. Ingrid had scant comfort in the fact that the ship was following along the Swedish coast and would be for some time yet. In the end, however, Sweden, Sigrud, and all she knew, would be left behind.

"Goodbye Sigrud," Ingrid whispered "Life will be so lonely without you."

Sigrud Olesson had been her bosom friend since early childhood and they had grown up together in the town of Olberg located deep in the interior of Sweden. Her father and Uncle Nils had run the Erlander

1

sawmill that employed most of the town's men including Sigrud's father. Ingrid had a comfortable childhood and had spent those idyllic days playing with Sigrud. Of course there were other friends such as Velma, Rudi, and her cousin Ivor but Sigrud was her best friend with whom she could share the secrets of her soul. Now at the tender age of fourteen all of this was being wrenched away from her. Ingrid thought again of the farewell scene on the docks where she and Sigrud hugged each other, sobbing on each other's shoulders.

"Oh Ingrid, things will never been the same without you," Sigrud sobbed. "Life will be so lonely."

"I know Sigrud," Ingrid sobbed. "I'll find a way to get back to you though. I don't know what caused Papa to decide to move to Canada, a huge empty place on the other side of the Earth."

"You must write to me as often as you can so I know that all is well," Sigrud said with watery eyes.

"I will write every day," Ingrid promised. "You will know every step of my voyage, and once we are established I will give Papa no peace until he promises to send me back to Sweden to visit you."

"And I will find ways to save money so I can come over to Canada and visit you," Sigrud assured her.

The bullhorn announced the last call to board the ship. Ingrid and Sigrud still held each other at arm's-length.

"Come on Ingrid," Agnes called, walking toward them.

"Oh Sigrud, I don't want to go! I'm afraid I'll never see you again."

"Go you must," Sigrud smiled, putting on a brave face. "We have a lifetime ahead of us and if you find you like it in Canada, I'll come to you."

Ingrid smiled feebly.

"Come on Ingrid," Agnes called, nearly grabbing Ingrid by the arm.

Sigrud reluctantly let go of her friend and whispered, "Bye."

"Goodbye Sigrud," Ingrid sniffed, as she turned to go with her mother. She turned and waved at Sigrud as they boarded the ship.

Ingrid glanced once more at the passing Swedish coastline then quickly went in to join her family. In the small lower-deck cabin she found her parents and Clarence going through a Swedish-English dictionary trying to teach each other some basic elements of the language of their new home. Clarence was an eager student. She heard him point out to his parents. "Remember in English the J is pronounced like G rather than a Y and the W sounds different from a V."

"Yes, Clarence," Alfred sighed.

"English is so complicated, I don't think I'll ever learn it," Ingrid complained.

"You'll have to learn it someday," Alfred said. "It is the language of our new home."

"It is in some ways similar to Swedish," Agnes added.

"They are related languages," Clarence chimed in. "English is easy."

"I don't care," Ingrid cried suddenly. "Why did we have to leave Sweden?"

"To build a new life," Alfred said quietly.

"Why couldn't you leave me behind with Sigrud while you build your new life?" Ingrid began crying. "Oh Papa, please put me off at the next stop so I can go back."

"We've been through this before," Alfred said sternly. "I will not have my family broken up."

"The ship doesn't stop till we get to Copenhagen in Denmark," Clarence added.

"That's enough, Clarence," Agnes said as she came over to comfort the sobbing Ingrid.

"It's just not fair," Ingrid sobbed, leaning into her mother's shoulder.

"Life is never easy," Agnes soothed. "Your father has our best interests at heart. Canada is a new land of opportunity. A chance for a better life for you, Clarence and Astrid."

"I don't want a better life. I liked the life we had."

"We all liked it but sometimes one has to change."

"I wish Sigrud could have come with us."

"I know dear, I know," Agnes said tenderly. "You can write to her and maybe when you father gets his new mill set up in Canada he will make enough money to send you back for a visit. Do you think that might be possible dear?" Agnes said, looking at Alfred.

"Yes, anything is possible," Alfred replied with a grunt.

Ingrid smiled for the first time since boarding the ship as she looked at her mother. This pleasant-looking woman with her hair also braided, seemed so full of wisdom and compassion.

"Show me where Canada is, Clarence?" Astrid asked with her nine-year-old curiosity.

Clarence eagerly pulled out his atlas. He had purchased one at a shop in Stockholm for the express purpose of tracing the journey to their new home. On the world map he showed her the approximate course they would be taking.

"Jiminy, Canada is a long way away," Astrid said, her large eyes showing amazement. "And it is so big."

"You could put a hundred Swedens inside Canada," Clarence added.

"Where in Canada are we going?" Astrid continued.

"To Alberta," Clarence explained as he pointed to the location of Alberta within Canada..

"Across all that land?"

"They say it takes a train four or five days to reach Alberta from the east coast," Alfred added.

"I'm going on deck for a while," Ingrid said. "I need some fresh air."

"Can I come?" Astrid asked, her interest in the geography of their journey having vanished.

"Sure, we'll walk around for a while."

"Maybe it will take your mind off home," Agnes smiled.

When they went up on deck, Ingrid glanced out the starboard side to make sure the shoreline of Sweden was still in view. The ship was about to go around the island of Oland. Soon they would be at the southern tip of Sweden.

With Astrid clutching her hand, Ingrid wandered through the salon and out on the promenade. It was a warm spring morning and the Baltic was calm. They stopped on the port-side near the bow to look out over the sea and observe the ever-present gulls that were on the alert for any garbage in which to forage. Ingrid overheard a group of people who also seemed to be emigrants.

One of them said, "They say that in the New World we have to learn how to measure all over again. Everything is *miles* and *feet*, rather than *kilometres* and *centimetres*."

"And you weigh everything by *pounds* and *ounces* instead of *kilos* and *grams*," another agreed.

"Come let's go," Ingrid said as she nudged Astrid along. "Is every-one leaving Sweden?" she mumbled in addition. By the time they made their way to the stern of the ship Oland was receding from them.

Clarence appeared, bright-eyed and cheery.

"We'll soon be going around the southern tip of Sweden," he said.

"I thought you were doing English lessons with Mother and Father," Ingrid snapped.

"Naw, I want to explore the ship. Hey, why so grouchy?"

"Why are you so happy to leave Sweden? Won't you miss your friends?"

"This is so exciting," Clarence bubbled. "We get to travel across the ocean on a ship. Go to a new land. Maybe even meet some wild Indians."

"Oh brother," Ingrid groaned. "Come Astrid, let's go back to the cabin."

"Did you have a nice stroll, dear?" Agnes said as Ingrid and Astrid entered the cabin.

"Humph." Ingrid frowned. "The more I hear about this Canada, the more it frightens me. I not only have to learn a new language, but it seems I also have to learn how to measure everything differently. How many miles is it to Canada, and how many pounds do I weigh?"

"It is very confusing to us too," Agnes assured her. "But we will get used to it."

"When I set up my new sawmill I will have to measure my lumber in something called board feet," Alfred laughed.

"I just don't know if I can get used to it," Ingrid sighed heavily as she flopped down on her berth.

"I think I'll go out on deck for a while," Alfred said, rising from his seat. "I might as well enjoy the Baltic air while I can."

As Alfred looked out over the hand railing, watching the coast of Sweden slip by, he thought of events over the past few years.

He and his brother Nils had inherited the saw milling company that his father had established in Olberg. Even though they got along quite well as partners, Alfred had a deep longing to strike out on his own. As the lumber business was in his blood, he could think of no other career but opportunities for starting up new lumber producing companies in Sweden were limited. Government regulations were beginning to be applied to help preserve Sweden's large, but finite forest reserves. Alfred had heard stories about Canada as a vast land of endless forests, both broadleaf and coniferous. Eight years ago Alfred's friend, Gunner

Elofson, had emigrated to Canada with his family. Gunner knew of Alfred's longing for adventure and opportunity and wrote him a letter that spoke glowingly of "endless forests of spruce, pine and birch, forests that beckoned a woodsman's axe and a saw blade" After reading Gunner's letter, Alfred had sat up all that night thinking about the prospects of starting a new life in Canada.

The next day when the children weren't present he discussed his plan with Agnes.

"Go to Canada? On the other side of the Earth?" she said incredulously.

"Yes, a lot of Swedes are going there these days," Alfred said with enthusiasm. "We will be neighbours to Gunnar Elofson."

"Out in the wilderness?"

"He says there is a town nearby and the railway has recently reached his area."

"Can we afford such a journey? It will cost a lot of money."

"I have several thousand kroner[1] in my savings and next time I'm in Stockholm I'll check the cost of such a voyage."

"You would spend our savings on a dream?"

"Not only a dream my dear, but an opportunity," Alfred insisted. "An opportunity to build a new life for us and, above all, a new life for our children. Canada is the land of the future, so they say, and that is why so many of our countrymen are going there."

"I suppose you have a point," Agnes sighed. "Opportunities are limited here in Sweden. If we can truly afford the voyage and the means of providing for ourselves when we get there. I'll not stand in your way."

Alfred considered his financial situation and checked his savings account to see if it was possible to take his family to Canada. The following day he went to Stockholm on a business trip and while there he inquired about the costs of such a voyage. He returned home satisfied that he could do it.

After he had carefully thought everything over, he spoke to Nils concerning his plan.

"Move to Canada?" Nils said incredulously. "It will cost several thousand kroner just to pay the passage for your family, let alone set up a sawmill when you get there."

"I have enough in my own savings to easily cover the passage if we

[1]kroner - name of currency used in Scandinavian countries (plural)

go steerage class. And if you buy my half of the family business, I should have enough either to ship the mill machinery from here or buy it over there."

"You want me to buy you out then?"

"Yes, it would be best in the long run," Alfred said assuredly "You will get to run the business exactly the way you wish without having to consult me."

"Yes, that is a good point. Even though we had few differences in our partnership it will be good to be able to do things independently." Nils laughed and added, "Who knows, maybe the business will fail without you."

"I think you will do better by yourself," Alfred assured him. "We'll have our solicitor start working on it this very day. I would like to take that small sawmill you are thinking of trading, and one of the planers as part of my buyout."

"My, you are impatient, brother," Nils chuckled.

"Well, they say Canada is a land of opportunity and a lot of our countrymen have gone there, including Gunner Elofson."

"So how is Gunner doing over there?" Nils asked.

"Apparently quite well. He says he has a lot of Swedes for neighbours, so that will be a plus," Alfred replied. "It was he who wrote me about the endless supply of timber waiting to be turned into lumber."

"I wish you well, brother, in your dream," Nils said. "I'll not stand in your way. We can have the solicitor draw up the papers as soon as you like."

"Very well, if you get going on that, I'll make arrangements for travel."

That night after supper, when all the family was relaxing in the living room, Alfred made his announcement. "Do you remember last week when I received a letter from Gunner Elofson? How would you like to be his neighbour in Canada?"

"You *are* sure we can afford the journey?" Agnes said. The cost of such a journey and establishing themselves in the New World was still her main concern.

"Everything has been worked out. I will use our savings for the journey and Nils will buy me out of my share of the mill. This will give me enough money to set up a mill over there."

"Are we really moving to Canada?" Clarence asked, wide-eyed with anticipation.

"Yes son," Alfred chuckled. "There is a great future waiting for you over there. One day you'll inherit a sawmill and lumber business far bigger than the one I now share with your Uncle Nils."

"Where is Canada?" Astrid asked.

Alfred picked his young daughter up and setting her on his knee he explained, "Canada is a great big country on the other side of the world."

"Is it like Sweden?"

"Very much like Sweden. It has forests and mountains like Sweden, but it is huge."

"Snow in the wintertime?"

"Yes, snow in the wintertime."

Ingrid sat glumly at one side. She couldn't believe what she was hearing. Her family was going to simply pick up and move to the other side of the Earth. All her plans for the summer with Sigrud were shattered. She and her inseparable friend were about to be pried apart. Finally, when the shock had worn off, she pleaded, "Please, Papa, can I stay in Sweden?"

"Where will you stay?" Alfred asked. "I will not leave you to the charity of our friends."

"I could live with Sigrud. I know she will say 'yes' if I ask her."

"We could not ask her family to keep you."

"Then leave me some money to pay for my lodgings."

"No. I will not have this family split up."

"Then let me live with Uncle Nils. He's family."

"We are your family - your mother, Clarence, Astrid and myself. We belong together and we must stay together," Alfred's voice became loud and firm.

"Then bring Sigrud with us."

"No," Alfred thundered. "If we take Sigrud with us, then she'll be taken away from her own family."

"Can we at least stay in Sweden until the Midsummer Festival?' Ingrid begged. "Sigrud and I are planning to go up to her Uncle Gustav's place at Ostersund. We were going to celebrate my birthday at the festival and watch the midnight sun. Oh please, Papa."

"I'm sorry Ingrid, but we must leave Sweden in the spring of the year if we hope to be established in our new home by winter. We leave Sweden on April 15th."

"It's just not fair," Ingrid cried, as she turned and fled to her room in tears. Her whole world was shattered.

"You should be gentle with her," Agnes said quietly to Alfred. "Fourteen is a difficult age to be taken away from your friends. And you know how close Ingrid and Sigrud are."

"Yes," Alfred sighed. "It will be hard for all of us to leave familiar surroundings but this chance to go to Canada is more important than anything."

As they sat down to their noonday meal in the dining room, the ship had rounded the southern tip of Sweden and was now plying the narrow channel between Sweden and the Danish island of Zealand. In this narrow channel several ships passed them going in the opposite direction.

"Where are all the ships going?" Astrid asked.

"Going to the ports of Russia or Germany, I expect," Alfred shrugged. "Maybe even back to Stockholm."

"If I knew which one was going to Stockholm, I'd jump overboard and swim to it," Ingrid remarked in a low tone.

"If you jumped overboard you'd drown or die in the freezing waters," Agnes replied gently.

"May I go out on deck and watch the ships?" Clarence asked eagerly as he wiped his face with a napkin.

"Finish your milk first," Agnes replied.

As Clarence gulped down his milk, so did Astrid, hoping to go with Clarence.

Ingrid excused herself with plans to return to their cabin so she could start a letter to Sigrud. Along the way she stopped and glanced at the coast of Sweden still near enough to see the trees and fields along with the occasional house. Ingrid turned and went down into the cabin.

She began her letter:

April 15, 1910
Dear Sigrud,
It has been only a few short hours but already I miss you terribly. We have passed the southern tip of Sweden but I can still see 'the golden shore.' It can't be more than a kilometre or two away. It is very tempting to jump overboard and swim back. Oh Sigrud I feel like we are sailing for the edge of the world.

Alfred and Agnes returned to the cabin and Ingrid put down her letter.

"Let's try to learn some more English," Alfred suggested.

They sat at the table and he got out the Swedish-English dictionary and Agnes got out a pencil and paper. As they murmured to each other over a few words and phrases, Ingrid continued.

"Everything will be so different in Canada. I have to learn a new language and they have a funny way of measuring everything. I have a question for you. How many pounds do you weigh? Or, did you know that your foot was twelve inches long?"

"Ingrid," Alfred said to her. "I have a couple of English words you must learn how to say."

"Oh, what are they?" Ingrid sighed. She did not want to learn any English now or in the foreseeable future.

"The words for *please* and *thank you*, I will say them and you repeat them."

Reluctantly, Ingrid repeated the words after her father.

"Another phrase is, *Help me, I am lost.*"

"Oh Papa, please, I want to finish my letter to Sigrud."

"Sooner or later you will have to learn to speak English," Alfred frowned.

"Let her be for now," Agnes said. "Eventually she will see that you are right."

"All right, but I will drill you on those basic words you need to survive."

Just then Astrid burst into the cabin, Momma Papa, Clarence said to come quickly. We can see Copenhagen." They all scrambled to the port-side deck to see the picturesque Danish capital approaching. Even Ingrid joined in the excitement.

To the south just a few kilometres away they could see the great city with its many colourful low buildings and numerous ships tied up at the wharves. Tugboats and fishing craft could be seen among great ships anchored at sea.

The ship made a brief stop at Copenhagen where some passengers got off and others boarded. A group of Danish passengers passed near to where Ingrid's family was standing and she observed that while she could understand what they were saying, their manner of speaking was quite different. They were talking of going to America.

'*Why is everyone leaving Scandinavia?*' Ingrid wondered.

The foghorn blew and the ship began to draw away from Copenhagen. They all remained on deck and watched the city slide out of view. One more piece of Scandinavia was getting left behind. Soon the land on both sides began to fall away as the ship headed up the centre of the Kattegat[2]

---

[2]Kattegat - the strait between Denmark and Sweden

Chapter Two

Ingrid worked on her letter to Sigrud for most of the afternoon describing their stop at Copenhagen and when she finally did go out on deck the shoreline on the starboard side had drastically changed. No longer a flat countryside of farms and forests, it was now one of jagged snow-capped mountains that seemed to come right out of the sea. The mountains were purple in the distance and the sun was beginning to slip behind them.

"Where are we Papa?" she asked Alfred as he came up alongside her.

"We're in the Skagerrak[1] and what you see ahead is Norway."

Ingrid swallowed with the thought that the last vestige of Sweden had passed by. She said, "Will we be in Stavanger soon?"

"Not for a few hours yet," Alfred replied. "It will be dark before then."

"If I put my letter in the postbox, will the mail be taken off the ship at Stavanger?"

"I expect so."

"Good. Then Sigrud will know about the first leg of our voyage."

"This has all been very hard on you hasn't it Ingrid?" Alfred said softly.

"Everything is so different, new language, the new way of measuring things and new money. How many kroner does it take to make a dollar?"

"I haven't been able to figure all of it out myself yet," Alfred chuckled.

"You will promise to send me back to visit Sigrud, when everything is set up over in Canada, won't you Papa?"

"I promise, but it won't be for a few years. Can you wait that long?"

"It will seem like forever, but if you promise, I will wait."

"I promise."

Ingrid smiled up at her father. For the first time since the voyage began she saw again the kind eyes that lie beneath those shaggy eye-

[1]Skagerrak - the strait between Denmark and Norway

brows. Alfred suggested that they find the others so they could have supper.

Everyone was in the cabin and thinking about going to bed when the ship's foghorn announced that they were arriving at Stavanger.

"Can I have a look at Stavanger before I go to bed?" Clarence asked.

"Me too," Astrid chimed in.

"Let's all go up on deck and say farewell to Scandinavia," Alfred suggested.

It was a dark, clear night with stars twinkling above as the ship drew into the harbour at Stavanger. Stavanger was a small city nestled in a shallow fjord on the southwest coast of Norway. The mountains rose up around it like giant shadows in the darkness. A call through the ship's bullhorn told all passengers to stay on board unless Stavanger was their final destination. Ingrid observed that few people get off but many got on.

"Why is everyone fleeing Scandinavia?" Ingrid asked.

"Opportunities in the new world," Alfred replied. "You see, we are not alone."

"I would have been happy to spend my life in Sweden."

"I know dear. I know."

They watched the gangplank being withdrawn and the foghorn again sounded to announce their imminent departure

"Farewell Norway, farewell Sweden," Agnes said quietly

"Goodbye Scandinavia," Clarence added.

"Goodbye Sigrud," Ingrid said in a small voice.

"Let us go back to the cabin and go to bed," Alfred said. "It has been a long day."

In the small hours of the morning Ingrid was abruptly awakened by the tossing of the ship in heavy seas. Her stomach began to churn.

"Is the ship sinking?" Astrid cried fearfully as a great wave crashed against the porthole.

"No," Alfred said from his bed. "It's just rough seas. The big waves just make the ship toss about."

Alfred switched on the electric light by his bedside and looked across the room for by now his whole family was awake. The ship sustained another heavy swell and Ingrid, who was on the outside of the narrow bed she shared with Astrid, nearly rolled out onto the floor.

"Oh, I'm going to be sick" Ingrid groaned. She scrambled out of bed and headed for the washroom.

"Papa the ship is sinking!" Astrid cried, as she ran over to her parents' bed.

Alfred pulled her under the blankets and put a reassuring arm around her. "The ship won't sink. We're out in the open sea now."

"The Atlantic Ocean?"

"Not quite. It's the North Sea and they say it is always stormy."

Ingrid staggered back from the washroom clutching her stomach. Another swell from the stormy sea caused her to nearly topple into Clarence's bed. A wave crashed against the porthole and Astrid clung to her father in terror.

"Is it going to be like this all the way to Canada?" Ingrid gasped as she crawled back into her own bed trying to cope with her churning stomach.

"I don't think so," her father assured her. "The North Sea is always the worst."

"And how long are we going to be on the North Sea?"

"About a day and a half," Clarence piped in.

"Oh no," Ingrid groaned. "I think I'll die before we get off it." She buried her head in her pillow.

"You will get used to it," Alfred assured her.

"I suppose we have to put up with that foghorn blowing away too," Ingrid complained, raising the pillow somewhat. The two-toned blare of the foghorn, which had been blowing since before they awakened, droned on in the background.

"There is probably dense fog outside," Alfred said. "The foghorn keeps ships from running into each other."

Ingrid did not go to breakfast but remained in her berth groaning in agony. Both Astrid and Agnes found they could only pick at their breakfast even though it was not served until the sea had calmed somewhat. Of the Erlander family, only Clarence ate heartily. Alfred joked that he must have a, cast iron stomach.

"It looks like we're sailing through a cloud," Astrid observed as she looked out the dining room windows at the dense fog enveloping the ship.

"I can see what Ingrid was complaining about with that foghorn," Agnes said. "Hearing that annoying sound all day is enough to drive one crazy."

"Oh well, it's all part of travelling by sea," Alfred shrugged.

By midday the skies had cleared, the sea had calmed and most thankfully the foghorn ceased to blow. Everyone but Ingrid adjusted to the rolling motion of the ship. Agnes persuaded her to take some fruit juice and milk, and by late afternoon Ingrid had ventured out on deck. She looked out over the sea and could see nothing but water stretching to the horizon in every direction. There were no other ships in sight and no gulls following. They were alone in the midst of vast ocean.

Ingrid returned to her cabin and began another letter to Sigrud.

Dear Sigrud,
This morning I found out what seasickness is. We woke up to rough seas and I felt so sick I thought I was going to die. It is not enough that I am tortured by being torn away from you, but it seems I will spend my voyage across the ocean in agony.

By supper she was both well enough and hungry enough to dine with the rest of the family. The sea was still calm when everyone prepared to go to bed and Astrid was finally convinced that the ship wasn't going to sink after all. While the children were preparing for bed Alfred had got out his violin. Alfred was a talented violinist who had taken lessons with the instrument in his earlier years. He could play both popular folk music and light classics.

"Are you going to play us a tune Papa?" Astrid asked. Alfred began playing *Swedish Rhapsody*. Astrid began to tap out the rhythm of its lively beat on the wall. Ingrid thought, *'Does he have to play something that reminds me of home?'*

"I'd like to play a musical instrument someday," Astrid said.

"Maybe in time I will teach you," Alfred chuckled. "What would you like to play?"

" A guitar," Astrid said.

"I'll look into it once we get settled," Alfred replied. "For now though, you should get some sleep."

"Play something restful," Agnes suggested. "It might help put the children to sleep."

He chose a very peaceful and beautiful piece called *Traumerei* to lull his family to sleep. They were all sleeping by the time he had finished, and Agnes who was also nearly asleep said, "It was very beautiful dear."

When the family awoke the following morning, again to a calm sea, Ingrid was ready to have breakfast with the others. Though her stomach was still slightly unsettled she felt she could cope. Clarence who, as usual, finished breakfast first went out on deck. He soon came hurriedly back to announce that they could see land. Everyone rushed up to the deck. Ingrid was pleased that they were within sight of land again. As they came to the railing on the starboard side they could see a slim veil of blue on the horizon.

"Is that Canada?" Astrid said pointing at the blue veil.

"No," Alfred laughed. "It's the coast of England."

"We should be seeing the coast of France soon," Clarence said excitedly. "Our voyage takes us through the Strait of Dover into the English Channel."

"I don't think we'll ever get lost with Clarence along," Ingrid said sardonically. "He seems to be plotting every step of the way."

"Maybe the captain should hire him as a navigator," Alfred chuckled.

"Can I go to the bridge and see the real navigator?" Clarence asked eagerly.

"I don't think the captain wants some know-it-all child telling him how to run his ship," Ingrid retorted.

"Ingrid, Clarence is only curious," Agnes said firmly. "But your sister is probably right Clarence, the bridge is not a place for a twelve-year-old."

"Aw!"

After watching the English shoreline slip by and move ever so slightly nearer, Ingrid returned to the cabin to continue her second letter to Sigrud.

"I feel a little better today. The sea is calm and I'm hardly sea-sick at all. More importantly I can see land again al-

though it is England instead of Sweden. Mom and Papa are busy trying to teach each other English but that language seems just too hard for me to learn."

"Ingrid, what are the English words for *please* and *thank you*?" Alfred asked abruptly.

Ingrid sighed and put down her writing pad, "I don't remember and please, Papa, I am trying to finish this letter."

"Say the words and I'll let you be," he said firmly.

Ingrid stumbled through the word *please* and so badly mispronounced the word *thank you*, that Alfred had to correct her. She turned back to her letter but couldn't concentrate. Finally Ingrid put down the writing pad and went out on deck toward the bow of the ship.

The coast line of England was much closer now. There were several craft in the water. She saw a large freighter go by and there was at least three fishing boats in clear view. Then gleaming white cliffs came into view on the English side.

"That must be the white cliffs of Dover that I read about," Ingrid said, as Astrid came alongside her.

"Look at the castle on top of the cliffs," Astrid cried as she pointed to the stately Dover Castle. Below the castle at the base of the cliffs she could see the town of Dover. "What's that land over there?" She asked, pointing to a coastline in the other direction which was much more vague than that of England.

"That must be the coast of France," Ingrid replied. "Clarence said we would be able to see France."

A small single-funnel ship was coming out of Dover heading across in front of them toward the distant shore.

"I bet that boat is going across to France," Ingrid said.

Dover quickly disappeared behind them and the coast of France began to recede over the horizon. They were now in the English Channel. Ingrid continued to watch English shore go by until Clarence came alongside her.

"Papa said to tell you we will be in Southampton in an hour or so and will have to be ready to leave the ship," he informed her.

"Oh my gosh," Ingrid replied. "I had better finish my letter to Sigrud so I can post it when we get there." She quickly returned to the cabin to tend to the task.

When the general announcement was made that they would be docking at Southampton in one hour, Agnes stressed that everyone should make sure that they put all of their belongings back into their hand luggage and then she bustled around tidying up the cabin. Ingrid hastily finished her letter and posted it on board the ship.

As the ship slipped past the great naval base at Portsmouth behind the Isle of Wight, the Erlander family were all on deck clutching their handbags.

"Look at all the warships," Clarence said in awe as they saw two cruisers in anchor with their huge cannons pointing forward.

"Why do we have to change ships?" Astrid asked.

"This ship is too small to cross the Atlantic Ocean," Alfred explained. "For that, we need a big, big ship."

"Oh," Astrid replied. "I hope the big ship is smoother to travel on than this one."

Soon the great ocean liner port of Southampton came into view. Moored to the wharfs were two huge three-funnel ocean liners that dwarfed their modest two-funnel ship.

"I bet we go on one of those ships," Clarence said excitedly.

"Or one like them," Alfred said modestly, though he was also impressed at the awesome size of the great ocean liners.

Announcements came over the bullhorns giving the passengers instructions. Those going on to the New World were to go one direction and those planning to stay in England to go another. The announcement was repeated several times as the ship was secured to the wharf and the gangplank lowered. Once on shore the passengers were ushered into a huge building for further sorting. As there were ships bound for several overseas destinations, Ingrid's family had to find the area where people who were waiting to board the ship to Canada was located. Although those doing the directing spoke in that incomprehensible English language to Ingrid, her parents and Clarence seemed to understand what was required and her mother never let go of Astrid's hand for a moment in the bustling crowd.

They found their way to a large room where their passports and tickets were checked, then struggled to find a place to sit on one of the many wooden benches available. The room was full of hundreds of people speaking a babble of many languages. Some were swarthy skinned, and some were fair. She noticed one group of people whose women had their heads completely covered with a cloth that was also drawn across their foreheads, and the men wore sheepskin coats. They seemed to stick together as a group and spoke an unusual language rich in *Y* sounds.

As the others sat Alfred and Clarence went to check on their main luggage to make sure it was safely off the ship and properly transferred. After a time, Ingrid decided to go to a nearby kiosk to get a cup of coffee for her mother and a glass of fruit juice for herself and Astrid. When it was time to pay, Ingrid unwittingly placed a one-krona[2] coin on the counter.

"Eh, what's this?" the vendor said. "We don't take foreign money here. I need a shilling for the drinks."

Ingrid looked bewildered. Although she didn't know what he had said, it occurred to her that he wouldn't accept Swedish money. She turned forlornly away from the counter.

"Eh, what about the coffee and drink? I already poured them."

"Do ye have no money, Miss?" said a pleasant voice beside her.

Ingrid turned to see a handsome lad in his late youth with a mop of curly brown hair showing beneath his tweed cap. He smiled at her. She didn't know what he said but his kind smile suggested that he was offering help.

"He won't accept my money," Ingrid held up her one-kroner piece.

The young man, who obviously didn't understand Swedish, wore a perplexed look at her reply, then held out an open palm saying. "Let me see yer money Miss, maybe I can help ye."

Sensing the gist of his words she dropped the coin into his palm. He looked it over and said, "Let me buy yer drinks, Miss."

Ingrid watched as the lad turned and paid the vendor with unfamiliar coins, then he gave her coin back saying with a wink, "Keep it Miss, dis one is on me."

"*Tack sa mycket*," Ingrid said automatically. Then, she repeated the phrase in faltering English, " Tank you much," as she picked up the drinks.

"So ye do know a few words of English," he laughed. "Let me carry da coffee."

[2]krona - Scandinavian money (singular)

"Tank you," Ingrid smiled again, as she turned to go to her mother and Astrid.

When they reached the place where Agnes and Astrid were sitting, Ingrid said excitedly to her mother, "This young man has bought us drinks because they don't take Swedish money here."

"Oh I forgot, we're in England now." Then turning to the smiling lad, in her own faltering English, Agnes said "Tank you sir, tank you much, wery much."

"Tis no problem ma'am," the lad replied. "I can see ye are strangers to da English tongue. Well I'll be on me way and leave you to yer drinks."

As he turned away Ingrid added again, "Tank you much Mr. sir."

The lad looked back and winked. In turn Ingrid flashed her beautiful smile. The lad smiled back before he vanished into the crowd.

Chapter Three

After several long hours of waiting, sitting on hard wooden benches in the huge crowded room, the call came to board the ship. The Erlander family, along with hundreds of others, filed out onto the wharf. They were directed to board the ship via a gangplank that seemed to lead directly into the heart of the great ship. Ingrid looked up and noticed another gangplank above them that led directly to the upper decks.

"Look at those people up there," Astrid said. Above them she could see ladies in fine dresses carrying their fancy umbrellas and men in shining top hats.

"They are the rich people in the first-class accommodation in luxury cabins," Ingrid said wistfully "We're travelling in steerage below decks."

They made their way into the vast interior of the ship down through a maze of corridors until they found their steerage cabin as directed to by a steward. Like their cabin in the small ship from Sweden it had one porthole for a window. There were, however, only two double-deck bunks, narrower than the ones on the other ship, on either side of the room, and a small storage space for their hand luggage.

"How are five of us going to sleep on four bunks?" Agnes wondered. "These berths are too narrow for Alfred and I to share one."

"We'll each have a berth except the girls, they'll have to share one," Alfred replied.

"They are so narrow," Ingrid protested. "How can Astrid and I fit on one berth?"

"We'll have to make do the best we can," Alfred replied. "They say it will only take four days, at most, to cross the Atlantic."

Once the ship had put out to sea, the family resumed a similar routine to that of the previous ship. From their cabin however, they could hear a mighty throbbing below them.

"What's that sound?" Astrid asked.

"It sounds like the ship's engines," Alfred replied. "They're somewhere deep in the bowels of the ship."

"How come we didn't hear them on the other ship?"

"I guess we weren't as close to the engine room as on this one."

"I suppose we have to listen to that noise all the way across the Atlantic," Ingrid grumbled.

"You'll get used to it," Agnes said with a soothing voice. "It's a steady background noise."

"I think I'll take my writing pad and go up on deck for a while," Ingrid replied. "It's time to start another letter to Sigrud."

"Let's see if we can learn some more English," Alfred said as he picked up the Swedish-English dictionary.

As Alfred and Agnes studied their English, Clarence alternated between helping them and satisfying his boyish urge to explore that part of ship in which steerage passengers were allowed to trespass. Astrid, meanwhile played with her rag dolls and picture books.

Ingrid began her letter:

Dear Sigrud,
As I sit and watch the coast of England slip past me heading toward the sunset I truly feel as if we are sailing to the edge of the earth. I just saw a point of land that someone said was called Land's End slip past us. It is an appropriate name as this is the last piece of land we will see until we reach the New World. So far on this journey I have, from time-to-time held foolish notions of jumping overboard and swimming for shore so that I might find my way back to Sweden and you, but now that can be put to rest as there is no more land until we reach Canada.

Ingrid was still busy writing when a cheery voice said. "Mind if I join ye Miss?"

Ingrid turned and saw the lad who had bought the drinks standing by the other end of the bench smiling at her. She quickly closed the writing pad.

She smiled back with her large violet eyes. Still uncertain as to what the lad had said she surmised he wanted to join her and replied in Swedish, "Yes please sit down."

"I can see dat if we are to have a meanin'ful conversation, we'll be needin' to learn da same language," the lad replied, as he sat down on the other end of the bench.

Ingrid gave him a perplexed smile.

The lad pointed to himself and said, "I Michael, " and pointing at her said "You. . ."

"I Ingrid," Ingrid replied. "You English?"

"Now don't go insultin' me, lass," Michael said with a frown. "I'm Irish."

"You Michael Irish?"

"No Miss, me name is Michael O'Brien. What is yer full name?"

Guessing at his question, Ingrid replied, "Ingrid Erlander."

"Er-lander, ye say, that sounds Scandinavian, are ye Swedish per chance?"

"*Svenska* ya," Ingrid smiled. "Or how you say Sved-ish."

"Are ye goin' to Canada? Ingrid Erl.. . . Swedish?"

Ingrid laughed as Michael had difficulty trying to pronounce her surname.

"Canada ya. You?"

"I am going to Boston. In America."

"America ya."

"Do ye not know any English at all?"

"*Talar ni Svenska?*[1]' Ingrid grinned. This drew a perplexed look from Michael.

Ingrid smiled her most beautiful smile with a glint of mirth in her eyes as she knew he didn't know how to speak Swedish.

"If I told ye, you have da most beautiful eyes, would ye tink dat I was fresh?" Michael said with grin and a wink.

"Are all Irishmen this bold with the ladies?" she laughed. Ingrid assumed that Michael had paid her a compliment.

"I have a feelin' we know what we're sayin' to each odder, even dough da words are different," Michael laughed. Ingrid laughed too.

Just then Clarence appeared on the scene.

"Do you want something Clarence?" Ingrid asked sharply. She was annoyed that he had trespassed on her conversation with Michael.

"Is he yer little brodder?" Michael asked.

"Ya," Ingrid sighed, guessing at what Michael had said.

"I'm Clarence," he announced. "Ya I am Ingrid's brodder. Who are you?"

"I'm Michael O'Brien aldough yer sister tinks me last name is Irish."

"Ingrid von't learn English," Clarence said with a frown.

Michael laughed.

"What did you say to him?" Ingrid demanded of Clarence.

[1]*Talar ni Svenska?* - Do you speak Swedish?

23

"I told him you were too stubborn to learn English," Clarence replied.

"You didn't tell him that," Ingrid said, flushing with embarrassment.

"Well, it's true," Clarence insisted.

"Why don't you go explore the deck some more," Ingrid said, as she didn't want her little brother around any longer..

Guessing the gist of their conversation Michael added with a laugh, "Aye, so ye have a little brodder checkin' up on ye do ye?"

"Ya," Ingrid sighed.

"Maybe we should be keepin' yer brodder around a while as an interpreter," Michael laughed. Clarence laughed too.

Again Ingrid looked to Clarence for explanation.

"Michael says I should stay and be your interpreter," Clarence explained.

"No thanks," Ingrid said bluntly. "We can manage without you."

"She do not vant me to," Clarence said to Michael.

"Maybe it is as well den," Michael winked. "Run along laddie and let me teach yer sister some English."

"Mom said to tell you were are going for supper soon," Clarence said to Ingrid.

Ingrid sighed. She looked at Michael and said. "I go eat now. Later Michael Irish"

"Tis alright lass," Michael winked. "It takes four days to cross da Atlantic. I'll see ye again."

Ingrid rose from the bench and said in faltering English. "Goodbye Michael Irish."

"Goodbye Ingrid Swedish," he laughed.

"Why does he call you Ingrid Swedish?" Clarence asked, as they walked away.

"I think he is making a joke because he has trouble saying my last name."

"Why do you call him Michael Irish?"

"You ask too many questions Clarence," Ingrid retorted.

At supper everyone noticed that Ingrid's mood had improved markedly. She even made an effort to grapple with a few more English words.

"This Atlantic air must be good for you," Agnes remarked. "You seem cheery this evening."

"Since we have passed Land's End, there's no hope of getting back to Sweden," Ingrid replied modestly.

"Ingrid has a boyfriend," Clarence blurted, unable to contain his observations.

Ingrid shot him a dark look.

"A boyfriend?" Alfred said sharply. "You are only fourteen."

"I don't have a boyfriend," Ingrid retorted, "Clarence is being a pest."

"Goodbye Michael Irish," Clarence mimicked.

"Michael Irish?" Agnes queried.

"Remember that young man who bought our drinks?" Ingrid said, trying to remain nonchalant. "I was sitting on a bench near the bow and he came along. He told me his name was Michael and I think he said he was Irish but I didn't get his last name. Obri or something."

"Was it O'Brien?" Alfred said. "That is an Irish name."

"O'Brien, that's it. He has as much trouble with my last name so he called me Ingrid Swedish."

"I see," Agnes replied. "But perhaps your father's right, you are too young to be involved with young men."

"Oh Mother, I'm not involved. He was just being friendly. Now if you will excuse me, I would like to go back to my berth and continue my letter to Sigrud."

"Sigrud is certainly getting a running monologue of our voyage," Alfred laughed.

"Yes. That is good, as writing to Sigrud helps Ingrid pass the time."

"You are right dear, it is a good thing she is writing to Sigrud. It also helps her feel that she is still in touch with her friend."

Lying on her berth, Ingrid continued:

As I watched Land's End at the western extreme of England slip by, I was in the depth of despair when a young man sat down beside me. Although I could not understand him, we became acquainted. There is music and laughter in his voice and it gives me a good feeling to talk to him. He is Michael an Irishman and I call him Michael Irish. He had trouble saying Erlander so he calls me Ingrid Swedish. I hope I will see him tomorrow, it will make our voyage much more bearable.

INGRID

Ingrid closed her writing pad and lay back on her berth and thought of Michael. The rest of the family had since returned to the cabin and she could hear the murmuring of her parents with their English lessons and Clarence was playing a game with Astrid.

After a time Ingrid announced that she was going up on deck for some fresh air before bed.

"You are not meeting that young Irishman up there are you?" Alfred said gruffly.

"No. He's probably in his berth somewhere," Ingrid said indignantly. "It would be hard for us to make plans when we can't even understand one another."

As the bow was the nearest deck area to them, Ingrid again went there. From the ballroom on the deck, two storeys above her, with its glass front and open doors, she could hear the din of general conversation punctuated by laughter. She wondered what it would be like to be one of the fine ladies dressed in satin dining on champagne and caviar. Turning away from the gaiety on the upper decks, Ingrid looked out over the ocean and the starry skies above.

"Out stargazin' are ye?" said a familiar voice behind her.

Ingrid whirled about and flushed with embarrassment at the sight of Michael watching her. He wore the usual grin on his face and there was laughter in his eyes.

"Michael Irish!" she gasped. Then in Swedish added, "Do you always sneak up on people like that?"

Michael came up beside her by the handrail and said "I'm sorry if I frightened ye." Then looking out at the starry sky, he added. "Do ye see da comet out dere?"

"Comet?"

Michael pointed to what appeared to be a bright star and said, "Dat's Halley's Comet. It's still too far away to see da tail yet. Some are sayin' dat it might hit da eart and it will be da end of da world."

"Comet, ya," Ingrid said. She remembered Clarence talking about the comet. He had pointed it out to her and Sigrud one night shortly before they had left Sweden.

"Comet bad," Ingrid said. She remembered the old stories about the appearance of a comet in the sky as bad luck. Certainly being uprooted from familiar surroundings was bad luck to her.

"I don't believe a word of it," Michael said as if he could sense her thoughts. "Da comet won't hit da eart, nor do dey bring on bad luck."

The sweet sounds of violins floated down from the upper deck as an orchestra began to play a Viennese waltz. Ingrid began to hum along and move as if she were about to start dancing.

"Would ye like to dance, Ingrid Swedish?" Michael said as he offered his hand.

"Dance, ya," Ingrid smiled as she slipped into his arms.

They twirled around the deck to the tune of the *Emperor Waltz*. Ingrid closed her eyes dreamily and imagined herself to be one of those fine ladies and Michael to be her escort dressed in a tuxedo.

"Maybe I don't know what ye say, Ingrid Swedish, but ye dance as beautiful as ye look."

Ingrid smiled back and could only say, "Tank you Michael Irish. You dance beautiful"

They twirled around the deck lost in their own world for several long moments until they heard a throat clearing. Ingrid froze at the sight of her father watching them.

"I thought you were just going for some fresh air," Alfred chided, scowling at Michael.

"Papa, we uh. . . The music is so beautiful I wanted to dance and Michael came along and asked if he could dance with me."

"It is getting late and you should be in your bed."

"Sorry gettin' yer daughter into trouble Mr. uh Erlan . . . uh Swedish . . . I mean"

"Mr Erlander," Alfred said sharply.

"Goodnight Michael Irish," Ingrid called over her shoulder.

"Goodnight, Ingrid," he replied.

"Papa, did you have to interrupt us?" Ingrid chided him, as they approached the cabin.

"I do not like my daughter lying to me," he rumbled.

"I didn't lie, Papa. I didn't know Michael would come along."

"You were hoping and that is almost the same thing."

As they entered the cabin Alfred said gruffly to Agnes, "I found her on the deck dancing with a young Irishman."

"Is this young man going to Canada too?" Agnes asked Ingrid.

"I think he said he was going to Boston. Is that in America?"

"Ya, Boston is in the United States near New York," Clarence informed them.

27

"So this ship must go on after reaching Halifax," Alfred wondered. "Probably a good thing that the Irishman will be going on."

"I think maybe you and I should go out on deck while the children get ready for bed," Agnes suggested.

"What for, woman?"

"Just come."

Out on the bow deck Agnes spoke to Alfred. "Don't be too hard on Ingrid. If she has found a friend it will be less lonely for her."

"It would be all right if her friend was a girl. She is not ready for a young man yet. She is only fourteen."

"She will be fifteen in midsummer."

"Still too young. What could she see in a young man whom she can't understand?"

"Some things don't need spoken language," Agnes said with a glint in her eye. "Maybe this will help her learn English."

"Well, I think she is too young."

"She will only see this young man for a few days until we reach Halifax."

"I suppose," Alfred sighed. "I will keep an eye on them though so there won't be any nonsense going on."

"Just make sure Ingrid doesn't know you are keeping an eye on her."

Alfred and Agnes put an arm around each other and looked out over the ocean. Above them was an awesome canopy of stars. From the ballroom above the sweet sounds of Strauss drifted down to them. In her berth Ingrid made herself as comfortable as possible with Astrid at her side. Her mind was whirling with the music of the *Emperor Waltz* and she dreamed she was swirling around the ballroom floor of some great castle in the arms of Michael.

Chapter Four

Ingrid woke the next morning just in time to save herself from falling out of her berth which was above that of her mother. The berth, which was narrower than the berth on the ship from Sweden, was simply too narrow for her and Astrid to share. Feeling decidedly cramped, she slid out of bed.

"You're up early," Agnes said drowsily.

"I can't sleep up there with Astrid, it's just too crowded," Ingrid complained.

"What is all the commotion?" Alfred said, switching on his bedside light.

"I got pushed out of bed," Ingrid grumbled. "Papa, can you see if they have any extra mattresses?"

"That would be a good idea, Alfred," Agnes added.

"Not this time of morning," Alfred grumbled. "Later, when I am wide awake."

Alfred switched off his light, rolled over and went back to sleep.

"Mom, can you turn your light on? I might as well get dressed."

Agnes mumbled something and switched her bedside light on. Ingrid gathered up her clothing and went to the washroom just outside the cabin door. Out the porthole she glimpsed the grey light of daybreak and thought it might be nice to watch the sunrise from the deck. She combed out her long blonde hair and decided to leave it free rather than do it up in the usual braids.

The air was cool as Ingrid went out on the bow. It lay in the shadow of the upper decks and since the ship was heading west she could not easily see the sunrise from here. She made her way along the outside passageway to the stern of the ship. The only person she saw along the way was a crewman who popped out of a side door.

"Morning Missy," he said. "Yer up bright and early today."

"*God morgon*," Ingrid instinctively replied in Swedish. She struggled in English to say "good morning" then continued on her way.

The stern deck seemed somewhat more sheltered than the bow. She went to the very back of the ship and looked down at the swirling waters being churned by the ship's mighty propellers. For a long moment she watched them, lost in thought, then turned her attention to the sunrise.

29

The orange orb of the sun was just breaking over the horizon and the thin layer of clouds provided just enough of a veil to allow one to look directly at the great luminous ball. The feathery clouds overhead were gathered in a manner that looked as if a great quilt had been drawn across the sky. The sunward side of each of these "quilted" clouds however, glowed orange as if they were the leftover embers from some celestial fire. Beyond the clouds, where the sky was visible, it changed from light blue to azure to nearly violet as one looked away from the sun. The glow of the sunrise reflected on the waters, broken somewhat by the waves, had the appearance of an orange cone pointing toward the receding ship. The awesome beauty of this natural wonder made the ship in the midst of the vast Atlantic Ocean seem of such little significance

'What artist could ever capture this wonder to behold,' Ingrid thought.

"I see yer out enjoyin' da beautiful sunrise, Ingrid Swedish," said a familiar voice.

Ingrid turned with a start, "Michael Irish! Do you always startle people like that?"

"Only very beautiful young ladies, out enjoyin' da sunrise," Michael grinned, guessing what she had said.

"You must wait around for me to appear just so you can surprise me," Ingrid replied.

"We are definitely goin' to have to work on da language problem," Michael said.

"My English, it not good, I not sure vhat say," Ingrid said with great effort.

"Maybe you're as well keepin' your language," Michael continued. "At least ye have da right to use it if ye wish. Back in Ireland dey make us speak English."

"I need English," Ingrid faltered. "Svedish no good for Canada."

"Would ye like me to teach ye?" Michael offered.

"Ya," Ingrid nodded, guessing at what he had said.

"Well den, let me start by tellin' ye dat yer hair is beautiful when it hangs down."

Ingrid smiled uncertainly, although she assumed he said something very pleasant.

"Ye didn't understand a word I said, did ye?" Michael laughed.

Ingrid laughed also.

Michael gestured to her hair that hung midway down her back. "I like yer hair, it is beautiful," he said again.

"You beautiful too," Ingrid said.

"No lass I'm not beautiful. I may be handsome, but not beautiful. Yer beautiful, I'm handsome," Michael explained with gestures.

"Ya, you handsome," Ingrid laughed.

"Clarence, what are you doing here?" Ingrid gasped, at the sudden appearance of her brother.

"Papa sent me to get you to come for breakfast," Clarence replied. "He would have come but I offered instead."

"Thank you for offering," Ingrid replied. She would much rather have Clarence catch her in the company of Michael than her father.

"Out spyin' on yer sister again are ye?" Michael said.

"I yust, I mean just, came to take her to breakfast," Clarence assured him.

"You won't tell Papa Michael was with me?"

"No, but remember when I need a favour sometime."

"I go eat ya," Ingrid said to Michael. "See you after, ya."

"Ya," Michael smiled. "I'll see you in a while." He headed for a doorway leading down into the ship.

"So, what were you doing wandering the decks at this time of day?" Alfred asked suspiciously.

"I wanted to see the sunrise so I went back to the stern," Ingrid replied innocently. "Oh Papa, it was a beautiful sunrise. I've never seen a sunrise over the ocean before."

"Indeed, I see you've let your hair down."

"Since I was pushed out of bed this morning and there wasn't a soul out on the decks. I just left it," Ingrid replied. "I'll braid it back up before we go to breakfast."

"Alfred, you must see about another mattress," Agnes reminded him.

"Yes dear, as soon as I see the steward who looks after us I'll ask for a mattress and some extra blankets."

Later in the morning, when Ingrid went on deck, Alfred suggested that she take Astrid with her. Ingrid reluctantly agreed. She knew this would probably blunt any chance of meeting or having meaningful conversation with Michael. This was probably the very reason that her father insisted that she take Astrid along.

"Will you take me to the back of the ship where you were this morning?" Astrid asked.

"What do you want to see back there?" Ingrid said. She didn't really want to take Astrid anywhere lest she run across Michael.

"Please, I've never been there and it's too far to go by myself."

"Get Clarence to take you."

"I want you to take me."

"Oh all right."

As they made their way along the passageway, they noticed that on stairs leading to the upper decks, signs were posted. Ingrid assumed they forbade entry by steerage passengers as they were told earlier to stay off the upper decks. In some cases the stairs were blocked with mesh gates.

"Why are there gates?" Astrid asked.

"They don't want us to mix with the rich people on the upper decks," Ingrid said in a disgusted tone.

When they reached the stern deck, Ingrid said to Astrid, "I'll show you how the ship moves."

She held Astrid up against the railing at the rear of the ship and told Astrid to look down.

"Look at the churning water," Astrid said, awed by what she had seen.

"Under that water are the propellers that push the ship forward."

"Wow!"

They sat down on a nearby bench and watched other passengers milling about. Some like themselves came to the back to observe the propeller action. Others came merely to sit on the aft benches. Even a few people from the upper decks came down to spend a brief time on the stern deck. Ingrid admired their fine cut of clothing.

Presently a young woman about Ingrid's age came from out of the lower decks. She was one of the curious people who wore a long dark dress and a head covering drawn tightly over her hair. She had a round face with wide cheek bones and a small concave nose. She seemed to walk listlessly around the deck. At one point when she came near the bench she looked directly at Ingrid. Ingrid gave her a radiant smile and the girl smiled shyly back. Ingrid gestured for her to sit on the bench with them and Astrid drew over tightly against her sister.

After a time Ingrid asked her if she spoke Swedish. The girl shook her head expectantly then Ingrid said, "Speak English?"

The girl shook her head and replied, "*Chy vy hovoryte po Ukrayinska?*"[1]

Ingrid tried another tack, "Vhat your name?" Then pointing as she spoke, "I Ingrid, dis my sister Astrid. You. . .?"

After a moment the girl said hesitantly, "I Olga."

"I from Sveden. Vhere you from?"

Olga did not comprehend.

Ingrid tried gestures and said, "I Svede. Vhat you are?"

The girl spoke in her own language which Ingrid noticed used a lot of *Y* sounds. Finally as she must have surmised Ingrid's question Olga said, "I Bokovinia."

They sat in silence for a while. Ingrid realized that trying to converse with Olga would be more difficult than with Michael.

Astrid produced a stick of rock candy from a pocket in her dress. Her father had bought her a stick of candy as a special treat the day before.

Ingrid noticed that Olga eyed the candy enviously.

"Give me a small piece of candy, Astrid, please?" Ingrid said.

"It's all the candy I have," Astrid protested. "Papa probably won't buy me another for a long time."

"You should be polite and offer a piece to our friend Olga."

Astrid broke off a piece of the candy stick and offered it to Olga.

"*D'yakou*[2]" Olga smiled as she took the candy stick.

"Do you like candy?" Ingrid asked

"*Dobre*." Olga replied as she licked the candy.

"Dobre. I guess that means good in your language huh."

Olga smiled shyly.

Presently Michael came along and Ingrid gave him a radiant smile. "Hello Michael Irish," she said eagerly.

"Hello Ingrid Swedish," he grinned. "I see ye have company, maybe I best be goin'."

Michael started to walk past them and Ingrid grabbed his sleeve saying, "No, not go, Michael Irish."

"Alright me lass, but you'll be needin' to be introducin' me to yer friends," Michael said gesturing to both Astrid and Olga.

---

[1]*Chy vy hovoryte po Ukrayinska* - Do you speak Ukrainian?

[2]*D'yakou* - thank you

"She Olga, come from Bokovinia," Ingrid said pointing to Olga.

"Olga from Bokovinia is it," Michael smiled. "Pleased to me ye."

Olga smiled shyly and looked at the deck.

"The odder I presume to be yer little sister." Michael said looking at the girl with the auburn locks and pigtail braids.

"Sister, ya," Ingrid smiled.

Astrid looked up and smiled shyly at Michael with her dimpled smile.

Olga stood up and smiled at Ingrid. She spoke her own language suggesting she was about to leave them.

"You stay," Ingrid said half-heartedly. She really wanted Michael's undivided attention but also wanted to be polite to Olga.

"*Do pobachemnya,*" Olga smiled as she turned away. Assuming she said goodbye Ingrid replied in Swedish, "*Hej da adjo*"

"Goodbye, Olga, at least I presume dat is what ye were sayin' to each odder," Michael laughed, as Olga turned to walk away.

"Is this man Michael?" Astrid asked, glancing at the handsome youth standing beside them.

"Uh, yes," Ingrid replied. "Can you promise not to tell Papa he stopped by to visit us?"

"Yes, Ingrid, if you promise to play a game with me after."

"I promise," Ingrid smiled as she hugged her sister.

"So what was dat all about?" Michael grinned, as he sat down in Olga's place.

"Just tell Astrid, not tell Papa ve see you," Ingrid faltered.

"Ah I see, keepin' da little sister quiet are ye? What did ye say her name was again?"

"Name, Astrid."

Astrid looked up at Michael.

"Pleased to meet ye Astrid," Michael smiled with a wink.

Astrid smiled shyly and turned to Ingrid. "What did he say?"

"I think Michael said he was glad to meet you. I think he likes you."

Astrid blushed brightly.

"Now what did ye go tellin' yer sister now?" Michael asked.

Ingrid laughed and replied, "I tell Astrid, you like her, ya."

"Ya," Michael replied, mimmicking her. "She's a pretty wee girl."

The skies began to darken, the waves started to get larger and the ship began to toss slightly while the wind became brisk. A voice over the bullhorn suggested that the passengers go inside.

Michael pointed at the darkening skies and said, "It's goin' to storm. They want us to go inside."

"Inside, ya," Ingrid replied as she took Astrid by the hand and led her to an inside corridor.

They stepped inside ahead of Michael and Ingrid turned to face him. "I find Papa and Mamma now."

"Why don't ye come to the salon tonight, we are puttin' on a show," Michael said.

Ingrid looked at him uncertain to what he had said

He pointed at the steerage salon as they went by.

"Salon, ya?"

"Salon ya, tonight," Michael said.

"Goodbye, Michael Irish," Ingrid said as they turned to go down the corridor.

"Goodbye Ingrid Swedish," Michael called after them.

"Remember, not a word about Michael to Papa and Mamma," Ingrid said to Astrid as they hurried down the corridor.

"Thank God," Agnes said as Astrid and Ingrid burst into the cabin. "I was about to tell your father to go look for you."

"Were you with your Irish friend?" Alfred asked suspiciously.

"I met another friend, a girl," Ingrid replied, evading a direct answer.

Astrid looked up at Ingrid and gave her a smile assuring her that her secret was safe.

"That's nice, who is she?" Agnes asked.

"Olga, from what I could understand she said she comes from Bokovinia."

"Bokovinia?" Alfred said. "Her name, Olga, sounds Russian or something."

Clarence, ever the student of geography, got out his atlas and scanned for an area called Bokovinia.

"It's in Austria-Hungary," he cried. On a map of Europe he pointed to an area in the southeastern part of the Austro-Hungarian Empire right next to the Russian border. The adjacent area of the Russian Empire was called Ukraine.

"She's Slavic. All the people in that area of Europe are Slavs."

A wave crashed against the porthole.

"Oh, I think I'd better lie down," Ingrid said as she crawled onto her berth. Although her stomach was unsettled the nausea was not near as acute as it was the first morning on the North Sea. Nonetheless, she declined lunch that day.

Ingrid lay in her berth for most of the afternoon and Astrid kept her company. Alfred and Agnes joined with some other Swedish emigrants to practice speaking English

Later in the afternoon, when she was feeling a little better, Ingrid continued her letter to Sigrud. She spoke glowingly of Michael and mentioned meeting Olga. Although Ingrid attended supper with her family she could only eat lightly.

During supper Clarence announced, "Charlie was saying that there is a party in the steerage salon tonight."

"A party in the salon?" Alfred asked.

"Can we go Papa?" he asked eagerly.

"A party in the salon? I don't know if that would be a suitable place to take children." Agnes replied.

The mention of the word salon, stirred a thought in Ingrid. *'Michael mentioned the salon, it must mean he'll be there.'* She held her tongue for the moment to gauge her father's reaction.

"They probably serve alcoholic drinks there," Agnes added.

"Please Papa, we've been cooped up in the cabin all day," Clarence pleaded. "My friend Charlie went to the one last night."

"And who is your friend Charlie?"

"He's an English boy about the same age as me. He's been teaching me English."

"I see," Alfred replied. Then he turned to a fellow Swede named Norman Anderson whom he had met during the voyage. He was sitting with his family at the next table.

"Say Norman, if you pardon my intrusion. . ."

"Go ahead."

"Do you know anything about a party in the salon tonight, and is it suitable for children to attend?"

"They have parties there every night where people from different counties entertain. They sing and dance. Some people bring their children, but the children have to stay with their parents."

"Do they serve alcohol?" Agnes asked.

"They serve beer and some of the men sneak something stronger from their cabins but it would be safe to bring your family. We are all going." Norman had two sons in their youth.

"I think the younger two at least should stay in the cabin," Agnes insisted.

Clarence's face fell.

"There is a children's show next door," Norman said. "I think there is a magician on tonight."

"We will go out tonight," Alfred said to his family. "We have all been too cooped up today. Clarence, you will take Astrid to see the magician, then you will go back to the cabin to bed. Ingrid, you may come with us."

"Thank you, Papa," Ingrid breathed. She was sure Michael would be there.

"Aw, I want see the party."

"You are too young for that and you will do as I say or you won't go out tonight."

"Yes Papa," Clarence said in a downcast tone.

As they approached the lounge they could hear lively fiddle music. Alfred commented that it sounded like Celtic music. Ingrid's heart jumped. She knew that Celtic meant either Scottish, or hopefully Irish.

The room was crowded and smoke-filled. As they entered there was a fiddler up on stage playing a lively tune backed up by a flute player. There were several people up on the floor doing a jig. They made their way to a table in the middle of the room. Much to Agnes' annoyance, Alfred ordered a mug of beer.

When the fiddler stopped, a young man jumped up on stage to sing a song. Ingrid's heart stopped. It was Michael. The flute player backed him up as he sang the haunting Irish ballad, *Raglan Road*. As he started singing he noticed Ingrid with her bright eyes rivetted on him, he smiled and continued as he looked right at her.

"Is this your Irish friend?" Alfred asked, noticing the moony look on Ingrid's face.

Ingrid nodded dreamily with her eyes fixed on Michael.

"He's old for Ingrid is he not?" Alfred said to Agnes.

"He looks to be only in his late youth," Agnes remarked. "He's got a beautiful singing voice."

When the song ended, a thunderous round of applause erupted with calls for more.

For his second tune Michael sang a lighthearted Irish love ballad.

When he came to the last refrain he substituted the word Swedish for Irish. Looking directly at Ingrid he smiled and sang:

"Oh she is my love me darlin' one
Her eyes dey sparkle like da sun
I love da ground she walks upon,
me pretty Swedish girl."

Ingrid smiled radiantly at him in turn, but Alfred frowned. He was not impressed at the way the young Irishman was charming his daughter. While a sound of exclamation ran through the crowd upon hearing his substitution, he nonetheless received strong applause. At the end of the song Michael bowed and stepped from the stage.

Alfred excused himself from the others as he spotted Michael go out a side door by the stage. Alfred was able to slip over to the same door without Ingrid noticing. The doorway lead to the mens public washroom and it was there he met Michael.

Michael recognized Alfred form the previous night and the usual mischievous glint in his eyes changed to one of apprehension.

"You are Michael da Irishman," Alfred said evenly.

"Dat I am sir," Michael replied quickly.

"You like, my daughter Ingrid, ya?"

"Indeed so sir," Michael replied. "Wit all due respects sir, she is a very beautiful young lady."

"Do you know dat she is yust fourteen-years-old?" Alfred said.

"Fourteen ye say," Michael's face dropped. "I took her for at least sixteen."

"How old are you?" Alfred asked.

"Nineteen."

"You are old enough to be a man," Alfred said with a calm firmness. "But my Ingrid is not old enough to be a voman."

"I mean yer daughter no harm," Michael replied. "It would be a cold day in hell dat I would, or let anyone else, harm one hair of her braided locks."

"If you respect my daughter," Alfred said. "You vould not give her false hopes. When ve reach Halifax in a day or two you vill never see each udder again. I don't vant Ingrid coming to her new home in Alberta vit a broken heart."

"I can understand what yer sayin' sir," Michael swallowed.

"So if it yust da same vit you, you vill not see my daughter again."

"I will try to avoid her, Mr. Elan. . ."

"Erlander," Alfred corrected him.

Alfred returned to his seat, with the simple explanation that he had gone to the washroom. Ingrid was searching the crowd for a sight of Michael, but he was nowhere to be seen. Michael had left through another door of the washroom and returned to his berth. The Erlander family stayed and watched a few more numbers from the Celtic entertainment, then gathered up Clarence and Astrid from their entertainment and returned to the cabin. Although Ingrid was disappointed that she didn't get to talk to Michael, she had a better night's sleep on a berth to herself. Alfred had earlier obtained the extra mattress and blankets. It was placed on the floor between the other berths and Clarence was assigned to sleep there.

Chapter Five

Ingrid spent a lot of time on the decks the following day, hoping for a chance to meet Michael. As the day wore on and there was no sign of Michael, Ingrid began to relay her thoughts in her ongoing letter to Sigrud.

> *As I told you yesterday I had met Michael, a young Irishman. I understand only a small part of what he says to me, but I know what he says is beautiful. Yesterday he even told me that I was beautiful. Last night I heard him sing, his voice was so wonderful. Though I couldn't understand the words his one song brought me to tears. I have been on deck all day hoping he would pop up and startle me like he always does, but I saw nothing of him. My heart pines for him.*

By late afternoon Ingrid returned to the cabin listless and despondent.

"Are you not feeling well dear?" Agnes said, as she sensed that Ingrid's feelings were down.

"I'm all right," Ingrid sighed. "I'm just bored."

"Your Irish friend didn't come around?" Alfred asked carefully.

"No," Ingrid said in a small voice as she flopped down on her berth.

"What about your, Bokovinian. . , is it, friend?" Agnes asked.

"No, not her either," Ingrid said in an annoyed tone as she rolled over with her back to them.

Alfred smiled quietly to himself. He assumed that Michael had heeded his request.

Later, after supper, when Ingrid announced that she was going up on the bow deck for a while, Alfred did not object. Ingrid however, walked all the way around the outside of the ship in a slow deliberate manner in hopes that Michael would find her. Finally she went she went through the midst of the steerage decks, past the salon.

She stopped by the doorway and listened, to the strange, exotic music that was coming from within. Although she knew that a girl her age shouldn't enter unescorted, Ingrid went in.

The salon was filled mainly with those curious people dressed in dark clothing with the ladies wearing their head covering. She thought of Olga, *'Was it the Bokovinian people's turn to entertain?'* As she looked around, Ingrid spotted Olga and Olga noticed her. Olga smiled and waved for Ingrid to come over. Ingrid came hesitantly over and sat beside Olga. The others around her smiled at the shy uncertain Ingrid.

"*Vitayu*,[1] Ingrid," Olga smiled.

"Hello Olga," Ingrid smiled and asked in Swedish. "What is going on?"

Olga replied in her own language about the entertainment. Ingrid smiled and decided to watch since there was no hope of Olga explaining to her in a way that she could understand.

The music was as enchanting as it was exotic. Two men on stage played mandolins and another a fiddle to a lively beat. Two men who were obviously under the influence of liquor got up and started to dance. They squatted down on their knees with the hands on their hips then kicked their legs out rapidly and they moved around the floor. They bobbed up and down and locked arms, revolving around each other.

The tempo changed and several women got up to dance also to a lively step that was totally alien to Ingrid. They held their hands above their heads as they twirled around. Nonetheless Ingrid found it all highly entertaining. A young man in the crowd got Olga up to dance and another asked Ingrid. Ingrid declined as she had no idea how to do this dance step. He was both drunk and persistent. Ingrid turned and fled from the room barely escaping his clutches. She slammed the door behind her and ran down the hallway Ingrid saw a young man ahead of her in the distance. "Michael, Michael Irish!" she cried out desperately. The young man vanished through a side door.

"Michael," she cried. Ingrid was sure it was him.

"Ingrid," called a firm but gentle voice behind. Ingrid turned to find that it was her father.

"Papa, what are you doing out here?" she gasped.

"What are you doing here, would be more to the point?" Alfred said.

"I was walking down the corridor and I heard strange music from the salon. I looked in. The Bokovinians were in there playing music," Ingrid gasped. " Olga called me in to listen so I did. Then, when they started dancing, I left."

[1] *Vitayu* - Hello

"You were calling this Michael."

"I thought I saw him in the corridor ahead."

"I see," Alfred said. "You shouldn't be prowling around through the ship at night. Not all people on this ship are gentlemen you know."

"Yes Papa," Ingrid said looking down.

"Come let us go out on the bow deck for a few minutes before we go to bed," Alfred said gently, as he put an arm around her.

"Sure, Papa."

Out on deck they looked ahead at the crescent moon on the western horizon. The ship seemed to be heading straight for it.

"It looks like we're sailing to the moon," Ingrid remarked.

"For you it must seem like we're going that far."

"Yeah," Ingrid sighed.

After a long moment Alfred said quietly. "This Michael, the Irishman, you are really fond of him are you not?"

"Yes Papa, very fond."

"I see. How do you come to be so fond of him when you don't speak the same language?"

"Papa, I don't need to know exactly what he says. I can see it in his eyes and feel it in his words. It makes me feel good just to be near him."

"Oh Ingrid, you are so young to feel love. Do you know that in another day or two you will never see him again?"

"I know Papa, I already feel I'll never see him again. I looked for him all day and he never showed."

"Perhaps he is staying away so not to hurt your feelings."

"If I could just see him one more time to say goodbye."

"Possibly you'll get a chance. We probably have another two days of sailing before we reach Halifax. You must however, control your heart, for even if you were a little older there can be no future for you with him. You are each going to a different part of North America, thousands of kilometres apart." Then, with a chuckle, he added, "I guess I should say *miles*."

Ingrid smiled and said, "There is so much to learn in this new life you are taking us to."

"But it will be a future for you. When we are settled in Alberta you will make new friends and probably find the real love of your life."

"Papa, you are so wise."

"Come, my daughter, it is time you went to bed."

The following day, Ingrid was not quite so desperate to see Michael. Though she longed to talk to him one more time, she knew in heart that her father was right. There could be no future for them together. As she sat on the deck Olga came along. Ingrid smiled and invited her to sit.

Olga looked at her with a sad pleading look and said in faltering English. "How you say, sorry last night."

Ingrid smiled as she realized that Olga was trying to apologize for what happened in the salon.

"Don't worry, it is not your fault," Ingrid said in Swedish, with a warm smile, as she stood up. Since neither of them really understood English, Ingrid felt it best to express herself in the best possible way.

Olga looked at her uncomprehendingly, smiled shyly, and said something in her own language. The two of them hugged briefly then sat silently for a long moment.

Finally Ingrid said in faltering English, "You go Canada too?"

"Canada *tak*[2]," Olga replied, then she continued talking in her own tongue.

Realizing that Ingrid had no hope of understanding her, Olga got up to go. Ingrid grabbed her arm and beckoned Olga to stay. Olga sat back down and smiled. "Friend you are." she said.

"Friend, ya," Ingrid smiled radiantly.

Meanwhile as Clarence was exploring amidships and looking for Charlie when a familiar voice said behind him, "Young Clarence is it?"

Clarence turned to find Michael behind him smiling with his broad Irish grin.

"My sister is vondering vhere you are," Clarence said innocently.

"I see dere's nuttin' wrong wit yer English," Michael laughed.

"I've been studying it since before ve left Sweden, and my friend Charlie has been helping me on da ship."

"I see. So how is yer sister doin'?"

"Ingrid? She vonders vhat has happened to you."

"I shouldn't be seein' her again," Michael said gravely. "I don't want to be breakin' her heart."

"Oh," Clarence replied. "Should I tell her I've seen you?"

[2]*tak* - yes

"Tell her dat I wish her well in her new life in Canada. I wish I was goin' dere meself."

"Hello Clarence," Charlie said, coming upon the scene. "I was looking for you."

"And I for you."

"So dis is Charlie is it," Michael grinned.

"Yes, Charlie, this Michael, he is a friend of my sister."

"Pleased to meet you Michael," Charlie replied without expression and without making eye contact. "Come on Clarence, let's go to the stern deck."

"Bye Michael," Clarence said as he turned to go with his friend.

"Does your sister like that mick?" Charlie asked when they were out of earshot.

"Mick! His name is Michael."

"My dad says all Irishmen are micks."

"Why?"

"Because they always cause trouble."

"I don't think Michael is a troublemaker," Clarence said defensively.

At lunch time, Clarence asked his father, "How come English people don't like the Irish?"

"Why do you ask?"

"I was talking to Michael and my friend Charlie came along. Later he called Michael a mick and said Irishmen were troublemakers."

"From what I read in the papers," Alfred said. "The Irish are not very happy being ruled by the English and are pushing for independence for Ireland."

"Why do people of different countries always fight?"

"I don't know. Sweden used to fight with Denmark and Norway, and now we get along. In fact, until two years ago Norway was part of Sweden. The Norwegians wanted to rule themselves, so our government let them go peacefully."

"They almost started a war." Agnes added.

"Yes, Norwegians probably call us something like micks, but our countries get along peacefully now."

"There is an old Norwegian saying," Agnes laughed. "It goes:
Ten thousand Swedes, crawled through the weeds, chased by one Norwegian."

"We can laugh about our differences with the Norwegians or Danes." Alfred added.

"Oh, I understand," Clarence replied as he digested the history lesson along with his lunch.

When they had an opportunity to speak privately Ingrid begged Clarence to tell her all about Michael.

"He asked if you were keeping well?"

"Why doesn't he want to see me again?"

"He said he doesn't want to break your heart."

"He is already breaking it," Ingrid said glumly. "If you see him again, tell him I wish to see him long enough to say goodbye before we reach Canada."

"If I see him again I will tell him," Clarence assured her, as he turned and bolted to find his friend.

That afternoon when Ingrid sat out on the deck reading a magazine she had brought from Sweden, she saw a couple of youngsters come down from the upper decks toward the bow. One was a well-dressed girl of about ten-years-old and the other a boy a few years older. They talked and acted in a manner that suggested they were brother and sister. They looked out over the bow for a few moments then came back along the deck. Ingrid set the magazine down on her lap for a moment losing interest in the article she was reading. A gust of wind caught the magazine taking it out of her hands. She scrambled after it and it blew against the girl on the bow. The girl grabbed it and smiled as she handed it back to Ingrid.

"Tank you much," Ingrid smiled as she took the magazine and went back to her bench.

The girl and presumably her brother came back along side the bench in front of Ingrid. Ingrid noticed that the girl had long ginger-coloured hair and large hazel eyes as she looked at her. She was very pretty and even at her prepubescent age she had very distinctive aristocratic features belonging to someone a few years older.

"Hello," Ingrid said pleasantly.

The girl smiled and said, "Hello," in return. The boy with her grinned awkwardly. Then the girl abruptly sat down beside Ingird, looking at her with an inocent smile. Looking over at the magazine Ingrid held, which was printed in Swedish she said, "Where are you from, that wiriting is different?"

"I from Sveden, you not understand vords," Ingrid laughed.

"I'm from Toronto," the girl stated emphatically.

"Toronto, in Canada ya,"

"Yes," the girl siad. "Are you going to Canada?"

"Go to Canada, ya," Ingrid replied.

"We should get going Ginny," the boy said. He was uninterested intrying to converse with Ingrid.

"Dat you name, Yinny?"

"Yes, my real name is Virginia, but everybody calls me Ginny," the girl stated.

"Yinny is nice name."

A well-dressed man came part way down the stairs and called out to them, "Paul and Ginny come back upstairs at once!"

"Bye." the girl said to Ingrid. Ingrid smiled her beautiful smile.

Although Ingrid didn't understand, the man, apparently their father, said to them as they turned up the stairs, "Now, you two know better than to associate with the people on the lower decks."

Ingrid was left with a strange feeling in regards to the little girl. She then shook her head. The girl was just some rich man's daughter who had wandered down to the steerage decks.

That night Ingrid went to bed again without seeing Michael. She seriously doubted that she would see him again. Again she thought of the girl with the large hazel-coloured eyes.

Mid-morning the following day, the announcement came that they were only two hours from Halifax. *"Everyone disembarking there should get all their belongings in order."* Ever the housewife, Agnes shooed the men out of the cabin so she and her daughters could tidy it up to the perfection in which they had found it. They even pulled the linen from the beds and piled it up ready for the laundry. When the chores were all done and her bags properly packed Ingrid announced she was going to have one last walk around the ship.

"Don't go too far," Agnes said. "It is not that long before we get off."

"I know, Mother."

"She's going to find Michael," Astrid said.

Agnes glanced at Ingrid and she replied. "Yes, I would like to say goodbye to Michael if I can find him."

"Run along dear, and mind the time," Agnes said.

Ingrid was about halfway to the stern when she saw Olga. Olga smiled at the sight of Ingrid.

"Goodbye, Olga," Ingrid said holding out her arms.

"Goodbye," Olga replied, and they embraced for a long moment.

Then, letting go, Olga said, "Go get ready, go." She turned and went back into the crowd.

Ingrid continued her search then finally she spotted Michael. He was along a railing watching the approaching coastline of Nova Scotia, still a thin blue hump on the horizon. He didn't see her approach.

"Michael, Michael Irish," she called.

He turned and smiled, "Ingrid Swedish, yer a welcome sight, but should ye not be wit yer family gettin' ready to disembark?"

"Michael I come, say goodbye," Ingrid fumbled.

"Well goodbye, my bonny Swedish girl," he grinned. "Wishin' ye all da best in Canada."

"And you in Boston," Ingrid replied with tears in her eye.

"Don't cry for da likes of me," Michael said with a brave face. "One day in Canada you'll find a young man who'll cause ye to forget all about da Irish mick ye met on da boat."

"Forget you never, Michael Irish," Ingrid sniffed.

"Aye, I must admit yers is a face I'll not forget either. If only ye were a little older and we were goin' to da same place."

They looked out over the sea for a long moment. The coastline was growing clearer now.

"Best ye be goin' Ingrid, yer family will be waitin'. You'll not want to be left behind."

"Maybe I go to Boston," Ingrid laughed weakly.

"No lass, you'll not want to go to Boston wit da likes of me. Now go to yer family where you'll be safe."

"Goodbye, Michael Irish," Ingrid sniffed.

Michael leaned over and kissed her gently on the lips, "Goodbye Ingrid Swedish, may da good Lord keep ye and bless ye."

In a moment, Michael turned and stepped in amongst the crowd.

Chapter Six

The Erlander family all stood on deck and watched the city of Halifax appear to grow steadily larger as the ship drew toward the docks. Smaller vessels that were in the harbour area seemed to scurry out of the way of the great ocean liner.

Upon docking, the bullhorn announced that all passengers disembarking who were not Canadian citizens or British subjects were to proceed to Gate Seven. As they moved down the gangplank, Ingrid turned and looked back. She could see Michael waving and she waved back. He then blew her a kiss before vanishing into the crowd on board.

The Erlander family along with dozens of other immigrants made their way through Gate Seven. Here they queued up in front of the wickets of customs officials who checked their passports and related documents.

"Stay close by," Alfred said to Clarence. "If I have trouble understanding the customs officer you can help me."

When it was Alfred's turn he presented both his and Agnes's passport. The customs officer looked at them and said, "Sweden, eh?"

"Ya," Alfred said hopefully.

"So you are Alfred Erlander, this is your wife Agnes, and these are your children, Ingrid, Clarence and Astrid."

"Ya."

"Your medical papers are in order, I presume?"

"Ya," Alfred said as he handed over the documents to show that his family had a clean bill of health and proper vaccinations.

"Are you applying as landed immigrants?"

"Ya."

"What part of Canada are you going to?"

"Alberta."

"Ah, a way out west. A lot of Scandinavians are going out there. What do you plan to do out there?"

"I vant to start a sawmill and lumbering business."

"Well, there is certainly lots of bush out there."

The customs officer stamped their passports and medical forms, then let them through the gate so they were now officially on Canadian soil. Alfred also signed a document verifying himself and family as landed immigrants.

When they retrieved their luggage, there were customs officers watching who did random checks asking people to open their luggage. Fortunately the Erlander family avoided this ordeal. Alfred went to a banking wicket to change his money into Canadian currency.

"Papa, can I have some money to post a letter to Sigrud?" Ingrid asked.

"Certainly my dear," Alfred replied handing her a twenty-five cent piece. Ingrid purchased a stamp and came back with a handful of change.

"Keep it," Alfred said. "When we get going on the train you can bring it out and we'll all try to figure out the value of the various Canadian coins."

Alfred and his family made their way to the railway station barely in time to catch the train to Montreal. Although it was an overnight journey, there were only four coach seats available. Fortunately they were together so the front two could be turned around to face the rear two. This allowed them to put their feet up on the opposing seat. This, together with being able to tilt the seat back slightly, would allow some comfort for the night, though it would be a far cry from a ship's berth.

Ingrid pulled out the change left over from the postage and began to examine it. The money looked as complicated as everything else in this new land. Clarence, who seemed to be a fountain of knowledge explained them to her. "Remember that twenty-five cent pieces are called quarters, ten cent pieces are called dimes, five cent pieces are called nickels, and the coppers are called pennies."

Alfred took some dollar bills out of his wallet for discussion purposes also.

The train left Halifax in the late afternoon and the Erlanders were afforded a view of the picturesque maritime countryside as the train chugged on. While the puffing of the locomotive sounded the same as those back home, the whistle had a much louder and lower-pitched sound. Always one to be on the prowl, Clarence decided to explore the train, but soon found he was not allowed in the rear part of the train beyond the dining car where the first and second class passengers were housed. Thus, the train was much less interesting to explore than the ship as they were so confined.

It was dark by the time they reached the Appalachian forests of New Brunswick and the lights in the coach were dimmed. Ingrid leaned over against the window and Astrid leaned against her as she attempted to get some sleep In the seat facing her, Alfred leaned against the window with Agnes leaning against him. Clarence first sat on aisle side of, first his parent's seat then on his sisters seat. His extreme uneasiness brought frequent grumbles from the others. Although the 'clickity-clack' of the train wheels against the rail joints and the gentle swaying motion of the coach had a tranquillizing effect, the discomfort of sitting nearly upright in cramped conditions virtually nullified the effect. Ingrid passed the night thinking about Michael, the soft kiss on her lips, his pleasing voice and strange words. She also thought of Olga and curiously the pretty little girl named Ginny. Ingrid could not fathom why this girl from the upper decks left such a strong impression on her. Finally she thought of Sigrud, but Sigrud seemed so very far away and it seemed so long ago since she saw her.

When daylight returned, the tired, sleep-deprived Erlander family could again look out at the countryside. They were running parallel to a broad river and passing through an endless array of long narrow farms.

"Are we in Alberta yet?" Astrid asked innocently.

"We have a long, long ways to go yet before we reach Alberta," Alfred said gruffly.

"I believe we are in Quebec," Clarence stated. He pulled out his atlas and checked. "And this river beside us is the St. Lawrence." He pointed to the map of Canada that he had open. "Do you know that if we got off in this part of Canada we would have to learn to speak French?"

"Oh Clarence," Ingrid grumbled irritably. "Must we always have a geography lesson? I almost feel like we're in a classroom or something."

"Did you say we change trains at Montreal?" Agnes said to Alfred.

"Yes, we catch the transcontinental Grand Trunk there."

"Then how long to reach Alberta?"

"About three days and nights."

"Oh no," Ingrid groaned. "Does this mean we have to sleep upright in the seats for three more nights?"

"When we get to Montreal, I'll see if we can get berths." Alfred assured her.

"Thank you dear," Agnes replied. "That would be much appreciated."

Ingrid tried to start another letter to Sigrud but soon found that she was too tired and irritable to think clearly.

They arrived at Montreal in the early afternoon. Once again their baggage had to be collected and moved to another train. Alfred secured four Pullman berths in a block, and the higher priced fare included their meals. The block of berths allowed them their own little semi private area of the train, with two double-seats facing each other on opposite sides of the car. Since Alfred and Agnes sat together on one seat, each of the children had their own seat.

They left Montreal in the early evening just in time for the first call to the dining car.

Later that evening, when the berths were made up, Alfred and Agnes together took one lower berth. Ingrid and Clarence moved to claim the other lower one simultaneously, while Astrid was happy to take the berth above her parents.

"I want the bottom one," Clarence argued as Ingrid moved to the inside and attempted to push him out.

"That will be enough, you two," Alfred said firmly. "I think Ingrid should have the bottom one since she's a lady."

"What's that got to do with it?" Clarence continued.

"You're a strong young man, you can climb up into the top berth."

"It's not fair. She always gets her way."

"That will be enough, Ingrid gets the bottom one," Alfred said resolutely. "We're all tired and need sleep desperately."

"Oh all right, " Clarence grumbled, as he made a face at Ingrid. He then turned and climbed the ladder into the upper berth.

Ingrid found the Pullman berths wider than those on the ship. She nestled down into the covers and the rocking motion of the train soon put her to sleep.

The entire family enjoyed a good night's sleep with Astrid and Clarence being the first to awaken. They poked their heads out through the curtains and spoke in loud whispers bringing grumbling from their parents and Ingrid. They could look up and down the length of the whole railway car and soon saw several other heads, children like themselves, poking out with similar curiosity. It was daylight when Ingrid awoke. She raised up in bed and looked out the window. Outside appeared to be an endless forest of small scraggly-looking evergreens that seemed to be growing out of bare rock. There didn't seem to be soil anywhere, just bare rock. The scenery still remained unchanged by the time they all went to the dining car for breakfast.

"Is this where you are going to put up your sawmill, Papa?" Astrid asked.

"No, I'm afraid I wouldn't get much timber out of this forest," Alfred laughed.

"Where are we, or dare I ask?" Ingrid said, looking at Clarence and fully expecting another geography lesson.

"Northern Ontario I think," he said lamely.

That afternoon Ingrid began her fourth letter to Sigrud.

April 22, 1910
Dear Sigrud,
We arrived in Canada two days ago and have been travelling steadily by train ever since. Papa says we will be travelling for at least two more days before we reach our destination. It is hard to believe how huge Canada really is. We have been travelling all day across a huge rock pile called the Canadian Shield. There is nothing to see outside except bare rocks and small trees growing out of them. I have never seen such desolation.

The monotony of this barren landscape, broken only by the occasional pristine lake, flashed past them all day as the train headed westward. It was still with them the next morning and continued till midday until they came abruptly to a treeless plain just before the great city of Winnipeg. The train stopped here for an hour or so and a large number of passengers got off, and an equally large number got on. Nearly everyone in their car were among those to disembark and only a few came into the car to claim the vacated seats. Among these was a young woman carrying a baby in her arms.

When the train left Winnipeg, the panorama offered a new type of monotony which was a vast expanse of endless plain virtually void of trees and alternating between rolling hills and great flat expanses.

"This must be what they call *prairie*." Clarence remarked as he looked out at the countryside going past him.

"At least people seem to live here," Ingrid remarked as the train passed several farms and a couple of towns within the space of an hour.

"Yes, just about anything is better than the Canadian Shield," Agnes added.

During the third day, as the train crossed Saskatchewan and after a time of looking out the window, Agnes said to Alfred. "Maybe we should have got off at the Canadian Shield, there is no timber here."

"There will be timber in Alberta. Gunner says there is lots of timber where he lives."

They were somewhere west of Saskatoon when Alfred looked out the window and noticed the occasional clump of small trees sprouting up out of the prairie. "See the bush is starting already," he commented confidently.

"Yes dear," Agnes replied.

As the Erlander family rode comfortably in their Pullman seats, far ahead of them the engineer was commenting to the fireman about how much time they had made as the train was travelling at about seventy-miles-per-hour. Then as the train came around a curve he noticed that the lantern on top of a siding switch, and its target, were red. His worst nightmare just came true.

"Oh My God, the switch is reversed!" he cried in terror, as he pulled the brake lever hard, and threw back the reverse lever. The fireman and brakeman looked out their side of the locomotive, their eyes also wide with panic. The locomotive squealed in protest at the enormous strain being applied in trying to suddenly reverse the forward momentum of several thousand tons of rolling steel. The locomotive resisted being thrown into reverse and a steam line broke from the strain, cancelling the dynamic braking effect of applying reverse. The wheels on all the cars locked up with full brake pressure and the train skidded helplessly forward amid a shower of sparks caused by the wheels sliding on the rails. The engineer pulled the whistle chain, clutching it for dear life, as to alert the countryside of the impending disaster.

When the locomotive reached the open switch it was still going much too fast to take the sharp turn into the siding. The forward momentum threw the locomotive off the rails and onto its side in a mighty crash. The tender was flipped on top of it, filling the cab with coal. There was a series of cascading crashes as the baggage cars and forward coaches folded up against each other like parts of a pocket ruler and piled up with ends sticking up in every direction. The people inside the forward coaches were, along with their hand luggage, tossed about like leaves in a high wind, crashing into each other and the seats amid terrified screams. The dining car didn't tip over but it jumped off the rails bringing it to an abrupt halt. Tableware flew off the tables amid the reverberating crash of smashing glass and earthenware, while pots of food flew off the stoves spilling all over. One of the cooks shrieked in agony as a pot of hot soup was spilled all over one side of his body.

As the train came to an abrupt stop, Ingrid and Astrid, who were sitting in the forward facing seats, were hurled against the opposing seats. Ingrid found herself sprawled on top of Clarence and Astrid crashed headlong into Alfred. Fortunately their car was near the rear of the train and was not derailed.

"Papa, Papa, what happened?" Astrid cried The others were too stunned to comment although the horrendous crash of coaches piling up ahead of them could still be heard. A baby, probably belonging to the woman from Winnipeg, began crying loudly, while the adults throughout the car sat in stunned silence.

A porter ran frantically through the cars telling everyone to remain calm and stay in their seats. Although visibly shaken, the porter's only comment was, "We've had a derailment."

The lady from Winnipeg complained of a broken arm, and the porter assured her that medical help was on the way. Her problem was multiplied with the howling infant that she struggled to hold in her arms. It had been rudely awakened when it flew from her arms as the car stopped and landed on the seat facing her. She had broken her arm trying to protect the infant as she nearly landed on top of it.

"Can we go see?" Clarence asked anxiously.

"No!" Alfred said emphatically. "There is danger out there and people are probably hurt. We best stay here like the porter says."

"I just want to go to the end of the car and look out the vestibule," Clarence insisted.

"Don't go outside," Alfred reminded him as Clarence got up.

"I'm just going to the end of the car and back," Clarence assured him.

"I think I'll stretch my legs too," Ingrid said as she also rose from her seat. "I'll keep an eye on Clarence." Clarence went straight to the front of the car and out into the vestibule so he could more easily witness the events outside. Ingrid started to follow him to make sure Clarence didn't disobey his father, but as she passed the lady with the howling infant she turned toward the lady. She could see the woman was in pain as she held the infant while still trying to comfort the broken arm.

With a feeling of great sympathy Ingrid spoke to the woman. She extended her arms, saying, " Hold baby, ya. You hurt."

The woman smiled gratefully and allowed Ingrid to take the baby from her. Ingrid sat on the facing seat cooing at the baby.

"What's your name?" the woman asked.

"Ingrid. Vhat baby name?"

"Edward."

Clarence came by looking downcast as one of the porters had told him to go back into the car.

"Dis brodder," Ingrid smiled.

"Hello," the woman smiled.

"Clarence," he replied. "Vhat happened to your arm?" He noticed the woman holding her arm tenderly.

"I think I broke it."

Ingrid said to Clarence in Swedish, "Tell Mom and Papa that I am helping this lady with the broken arm and I need Mom to talk to this lady in English for me."

As Clarence turned to do the task, Ingrid noticed the perplexed look in the woman's eyes.

"I not talk English," Ingrid added as she gently rocked the baby causing it to settle down .

"It is alright." the woman assured her. "You are a great help to me."

She struggled with one arm to dig around in her handbag finally producing a baby bottle. She handed the bottle, half-full of warm milk, to Ingrid.

The baby seemed comforted with the bottle in its mouth and snugly tucked in the crook of Ingrid's arm.

Agnes appeared. She became curious when Clarence told her that Ingrid was caring for someone's baby.

"I see you have found a baby to hold," Agnes laughed as she spoke to Ingrid.

"This lady is hurt, and I am helping look after her baby," Ingrid replied. "And since you speak English better than me, you can explain that I want to help her."

"Hello," Agnes said pleasantly to the woman. "I am Ingrid's mudder, I'm sorry dat my English is not good eder, but ve are from Sveden. Ingrid vants to help you vit da baby. She says you are hurt."

"Yes, I think I have a broken arm," the woman replied with a painful smile. "By the way, my name is Flora McDonald. I am most grateful of your daughter's kindness. Please tell her, she is more than welcome to help me with the baby."

Agnes translated to Ingrid and Ingrid smiled and struggled to say *Mrs. McDonald*.

"Tell her to call me *Flora*," Flora laughed. "It is easier for her and it is not disrespectful."

Ingrid smiled and said Flora with much less difficulty.

"Your daughter is very beautiful," Flora said to Agnes. "And a perfect mother."

Ingrid stayed with Flora for the rest of the time they waited at the train wreck caring for little Edward. At one point she event brought the infant back to her family. Astrid also made a fuss over the baby and briefly held it.

Agnes went forward to Flora's seat and invited her to sit with the Erlanders.

Flora reluctantly accepted as she felt she would be imposing. Agnes however, insisted.

"So vhere are you going to?" Alfred asked Flora, as she sat on the seat facing them.

"Edmonton. I live there," Flora replied. "We were down at Winnipeg visiting my mother, when we ended up in this mess."

"Isn't dis yust terrible?" Agnes added.

"So where are you folks going?" Flora asked.

"Ve are going to a place called River Bend, I tink is vest of Edmonton, Alberta," Alfred said.

"My husband vants to start up a sawmill," Agnes added.

"What a coincidence," Flora laughed. "My husband owns McDonald Lumber in Edmonton. Maybe he will buy lumber from you."

"Maybe so," Alfred said.

"What is your full name?" Flora asked. "I'll tell him about you." She struggled to get a pencil and paper from her purse. Agnes helped her and gave them to Alfred.

"Alfred Erlander," he smiled as he wrote his name down. "River Bend, Alberta."

He gave the notepad and pencil to Agnes, who then placed it back in Flora's purse.

Clarence and Astrid watched events unfolding outside. They saw horses and wagons converge on the scene. Some of the wagons carried water tanks, apparently from the local fire department. Several North West Mounted Police officers with their snap-rim Stetsons arrived on horseback to take charge of the situation. Also from their windows the Erlander family could see people, apparently passengers from the forward cars, coming out. Many were limping and bleeding, others wailing, and others were being carried on stretchers or helped along by the uninjured. Some were laid out on the ground and covered completely with blankets.

"Are those people being covered up, dead?" Clarence asked innocently.

"Yes, Clarence," Alfred said quietly.

"Try not to look," Agnes advised.

Clarence was too fascinated as to what was happening outside to be frightened of the horror of it all. Astrid turned away from the window with the mention of dead people being outside. Ingrid's attention was totally focussed on the baby.

'*Thank God we weren't in the coaches on this leg of the journey,*' Alfred thought.

After a time, the porter came by again and various people in the car bombarded him with questions.

"Another locomotive is coming, to pull us back to Saskatoon, and to transport the injured," he said assuredly. "You may have to double-up as we will need space in the usable cars to transport the passengers from the coaches."

"Ve can all sit togedder on dis side," Alfred said.

Flora gave up her seat as she was the only one in that section. The entire Erlander family and Flora crowded into one section. Flora Ingrid and Astrid sat on one seat while Alfred Agnes and Clarence sat facing them. This allowed for eight more passengers. Clarence helped Flora fetch her remaining hand luggage.

The whistle of an approaching train from the rear could be heard. This followed with a gentle thud of it being coupled to the cars still on the rails. Teams of people went busily by the windows helping the badly injured into the extra cars brought with the locomotive. The uninjured and slightly injured were placed in those cars of the original train that were still usable. Three members of a family with bloodstained clothing and visible scrapes on their bodies took the seat vacated by the Erlander family. They sat, staring straight ahead, too stunned to be fully aware of their surroundings.

Soon the train was on its way heading eastward to Saskatoon. The wheels beneath them banged noisily as nearly all of them had flat spots from skidding on the rails.

Once in Saskatoon, the uninjured passengers were given dinner at a hotel at railway expense and rooms for the night. As Flora was taken to the hospital to have her arm attended to, The Erlanders offered to care for her baby.

By morning the luggage, from the wreck, that could be salvaged was brought to Saskatoon station for the passengers to reclaim, The Erlander family was pleased to discover that none of their luggage was lost, although some of their suitcases had been battered and one was now bound together with twine. It had sprung open and the contents had been hastily stuffed back inside. Those passengers able to travel were to be put on a special train that was to be rerouted over the Canadian Northern line to get around the derailment.

"I had better look for Flora's luggage too," Alfred said, after he finished reclaiming the their family luggage. "She will not be able to pick through all this stuff with a broken arm."

"Good idea," Agnes replied. "We must get her baby back to her though." She looked over at Ingrid who was holding the baby as if it was her own. With a laugh she added, "Before Ingrid kidnaps it."

"There's Mommy now," Ingrid said as she saw Flora coming toward them with her arm in a sling.

"How's my little baby," Flora said as she attempted to take the child in one arm. Ingrid supported her effort as Flora held the infant with one arm and smothered it with kisses.

"You coming on train?" Ingrid asked.

"Yes. I was lucky, I only had a minor fracture. But I'll have a hard time retrieving my luggage."

"Papa get bags."

Alfred had gathered up what he could find of Flora's luggage and put it beside that of his family as Flora and Ingrid approached.

"Thank you very much, Alfred," Flora smiled gratefully. As she looked over her luggage she said, "There is one suitcase missing."

"Dat's all dere is vit your name on it," Alfred said with a concerned look. "Dey say some got destroyed in da wreck."

"I can have my husband look into it when we get back to Edmonton." Flora sighed. "I wired him to tell him of my predicament. My mother-in-law will help me with the baby until my arm mends, though I am tempted to steal your daughter."

As the luggage was carted away to the baggage cars, the others boarded the train. Flora agreed to take a seat in the same block as the Erlanders.

"I'm afraid to go on the train again," Ingrid said. "It might crash."

"We must get on the train to get to our destination," Alfred said calmly. "Accidents like train wrecks don't happen often and even if we ride the train many more times in our lifetime, we'll probably never see another wreck."

"I sure hope not," Agnes chimed in.

The train continued on to Edmonton without incident, reaching the Alberta city by midday. Ingrid followed Flora off the train, carrying the baby. Clarence came behind with Flora's hand luggage. Flora's husband and mother-in-law were there to greet them. Flora introduced Ingrid to her family amid much praise for Ingrid's kindness and her mother-in-law smiled greetings. Flora explained that Ingrid could not speak English.

Finally she turned to Ingrid and smiled, "Edward's grandma will look after him now, she nodded toward her mother-in-law, "though I am tempted to hire you as a maid." Ingrid smiled uncertainly, but sensing what Flora had said, she kissed the infant with a teary smile and handed him over to his grandmother.

"I will never forget your kindness," Flora said as she hugged Ingrid.

The conductor cried, "All aboard!" Ingrid and Clarence stepped into the vestibule and turned to wave at the McDonalds. They waved back.

After the train had left Edmonton, the Erlander family decided to spend some time in the recreation car. This car had large soft seats and a partitioned off area where the men could sit and consume spirits. Alfred elected to go here as he had a craving for a glass of beer. Agnes and the girls sat in the main area while Clarence continued to prowl the train. A small pleasant-looking woman came along and sat at chair near Agnes. She smiled briefly upon eye contact with Agnes then pulled some knitting out of a bag and began to work at it.

"Are you knitting a pair of socks?" Agnes asked both for the sake of conversation and to practise her English.

"Aye," the woman replied. "I'm knittin' them for my man."

"Your husband?"

"Well, I hope tae be his wife," she laughed.

"Are you going far?" Agnes asked.

"Just ae wee ways further,." she said. "Tae ae place called Mornin' Glory. Alistair is waitin' for me there. Thah's thae man who sent for me tae be his wife."

"I see, you are a mail-order bride den?"

"Aye sort ae, although Alistair and I knew each other in thae Old Country."

"You Irish?" Ingrid interjected. She sensed the woman's manner of speaking to be similar to that of Michael.

"Nay lassie, "I'm Scottish."

"Dis is my daughter Ingrid." Agnes said. "I am Agnes and the udder girl is my daughter Astrid."

"Please tae meet ya's," the woman smiled. "My name is Effie. Is this yer family?"

"No my husband is in da lounge drinking beer and I have a son prowling da train somevhere."

"How far are ye going?"

"I tink Alfred, dat's my husband, said ve are going to River Bend. He vants to start a sawmill."

"By yer names and manner ae speakin', are ye Scandinavians?"

"Ya, ve came from Sveden. Vere you in da wreck?"

"Wreck, whah wreck?"

"Da train yumped da tracks somevere in Saskatchewan and ve vere lucky ve didn't get killed."

"I came on thae Canadian Pacific by way ae Calgary," Effie said. "Come tae think of it. I thought I heard some folk talkin' about ae train wreck in Saskatchewan. Ae lot ae folk got killed."

"Ya, ve vere right in da middle of it."

"Ach whah ae terrible thing tae witness. I trust ye all survived in good form."

"Ya, it makes von vonder if dey should ride da train again."

"Aye."

Ingrid grew disinterested in the conversation which she could scarcely understand and began to thumb through a magazine on a side table. It was even more incomprehensible. While the alphabet was the same, the words were totally alien. Although Clarence was always finding similarities between some Swedish words and their English equivalent, Ingrid could see no relationship. Ingrid was glad they were going to be living among other Swedish settlers when they reached their destination. She might not have to learn English at all. She probably would have learned to speak the language had she been around Michael longer, if only to be able to speak to him, she doubted she would ever learn how to read it.

Ingrid looked out the window and saw a long silvery lake come into view. A porter appeared and announced that Morning Glory was the next stop.

"Well, you'll have tae excuse me," Effie said. "This is where I get off tae meet my appointment wi matrimony."

"Vell, congratulations," Agnes said. "Maybe ve vill meet again. I tink dat River Bend is not far avay."

"It was ae pleasure meetin' ye, and I hope all finds ye well."

Clarence appeared in time to hear Effie's farewell. "Is she Irish?" he asked.

"Is this yer young laddie?" Effie said.

"Ya, dis is Clarence. Clarence, dis is Effie. She is Scottish not Irish."

Effie chuckled and replied, "I suppose our way ae speakin' is similar. It's better tae be called Irish than English."

"Vhy don't da udder British people like da English?" Clarence wondered.

"It's ae long story. Ae long sad story."

The train began to slow down and Effie hastily said, "Well, *goodbye thee noo.*"

"Goodbye Effie," Agnes replied. Ingrid also smiled and said goodbye.

The train squealed to a halt in front of Morning Glory station. Agnes observed two men on the platform. One wore a pastor's collar and the other a suit. The man in the suit seemed quite nervous. '*It must be Alistair,*' Agnes thought. She wondered if the wedding ceremony was going to be performed right on the station platform.

The train was barely underway, when the porter again appeared. He announced River Bend as the next stop.

Chapter Seven

As they stood on the platform at River Bend station and watched the train pull away, the Erlander family felt both the relief that they were at the end of their journey and apprehension about the unknown that faced them. All their worldly possessions seemed to be in the pile of luggage on the station truck.

"So, we're finally at the end of our journey," Ingrid remarked.

"We won't have to worry about any more train wrecks," Astrid added.

"As long as we were travelling though, we had some security such as our meals and lodgings. So now what are we going to do, Alfred?" Agnes wondered.

"I will go in and see if Gunner has been here," Alfred said. As it was a warm afternoon the others settled on the bench in front of the station.

"At least we have some civilization," Agnes remarked as they looked around.

In front of them they could see a sprawling village of several dozen houses and shops. Some buildings were made of logs while others were frame. The streets were dirt tracks without street lamps. There were a few horse-drawn wagons and buggies along the main street. Also on the main street was a large two-storey building that looked like a hotel. In the background was a tipple, a large slag pile and the pithead machinery, all indicating an underground coal mine.

"Has Gunner Elofson been here looking for me?" Alfred asked the station agent.

"Who are you?"

"I am Alfred Erlander. Gunner Elofson vas expecting me."

"Come to think of it, there was another Swede in here a couple of days ago. What did you say your name was?"

"Alfred Erlander."

"Yes, I believe he asked if an Alfred and family had arrived yet. He asked questions like how it would take the train to come from down east. Then we heard about the wreck."

"Ve vere in it."

"Oh My God! Were any of your family injured?"

"No, ve vere lucky. A lot of people vere killed."

"That must have been some experience."

"Ya, I don't vant to see anudder train wreck," Alfred said. "So Gunner didn't say vhen he vould be back."

"I have no idea," the agent shrugged Then as he heard the voices of Alfred's children, he added in a more compassionate tone, "No doubt you are looking for a place for you and your family to stay till he comes back."

"Ya, I don't tink ve vould like to sleep outside dis time of year."

The agent laughed and said, "Why don't you and your family go down to the Immigrant Hall? That's that big building that looks like a hotel."

"Immigrant Hall?"

"Yes, it is a hostel for new arrivals. People like you can stay there temporarily until you get established. It's a lot cheaper than staying in the real hotel."

"Tank you, ve vill go dere. Can ve leave our luggage here?"

"No problem, your luggage will be safe in the storeroom until you're ready to pick it up."

"Tank you."

The Erlander family walked down the wooden sidewalk on the main street toward the Immigrant Hall. They felt a little more secure as they passed a general store, a post office, and a barbershop along the way. Clarence identified a doctor's office across the street.

"They have a doctor away out here?" Agnes said. "Maybe we are not so far from civilization after all."

"I think they have doctor because there is a mine here," Alfred remarked.

"Can I help you?" the clerk at the main desk of the immigrant hall asked as the bedraggled-looking Erlander family approached the front desk.

"Ya, my name is Alfred Erlander and dis is my family. Ve need a place to stay and someting to eat."

"You can stay her for up to a week at twenty-five cents a night plus supper and breakfast. After that you must move on. This is a hostel for people like you who need a temporary place. We also have an office where you can file a homestead claim, or purchase land without having to go all the way to Edmonton."

"Ve vill be staying only until our friend Gunner Elofson comes for us."

"Gunner Elofson, he's another Swedish fellow, is he not?"

"Ya."

"He was here the other day looking for an Alfred. What did you say your name was?"

"Alfred Erlander."

"Yes, I guess it was you that he was looking for." The clerk looked at the ledger and said, "We have one room with two three-quarter beds in it." Then looking at the weary-looking Erlander family he added. "We can probably get a folding cot for your son. I hope you don't mind the crowding."

"Ve are used to it. Ve all slept in von room bot on da ship and on da train."

"There are baths down the hall. I'll arrange for the ladies to get their baths first."

"Tank you very much," Agnes said. "Ve haven't had a bat since ve got off da ship."

"Supper will be between six and seven in the diner."

The women each had time for a much appreciated bath before supper and they all went to the hostel diner for their supper. Supper consisted of potatoes, beans, salt pork and a small slice of bread without butter. For drinks they had a choice of coffee or water. The meal was simple but very filling. That evening after the men had their turn at the bath all settled down to a good night's sleep.

Breakfast was an oatmeal gruel with which they were allotted a small quantity of brown sugar for flavour. This meal also came with a slice of bread and coffee. There were several people in at breakfast and a babble of several different languages filled the room. Alfred identified Finns, Germans and Norwegians among them.

Alfred commented, "I hope there are lots of Finns in the area. They are expert loggers and mill hands."

"Finns are wild and crazy people," Agnes grunted. "All they do is drink and fight."

"They are good in the bush. If you stay out of their way when they go to town, you'll have no trouble with them," Alfred replied.

After breakfast Agnes and the girls spent their time visiting the various shops while Alfred and Clarence went to the station and back keeping an eye out for Gunner Elofson. They even went to the mine area and briefly watched the pithead machinery haul up loads of coal and dump it into railway cars.

"Would you like to be a miner, Papa?" Clarence asked.

"No thank you," Alfred replied. "Crawling around down in some dark hole breathing coal dust, or to risk getting buried alive is not for me."

"Why do people do it?"

"Some people don't mind working in tunnels and the pay is usually good. Anyway, we should head back in case Gunner shows up."

As they came back down the main street, they spotted a young man driving a team of horses that were pulling a high-wheeled lumber wagon. He wore a workman's cap and he looked vaguely familiar to Alfred. The young man driving the team noticed Alfred studying him and stopped.

"Are you Alfred Erlander?" he said in English.

"Ya, did Gunner Elofson send you?" Alfred replied in English.

"Ya, I am his son Lars."

"Lars Elofson!" Alfred exclaimed. "You vere yust a boy vhen you left Sveden."

"Ya, dat vas eight years ago."

"Clarence, go find da odders," Alfred said excitedly. "So vhat is your plan for us?"

"I am to take your family out to our place, Dad built a cabin for you. From dere you can plan your future. Dere is plenty of land near our homestead vit lots of timber."

Clarence and the rest of the family came down the street to where Alfred was standing. Lars stared dumbfounded at the sight of Ingrid. He was totally captivated by her graceful beauty with her large bright violet eyes and blonde hair done up in braids.

Ingrid was aware that he was staring after her and she felt uncomfortable.

Alfred introduced his family in English but Agnes asked Lars if he could speak Swedish.

"Yes I can, Mom and Dad still speak Swedish a lot at home," Lars replied in Swedish.

"We are all trying to speak English, but it is easier to talk in Swedish. Neither of the girls can speak English," Alfred replied.

"We can speak Swedish if you like but the children will have to learn English in school. Meanwhile let us get your things so we can head out. We have a seven mile trip ahead of us."

"Seven miles," Clarence muttered. He did a calculation to translate into kilometres.

"Everything is miles and feet, or pounds and ounces," Lars said. "If you talk about kilometres no one will know what you are talking about."

The Erlander family gathered their belongings from the immigrant hostel and the station, piling their luggage into the box of the wagon.

"Maybe the girls would like to ride beside me," Lars said, looking at Ingrid. "The seat has springs, and it won't be so rough."

"I'll ride back here," Ingrid said curtly as she sat on a steamer trunk. Astrid sat down beside her. A disappointed look swept across Lars' face as Agnes and Alfred climbed on to the seat beside him.

They set out on a trail that meandered through the bush, snaking from one ridge to another in an effort to avoid crossing any swamps. Alfred was busy casting calculating eyes on every large tree they passed by.

"This country is a logger's paradise," he remarked as he looked around. "There seems to be no limit to the amount of lumber I can make, once I got my sawmill set up."

"Well, dear, it looks your dream is going to come true," Agnes replied.

"Yes, there are plenty of big trees around," Lars added.

As they penetrated further into the vast aspen forest, punctuated by the occasional stately spruce, the passengers in the wagon found a new annoyance.

"Ouch!" Astrid exclaimed as she swatted a tiny insect on her arm. She swatted another. Soon they were all swatting.

"Mosquitoes," Lars commented dryly as he noticed the plight of the Erlander family. "If they get too bad we may have to skin a black poplar tree. If you rub the sap on your arms it will usually keep them away."

"Your father never told us about mosquitoes," Alfred grumbled.

"He probably didn't want to scare you away," Lars laughed. He turned and said, "Are the mosquitoes bothering you back there, Ingrid?"

"I'm doing fine," Ingrid assured him with an indifferent tone.

They came down a steep hill, so steep that it made everyone lean backwards, at the bottom of which was a huge mudhole. As they reached the mud hole, Lars slapped the reins on the horse to goad them through the mire. The horses ploughed into the murky water with a great splash that showered everyone on board with black sticky mud. The wagon soon followed, sinking to the hubs of the wheels in the oozing black muck..

"The water is coming in!" Astrid cried as black soupy water began to seep in between the floorboards.

Lars continued to slap the reins and yell while urging the horses forward. Once on dry land the horses easily pulled the wagon out of the muck with a great slurping sound. They would cross several more mud holes in the course of their journey but none were as severe as that first one.

Observing that they were generally heading east, Alfred asked, "Are we heading back towards that last place, Morning. . ?"

"Morning Glory. Yes we live only about five miles from there."

"Why didn't we get off at that station? Our wagon journey would have been much shorter," Agnes wondered.

"Dad probably told you to go to River Bend because there would have been nowhere for you to stay at Morning Glory, if we were not at the station to meet you."

"We met a Scottish woman on the train who got off there," Agnes said.

"That must be Alistair's bride," Lars chuckled.

"Who is Alistair?"

"He has the Morning Glory General Store. It used to be a trading post but he bought it and turned it into a store."

"Is that all there is in Morning Glory, a store?"

"That's all, but there is getting to be a fair number of settlers around there so it will probably get bigger."

They passed two other homesteads during their torturous journey through the forest before the wagon turned into the farmstead of Gunner Elofson.

"So this is your father's homestead," Alfred said.

"It's a full-fledged farm now," Lars said proudly. "Dad proved it up last year and now has the deed. I have a homestead just across the way I hope to have proved in a year or two." He pointed to a cleared patch on the opposite side of the road. He glanced back at Ingrid but she ignored him.

As they approached a large two-storey house built of logs a barking dog came out to greet them. The door opened and a woman appeared. Several children of various sizes followed her out.

"I finally found the Erlanders," Lars announced.

Lars brought the horses to a halt and jumped off the wagon to come around and help the girls climb down. As he helped Astrid off the wagon Ingrid climbed off by herself, much to his disappointment. Alfred helped Agnes down.

"It's good to be on solid ground again after bouncing around in that wagon," she remarked when she was firmly on the ground. Then turning to their hosts she cried, "Myrtle Elofson!"

"Agnes Erlander!" Myrtle exclaimed, "you haven't changed at all over the years." They hugged for a moment.

Then Agnes drew back and said, "Do you remember my daughters are Astrid and Ingrid, and my son is Clarence?"

"Pleased to meet you. You were just little and Astrid was a baby when we last saw you. You have already met Lars, and my other children from oldest to youngest are Signe, Elfin, Albert, Sylvia, and Dag. Come right in and I will make some coffee."

"They have all grown so much," Agnes said as she followed Myrtle into the house.

"Alfred Erlander," called a male voice from behind them. They all turned and a man came toward them.

"Gunner Elofson!" Alfred cried extending his hand. "It has been a long time."

"About eight years," Gunner said clasping it. "And this is your family?"

Alfred introduced them and they all went inside for coffee. As they settled on homemade chairs, around a large kitchen table, Gunner remarked. "What did I tell you Alf? There is more timber here than you will know what to do with."

"Yes, I see. I will be able to saw lumber for the rest of my life and still not run out of timber. What kind of wood do they have here?"

"Mostly aspen, which they call white poplar, spruce, and some pine.

If you look real hard you can find birch trees big enough to make lumber. The biggest demand is for the conifer trees but they use aspen for boards."

"I see."

"So, were you people in that train wreck in Saskatchewan?" Myrtle asked.

"Yes, it was terrible," Agnes said with a pained look. "There were injured people and dead bodies everywhere."

"We were worried you might have been in on it. We heard there were about fifty people killed."

"We were lucky that I had enough money to get berths near the back of the train," Alfred said. "The car we were in stayed on the rails."

As the others talked, young Dag, who was the same age as Clarence, invited him outside to play. When outside Dag asked him in English, "Do you speak English?"

"Ya, I have been teaching myself and Mom and Dad since ve left Sveden."

"That's good you will have to know it when you go to school."

"Ya, I vill perfect it den," Clarence replied.

"I prefer English," Dag said. "Our whole family can speak it since us kids started going to school."

"Dat's good," Clarence said. "Ve vill speak English vhen ve are togedder and vhen I start school I vill be ready. Vhere is school?"

"There is a school about two miles from here we go to."

"Two miles, dat is about five kilometres."

"What are kilometres?"

"Dat is how ve measure in Sweden, but I guess I vill have to learn about miles."

The Erlander family was put up in a two-room log cabin Gunner had built in his yard.

"You built this cabin especially for us?" Agnes asked incredulously, when Gunner showed them the cabin.

"Actually, I have to confess," Gunner said. "Lars and I built it for him. He plans to move it over to his own homestead later. Since we knew you were coming, we decided to build it in my yard so you could use it until you established your own place."

"That is still very generous of you, Gunner," Alfred said.

"Well, we couldn't expect you to stay outside," Myrtle said as she lugged along some blankets.

"You can see through the walls," Ingrid observed. The logs had not been chinked yet.

"Ya you might have trouble vit mosquitoes tonight," Lars said.

"Well, they say beggars can't be choosers," Agnes said. "And we are beggars."

Just then they heard a howling from the depths of the forest joined by a chorus of similar howls.

"Wolves?" Ingrid said fearfully.

"Just coyotes," Lars laughed.

"What are coyotes?" Astrid wondered.

"Coyotes are similar to wolves but much smaller," Lars assured them. "They are mostly scavengers that eat dead things or little animals like mice."

Clarence and Dag appeared and Dag asked, "Can Clarence sleep with me in our house?"

"Please Papa," Clarence pleaded.

"It is alright if he sleeps with Dag," Myrtle said. "They are becoming good friends."

Agnes looked at Alfred and he sighed saying, "I guess it would be alright, but you had better behave yourself, Clarence."

"Thank you Papa," Clarence said. He and Dag turned and bolted.

The cabin contained two small rooms, one of which served as a bedroom for Alfred and Agnes. The girls slept in the main room which also served as the kitchen. The cabin wasn't quite finished and mosquitoes came in through the cracks between the logs and around the windows to attack them mercilessly as they tried to sleep.

The following day, Gunner took Alfred around to show him some land that was still available. Unlike the homesteaders who looked for burned-off land with small trees that were easy to clear, Alfred looked for timber. By afternoon he found a quarter-section about two miles northeast of the Elofson place that abounded in timber.

"Look at the spruce," Alfred said with eyes aglow as looked over stand after stand of tall upland spruce trees. "And aspen, or white poplars as you called them." Alfred placed his arms around one old-growth aspen and found he couldn't reach all the way around it.

"I told you this was a lumberman's paradise," Gunner laughed.

"Paradise, it is logger heaven," Alfred gasped. "I'm definitely going to buy this quarter."

"Okay, we will have to find the surveyor's pin, so you can identify it," Gunner said.

In the course of finding the surveyor's pin which gave the legal description of the property in question, they came near a muskeg area. "Look at all the birch!" Alfred exclaimed. "Some of them are big enough to make lumber with."

"You are lucky," Gunner remarked. "The birch growing around the swamps usually dies before it gets too big. But it looks like you've got tamarack, too."

"Tamarack?"

Gunner showed him a coniferous tree growing in the muskeg with smooth bark and fine soft needles. "This is tamarack. It is no good for lumber because the grain is twisted, but tamarack makes excellent building logs, fence posts and telegraph poles."

"There is a market for all this?"

"Absolutely, the railways will buy the telegraph poles and you'd have no trouble shipping out large quantities of fence posts with your lumber."

"What is so special about tamarack?"

"It doesn't rot," Gunner explained. "Once you peel it and let it dry it turns really hard. Fungus won't even grow on it."

"Remarkable," Alfred said. "Let's find that pin so I can claim this land of standing gold."

The next day, Alfred went back to River Bend. He borrowed a team and wagon from Gunner to fetch supplies. At the Land Office in River Bend, he purchased the quarter outright and then wired back to Sweden for Nils to ship the sawmill and planer. He then went to the Immigrant Hall to hire a couple of helpers.

"I vant a couple of men who are good in da bush," he told the proprietor. "I saw some Finns here da udder day; dey are usually good in da bush."

"Well then, I think I know just the man for you. He's sitting in the diner having coffee with a couple of others," the proprietor said

The proprietor took Alfred to the diner and pointed out a massive, hairy man with a full beard and long hair, sitting at a table hunched over his cup of coffee. "That man over there with the beard is called Kangas the Finn. They say he's the best logger around, but I don't think he's working just now."

"Kangas da Finn, you say," Alfred replied.

"Yeah, I must warn you though, he's got a formidable reputation."

Alfred looked at the proprietor.

"They say he's a good worker, but no one has ever beaten him in either fighting or arm wrestling. He drinks like a fish and he's about the strongest man around."

"I can see vy," Alfred replied, as he again studied the formidable-looking man. "I tink I vill go speak to him."

"Are you Mr. Kangas?" Alfred asked in Swedish as he approached the huge hairy man whose sleeves were rolled up exposing his massive muscular forearms. He assumed that Kangas, like many Finns, could also speak Swedish.

"Yes, Kangas is my name," the man replied, also in Swedish, with a rasping voice as he turned to face Alfred directly. Alfred could see that his eyes were bloodshot. "My full name is Yrjo Paavali Kangas." He laughed heartily and added. *"Puhutteko Suomea?"*[1]

Alfred looked perplexed and said, "I presume you are Finnish?"

"That I am and I also speak English. Since nobody over here can pronounce my other names, they call me Kangas the Finn. And you are obviously a Swede."

"I am so. My name is Alfred Erlander. Are you good in the bush?" Alfred asked. "I need a couple of good loggers who are also good at building log houses."

"Good in the bush," Kangas laughed. "I have to be. In the old country there's nothing but bush. I used to build log houses back home."

"Then you are the man I'm looking for. I'm going to be setting up a sawmill operation and I need some good hands," Alfred grinned. "I know that Finns are good in the bush."

"I got some friends here looking for work," Kangas said.

"I can only afford two at this point, but once I'm ready for business I'll need more."

Kangas turned and spoke to a slim, handsome, youthful-looking man beside him in Finnish, then turned back to Alfred. "Esa Kekkonin here will come along. As long as you feed us and give us a little whiskey money we'll cut down all the trees you want."

[1] *Puhutteko Suomea* - Do you speak Finnish?

73

"Esa is it?" Alfred said to the young man who appeared to barely out of his teens. "Do you speak Swedish or English?"

"Yes, I speak both but my English is not too good yet," Esa said pleasantly. "I've only been in Canada a few years."

"My family doesn't speak much English yet either," Alfred replied. "So you and Kangas come home with me and bring all your gear. I'll be over at the general store getting some supplies. If either of you men are as good as I believe you to be, you will be both paid and fed well."

Alfred was just finishing loading his supplies, which included a large tent along with a big order of non-perishable groceries, when the two Finns arrived. They threw their gear on the wagon. The gear for each of them was the same - a bedroll with spare clothes rolled up inside and a double-bladed woodsman's axe. Alfred also noticed the butt of a rifle protruding from Esa's bedroll.

Noticing Alfred's observation Esa said, "I like to hunt, and I will supply you with venison to eat. It will also be handy to keep the bears away."

As Alfred headed back home with the two Finns, he asked of Kangas in Swedish. "How long have you been in Canada?"

"I have been here ten years," Kangas replied. He then went on to relate his story. " When I left Finland I worked in Sweden for a couple of years then came to Canada. I worked in the bush first in Ontario then here. They said Alberta was the new land so I came here about five years ago. One day though, I'm going to go to BC where the real timber grows."

"So, you were a lumberjack all your life," Alfred said.

"Yeah, well there is not much else to do in Finland, though at one time I had hopes of going to university at Turku."

Alfred glanced over at the huge hairy man. Somehow Kangas didn't seem like the scholarly type. "What changed your mind?" he asked.

"I got involved with a group seeking freedom for Finland. The Russian police were coming down on our group so I fled to Sweden. I gave up all notions of higher education and stuck to my original trade as a woodsman and here I am."

"I guess a sharp turn of fortune can change the character of a person," Alfred mused as the story put a new light on the background on the nature of this apparent ruffian. "Is it really that bad in Finland under Russian rule?"

"Finland is almost treated as a separate country but the Russians will only let us go so far." Kangas replied.

" We want to be independent like other countries." Esa added. "Even when our country was part of Sweden, we Finns were the poor relations."

"Were we worse than the Russians?" Alfred asked carefully.

"No, I don't think so but it was long before my time when Finland was part of Sweden."

"It's just that you Swedes gave us your culture and most of us ended up learning your language, so our culture and language was nearly lost." Esa added.

"I see," Alfred said. "So tell me Esa, did you flee from the Russians too?"

"No, I left three years ago on my own as part of a crew on a tramp steamer. I could not see any future there so I came to Canada, because I heard it was a land of opportunity."

"You were quite young."

"Just seventeen," Esa laughed.

"So you were a woodsman too," Alfred laughed.

"I come from the interior, a village near Tampere. So I've been around sawmills all my life." Esa laughed.

"That's good," Alfred said. "Lumbering is in my blood too. Back home my brother Nils and myself were partners in a sawmill we inherited from our father."

"Did you have a disagreement?" Kangas laughed.

"No, I also heard that Canada was a land of opportunity with endless forests. So I brought my family over here to start my own lumbering business."

"Well there is no end to the bush around here," Kangas laughed.

"So, did you just arrive at River Bend or. . ."

"No I worked for another logger, but we had, shall we say, a disagreement and I quit so that's why you found me unemployed."

Alfred observed, out of the corner of his eye, that Esa and Kangas exchanged looks. He had a feeling that there was a bigger story behind this *disagreement* of which Kangas spoke. As he drove along, he wondered if hiring Kangas was a wise choice after all.

Chapter Eight

When Alfred pulled up to the cabin at the Elofsons, the rest of his family came out to greet him. They saw two dark-haired strangers on the wagon, both wearing checkered shirts and floppy caps. One was a huge bearded man and the other a slightly-built, clean-shaven, handsome man. At a glance, the bearded man reminded Ingrid of a huge lumbering bear.

"I would like you to meet Kangas the Finn and his partner, Esa Kekkonin," Alfred said indicating who was who. To them he said, "This is my wife Agnes, son Clarence, and daughters Ingrid and Astrid. Kangas and Esa are going to stay with us and help us build our house."

Both Agnes and Ingrid were repelled by the sight of Kangas with his long hair and beard. He grinned at them when introduced but Esa appeared quite reserved. Astrid smiled shyly at Esa and he gave her a friendly wink.

"Ingrid is a pretty name," Kangas said with his rumbling voice and lusty grin. "It suits your looks."

Ingrid blushed uncomfortably and looked away from him

"I am taking Kangas and Esa over to our property," Alfred said. "We are going to set up a large tent for our family and my two helpers can start felling logs. I will come for you later."

As Alfred drove away with the two Finns, Ingrid asked her mother in a quiet voice, "They're not going to stay in our house, are they?" She was repelled at the notion of boarding the two strangers, particularly Kangas.

"I surely hope not," Agnes replied.

When Alfred showed Kangas and Esa the great stands of timber on his property, Kangas remarked, "You picked the right property to set up a sawmill. You'll come out of this with money in your pockets."

"First I need a house for my family. We can do that while waiting for the mill to come."

"Where are you getting the mill from?"

"The old country."

"All the way from Sweden? You must be rich already."

"Well, I won't be by the time I get set up. But don't worry, you and Esa will get paid."

Later that afternoon, the Erlander family moved to their own property and into the large tent which would serve as their home until the house was built. The two Finns built a crude lean-to shelter of brush and boughs and used this for their sleeping quarters. Agnes, with the help of her daughters, cooked for everyone.

As Alfred set about in earnest to build his new home, the forest rang with the sound of axes at work as Alfred and the two Finns cut down the large tamarack logs. Lars brought his team and skidded the logs to the building site. The logs were peeled, and squared with a broad axe. The Finns made dressing the logs look like a fine art.

Camping out in the forest while their house was being built afforded the Erlander's plenty of opportunity to view the night sky. During that spring of 1910 it held a wonder to behold, seen only twice a century at most, the passing of Halley's Comet. They watched nightly as the comet grew bigger and brighter. Its tail grew longer and longer stretching nearly halfway across the sky.

One night in mid-May when the comet was at its brightest and they were all standing watching it in awe. Agnes said fearfully, "Do you really think it will hit the Earth and bring the world to an end?"

"That's what some newspapers are saying," Alfred said. "But I think they like to make up stories just to frighten people."

"I read in the astronomy book that Halley's comet comes by every seventy-six years," Clarence piped in.

"Maybe you'll be alive to see it again," Alfred laughed. "If you live to be eighty-eight years old."

Over the next few nights the comet appeared earlier in the evening and was soon lost in the sun's glow indicating that it had clearly passed the earth without hitting it. Everyone was relieved. However as the Earth passed through the tail of the comet, the night sky was lit up with multiple meteor showers.

Soon the house was beginning to take shape. It was a large three-roomed house with a high-pitched roof and built of squared logs. The main room served as both the kitchen and living room and took up over half the house. The door was on the end opening into the main room and there was a large window on each side. On one end were two bedrooms each allotted one small window. One bedroom was for Alfred and Agnes, and the other for the girls. A flat ceiling above the bedrooms allowed for a large loft. This served as both a storage area and Clarence's bedroom. A vertical ladder was installed on the end of the partition between the bedrooms as a means of access. Alfred installed another small window at the end of the loft so Clarence too could have a window by his bed. The floor was for the present, dirt. Alfred said that once the mill was running, planks for the floor would be the first lumber to be cut.

The necessary furniture was purchased and now the Erlander family had a home of their own in Canada. Ingrid was overjoyed to receive her first letter from Sigrud. Although this served to remind Ingrid somewhat of what had been left behind, it seemed to be a long time ago since she was in Sweden. On their first night in the new house Ingrid answered her friend's letter:

June 30, 1910
Dear Sigrud,
We once again have a house of our own and a bedroom that is almost my own. I share it with Astrid. Papa built a log house on our new land and we all helped him build it. He hired two Finns to help also, one of them named Esa seems like a nice quiet man, but Kangas is a wild-looking hairy man. They call him Kangas the Finn but I call him Kangas the Barbarian.
I remember how we were going to celebrate my birthday at the Midsummer Festival. I spent it instead plastering the cracks between the logs with mud and grass. This will keep out the cold drafts in winter and the mosquitoes in summer. Mosquitoes are horrid little insects that attack you constantly, especially in the evening. I noticed on Midsummer's eve, the sun actually goes down below the horizon and it almost gets dark. We do not get the midnight sun here, Clarence says it is because we are further south. Clarence has been giving us a running geography lesson ever since we left Sweden. Did you see the comet in Sweden? We watched it get bigger and bigger in the sky every night in early May. Clarence

says it comes back every seventy-five years. I wonder if I'll live long enough to see it again. If I am alive, I will be ninety-one years old. Can you imagine where you'll be in 1986?

I find the English language hard to learn and I don't think I'll ever learn how to read it. I am lucky that our neighbours and friends are mostly Swedes so maybe I won't have to learn it at all. Everything here is so new and frightening but there is a certain sense of freedom being on the very edge of civilization. Papa has said that in a year or two when he starts making some money he will send me back to visit you, although I'll not look forward to riding a train again after the wreck. The sun has gone down behind the trees and it is getting too dark to write so I will close for now. Goodbye Sigrud, I miss you terribly.

Your Loving Friend
Ingrid.

With his family now established in their new home. Alfred began in earnest to build his dream. The daylight hours around their home were filled with sounds of axes at work and the crash of falling timber as the big trees were knocked down. Alfred bought a team of horses for skidding and often hired Lars to do skidding with his team as well. Alfred also went to Edmonton and purchased a steam tractor. He had it shipped out to Morning Glory on a railway flatcar. It was difficult to negotiate this huge unwieldy machine along the forest trails but Alfred managed to get it home. The steam tractor was needed to drive the sawmill. He also purchased a one-cylinder gasoline stationary motor with its two huge flywheels. This would be used to drive both the planer and a buzz saw that he had set up for bucking up fence posts from the tamarack. Ingrid and Clarence spent much of their summer skinning tamarack posts and telegraph poles. By mid-August he had shipped away two railway car loads of poles and posts.

Kangas and Esa were made permanent employees and they built themselves a cabin near the main house. Later, Kangas began to build a curious addition to the cabin. It was built from carefully skinned and hewed small spruce and pine logs. Then, on a trip to River Bend with the team and wagon, to fetch supplies, Kangas came back with several large flat rocks that he had gathered from the riverside and, he and Esa carried them into the addition. All of this had the Erlander family curious as both Finns were mysterious about it all. That evening when Kangas came in for evening coffee at the Erlander house to discuss the next day's activities, Clarence asked him;

"Mr Kangas, what are you building on your cabin?"

"A sauna."

"I thought that was what you and Esa were up to," Alfred chuckled.

"A sauna, what's that?" Clarence asked.

"A steam room." Kangas replied. "It is good for your body after a day's work to sit in a sauna for a while."

"It must be awful sitting in a room full of steam with your clothes on," Clarence ventured.

"You don't. You take your clothes off before you go in there."

"A steam room," Ingrid grimaced. "Who would want to sit in a room full of steam?"

"Now Ingrid," Alfred said. "Finnish people love having a sauna."

"You should try it sometime. It's good for you," Kangas grinned.

"No thanks," Ingrid said icily. She would never feel safe sitting naked in a steam room if Kangas was anywhere around even if the door was locked.

"I'd like to try your sauna sometime, Mr. Kangas," Clarence said eagerly.

"Sure, Clarence, Esa and I will be trying it out tonight and you can join us if you like. Your whole family is welcome to try it."

"I'd like to try it," Astrid added.

Kangas chuckled and replied, "That would only be if you could convince your sister or your mother to join you."

Ingrid's and Agnes's eyes rolled upward

"Say, Mrs. Erlander," Kangas said to Agnes. "Could you save your potato peelings for me?"

"Sure. What for?"

"Let's say I have a use for them," Kangas said mysteriously.

Kangas collected the potato peelings in a small barrel in the cabin where they were allowed to ferment. Then at the proper time he distilled the mash in the sauna room, often while he was having a sauna, to produce his own brand of moonshine.

As the work involved in setting up a full-fledged saw milling operation unfolded many more men were required. A dining hall was set up outside the house to feed the various people Alfred employed. It was, at first, just a roof supported by four poles, attached to the front of the house. As cooking became a major undertaking, Ingrid's duties gravitated more toward the kitchen as the summer wore on. Esa would often take his rifle along when he went out logging and sometimes when he was skidding logs back to the planned mill site he would have a freshly-killed deer lying on top of the logs. Other times he would bring home a jack-rabbit or a couple of grouse.

By late August, the sawmill and planer had arrived at Morning Glory via train. It took several horses to drag the mill to the Erlander place. Alfred practically worked day and night to get the mill set up and soon the air was filled with the shrill whine of the great saw blade in action.

As the new life in Canada of the Erlander family began to unfold, Agnes made a surprise announcement one evening at dinner. The Erlander family always ate their evening meal together in the house while the crew ate in the dining hall. She expressed herself in Swedish.

"I have studied all the signs and have come to the conclusion that I am again with child."

"You're what?" Alfred said, dumbfounded. "It has been nearly ten years since you last had a child."

"I thought you were too old to have more children," Ingrid said.

"I'm only thirty-five," Agnes said indignantly. "Lots of women still have children when they are forty."

"True," Alfred said. "It's just that it has been so long since Astrid was born, I didn't think we were capable of having more children."

"It must be all this fresh Canadian air," Agnes laughed. "Our new child will be a true Canadian."

"Will we really have a baby in the house?" a wide-eyed Astrid asked.

"Yes, we certainly will, dear," Agnes smiled. "Probably about next March.

"Maybe I'll have a brother," Clarence added. Then with a frown he added, "I have two sisters already."

"It will be what it will be," Agnes added. "And we'll all love it just the same."

"Yes, well that puts a whole different light on things," Alfred grinned, pleased to know that he would be a father again.

INGRID

Mid-morning, one early autumn day, the dog announced the arrival of a two-seater carriage with a driver alone in the front seat. Agnes went out to greet the carriage, curious as to who would be coming to out their place in such fine style. Ingrid watched from the doorway. A well-dressed man stepped from the rear seat, turned and smiled at her.

"Good morning," he smiled. "I'm Jim McDonald. I believe you've met my wife and son."

"Flora!" Agnes gasped as he helped a familiar figure, carrying an infant, from the carriage.

"Agnes?" Flora replied, uncertain if she had remembered Agnes' name correctly. Agnes moved to embrace her and Flora returned the embrace with her free arm. Upon recognizing the woman and child, Ingrid rushed to hug them.

"Oh Ingrid, you're just as beautiful as ever," Flora said.

Ingrid smiled uncertainly but looked longingly at little Edward.

"Oh, take the child," Flora laughed handing her infant to Ingrid. Edward gurgled as Ingrid fussed with him. "Vhat you do here?" Ingrid asked.

"I came to see your father about lumber; the others came to see you," Jim laughed.

"Did you come a da vay from Edmonton in dat buggy?" Agnes asked.

"No, we took the train out to River Bend and hired a carriage from the livery," Jim laughed.

As Astrid emerged from the house, Agnes told her in Swedish, "Go fetch your father. Tell him we have a special guest who is interested in his lumber."

As Astrid turned to do the task, Agnes said to the others "Come in da house, I have some fresh coffee on."

"I'll head out to the mill to find, . . Alfred, is it?" Jim replied.

"Ya, I am sure he vill be glad to see you," Agnes smiled. "He has already cut lots of lumber."

"Good," Jim replied, as he headed toward the sawmill.

Flora followed Ingrid and Agnes into the house, looking curiously at the dining hall as they walked through it.

"Many men eat," Ingrid fumbled in explanation.

"Ya, ve have a big crew to feed." Agnes added.

When they entered the house, Flora looked around at the plainly furnished main room with its homemade furniture and rough plank floor.

"You vill have to forgive da house," Agnes apologised. "Ve yust finish building it. Please have a chair." Ingrid drew a chair away from the table with her free hand as she flashed her beautiful smile.

"This is all, very rustic," Flora laughed as she lowered herself into the chair. "I was born and raised in Winnipeg so it's a bit hard to imagine someone carving a home in the wilderness from nothing."

"Von day ve vill have a fine house," Agnes declared.

"I'm sure you will," Flora laughed. "Your husband appears to be an ambitious man."

"He has a dream," Agnes said. "He and his broddder had a sawmill in da old country."

"It is people like him, that will make this country great one day," Flora stated as Agnes. poured her coffee.

She looked across at Ingrid cooing at the baby as she rocked it gently. "I take it Ingrid has not yet learned to speak English."

"No she is a little stubborn dat vay," Agnes sighed. "But von day she vill learn."

As the women visited in the house, Alfred came to greet Jim. Astrid had explained who their guests were.

"Mr. Erlander I presume?" Jim said as Alfred approached him.

"Ya, I am Alfred Erlander."

"I'm Jim McDonald from McDonald Lumber in Edmonton. Your daughter helped my wife when she was injurred in the train wreck." Jim said extending his hand. "I was told you have a sawmill."

"Ya, is your vife's broken arm better now?" Alfred asked shaking his hand.

"Oh yes, I brought her and our son along. They wanted to see your wife and daughter. I want to see your milling operation. Since you showed such kindness toward my wife that time, you are my first choice to supply us with lumber from this area.

"Vell tank you for tinking of me. I have a sawmill and planer, and ve have lots of lumber and I vas yust about to look for somebody to buy it."

"Well, here I am. Show me your lumber."

"Vell den, let's go down to da mill and you can see vhat ve are doing."

"Thank you Mr. Erlander, that sounds like a good idea."

"Yust call me Alfred," Alfred said.

As they approached the sawmill, Jim observed the big steam tractor chugging away, driving the sawmill with a long belt. As they walked past the mill, its great circular blade was ripping its way down the length of a large spruce log.

"Dat is my main man, Kangas da Finn," Alfred said pointing to a huge bearded man who was presiding over the sawing crew.

"Kangas the Finn?"

"Ya, he is a Finn and ve can't pronounce his udder names, so everyone yust calls him Kangas da Finn." Alfred laughed.

"So you were fresh from the old country, during that time of the wreck?" Jim asked.

"Ya, ve came from Sveden to start da sawmill. Ve are yust learning to speak English."

"There seems to be a lot of Swedes in this area."

"Ya."

"I'm impressed with your operation here," Jim said looking around at the piles of neatly-stacked lumber. "You have been quite busy. Anyway, Alfred, we are looking for four basic types of lumber."

"Yust a minute, I vill call my sawyer man." Alfred waved at Kangas to come and join them.

"Did you say you have a planer as well?" Jim asked.

"Ya, I vill show it to you ven Kangas gets here."

"Excellent. I was prepared to buy rough lumber, but if you plane it for me it would be better and you will get a higher price."

Kangas caught up to them and Alfred introduced him to Jim. Jim winced from his bone-crushing handshake as he looked up at the huge, hairy man.

They walked along toward the planer and Jim explained the various kinds of lumber cuts his business wanted, and from which kinds of wood. Wall studs and planks were to be cut from spruce or pine but boards could be cut from aspen wood. They approached the planer. Here they watched Esa and his crew run boards through the machine that was driven by the chugging one-cylinder gasoline motor with two huge flywheels. Jim looked at some of the planed boards and said. "I see you have cut shiplap grooves along the edge of the boards. Just what we want for wall and roof boarding."

"Ve can provide any lumber dat you vant," Alfred said. "Don't you tink, Kangas?"

"Ya, no problem. Vit da timber around here ve give you all you can take."

"It looks like you are set up to turn out lots of lumber and you seem to know what you are doing."

"I owned a sawmill in da old country vit my brudder Nils," Alfred said.

"Dat all dere is in bote Finland and Sweden, is bush," Kangas laughed.

"Well I think we can make a deal for you to supply me lumber," Jim laughed.

"How do I send it to you, by train?" Alfred asked.

"Yes, when you have enough lumber for a flatcar load, make arrangements with the station agent for shipping. Since you already have cut a large amount of lumber we will pay you for one load in advance if you can give us a delivery date."

"Dat can be arranged. Right Kangas?"

"Right," Kangas replied with his rumbling voice.

"Alfred, I have a contract here for you, in my briefcase," Jim said.

"Let's go back to da house for a cup of coffee and ve can talk business," Alfred said as they started back to the house.

"Vell I should get back to saw," Kangas said.

"Ya, maybe get some of da boys to use some of da slabs to build sheds for da lumber. Da pile keeps getting bigger and ve should be trying to keep da lumber out of da wedder."

"Vill take care of it, boss," Kangas replied.

When Alfred and Jim entered the house, they found Agnes and Flora chatting as if they were old friends. Ingrid sat back trying to fathom their conversation as she continued to hold the baby. Astrid was at her side fussing over the baby also.

"You had better vatch my daughter," Alfred laughed. "She might try to steal your baby."

"I know," Flora laughed. "If I were richer, I'd hire her as a nanny."

Ingrid looked perplexed and Agnes explained. Ingrid's eyes lit up with the prospect, but then she realized that she didn't speak English and also, her mother needed her help.

"No, Mom need help, cook for men," Ingrid faltered. "She have baby soon."

"You are having a baby?" Flora gasped. She was astonished that Agnes was expecting another child with her youngest being nine years old.

"Ya, I fool everyvone," Agnes laughed "It must be da Canadian air."

"So you will soon have a baby in your own house," Flora said to Ingrid. "Your mother needs you much more than I."

When they were settled around the kitchen table, Jim presented the contract to Alfred. Alfred picked it up and then said. "I don't read English too vell."

"I suggest you have someone read it before you sign it," Jim said. "Someone back in River Bend could probably do that for you."

"You look like an honest man," Alfred said. "I tink I can trust you."

"Thanks for the confidence," Jim said. "Tell you what, if you can spare the time, come back to River Bend with us and you can have it read, maybe at the bank. If you agree to the terms and sign it, I will give you a draft for a thousand board feet of mixed lumber."

"Good idea, I should go dere for some supplies anyhow," Alfred replied.

Agnes spoke to her daughters in Swedish, telling them to start preparing the noonday meal for the crew. Ingrid reluctantly gave the baby back to his mother as she and Astrid began to organise tableware to be taken out to the dining hall. Agnes checked some pots that were cooking on the stove.

"Well, Flora, best we be going. It looks like everyone here is getting busy," Jim said rising from his seat.

"Stay for dinner," Agnes said. "If you don't mind beans and potatoes. Ve vill eat in here vhile da crew eats out dere."

"We'd be putting you out," Flora said.

"You stay," Ingrid frowned.

Jim and Flora glanced at each other.

"Please," Alfred said. "Vhen we are finished eating I vill follow you back to River Bend on horseback."

"What about our driver?" Jim said, thinking of the almost-forgotten carriage driver.

"Tell him to eat vit da crew."

Chapter Nine

Cooking for, and cleaning up after, this large crew of hungry men soon became a full-time job for both Agnes and Ingrid. Even Astrid was employed as a dishwasher. Meals were simple. Breakfast was either oatmeal gruel or buckwheat pancakes with a large homemade bun allotted to each plate. The other two meals were either beans and potatoes with salt pork, or stew and potatoes. The stew was usually venison, but occasionally it was chicken or jackrabbit. A couple of times a month they might get a roast haunch of venison for supper. Alfred had built a chicken coop and bought a milk cow to help with the food requirements though most of the milk was consumed by the family. Next year he planned to build a small piggery as well

Clarence had a variety of jobs from fetching wood and water for the house to shovelling sawdust away from mill and shavings away from the planer. Both sawdust and shavings were used to stoke the boiler of the steam engine while the growing pile of waste slabs from the mill became their principal source of firewood.

When school had started that fall, both Clarence and Astrid were relieved of many of their chores so they could attend school. Ingrid was also offered the opportunity to go to school. They discussed it one night at supper.

"I have enough to do around here. Mother needs a full-time helper, especially in her condition." Ingrid insisted.

"I could manage," Agnes said wearily. "This would be a real opportunity for you to learn English."

"I don't want to learn English," Ingrid persisted "I don't need to learn English. Everyone I know can speak Swedish."

"English is the language of Canada so you will have to learn it sooner or later," Alfred added.

"Rather it be later," Ingrid retorted. "I definitely don't want to go to school with a bunch of children much younger than me. I am fifteen and nearly old enough to be out of school, even if we were still back in Sweden."

"Let her stay and help," Agnes relented. "I will sorely need her, especially as it draws nearer the time for the baby."

"Thank you Mother," Ingrid said firmly.

As Fall advanced the dining hall was walled in with a double layer of slabs, and a layer of shavings in between. Also a heater was installed along with a large washstand. A bunkhouse, built from logs, was erected for Alfred's growing crew. Shortly after the first snowfall, Alfred shipped out his first consignment of lumber. The lumber was hauled by teams and sleds to the railway siding at Morning Glory and loaded onto a flatcar. With steady money now coming in, Alfred kept several men on payroll full-time. Kangas was appointed as foreman over the whole crew. Esa ran the planer when it was time for planing but otherwise helped fell and skid logs.

In addition to the permanent men, several homesteaders from nearby worked piecemeal either for wages or for quantities of lumber. The most persistent of these extra hands was Lars Elofson. He spent so much time at the mill one wondered when he had time to develop his homestead. At meal times he watched Ingrid with longing eyes but was shy and clumsy in efforts to court her. Ingrid on the other hand found no attraction to him whatever and the way he always watched her was somewhat unnerving to her. He seldom spoke but once in a while he would make a comment like, "I like your hair," or "You have a nice apron on today." His words came out in a most unromantic way. She often thought of Michael with his cheery smile and musical words that she couldn't understand. While she could understand Lars, his slow and awkward words did not light her heart like those of Michael.

One morning after having a dream about Michael, Ingrid came to the dining hall with a large platter of pancakes. As she set the platter down on the serving table she thought she heard Michael. Although she didn't understand the words that Irish accent was unmistakable.

She wheeled and unthinkingly said, "Michael?"

Behind her in the lineup for pancakes and just ahead of Kangas was a big muscular man in his mid-thirties.

"No, Miss, me name is not Michael," he laughed. "It is Patrick."

"I sorry," Ingrid faltered in English. "You talk like Michael."

"Indeed. Was dere a Michael workin' here?"

"No," Ingrid replied in a small voice.

"I tink dat Michael vas lost love," Kangas laughed, as he spoke in English.

"Just you never mind about Michael, Kangas the Finn," Ingrid snapped in Swedish. She didn't know exactly what Kangas had said but gathered he was making a joke about Michael She turned and went back into the house.. When she composed her thoughts and came back into the mess with more pancakes, she wondered if she would ever meet her true love. None of the crowd of hungry men in the room looked like likely prospects especially the two most prominent in the crowd, Lars Elofson and Kangas the Finn.

By early winter Alfred had cut most of the prime timber on his own land and began to poach it from the surrounding crown land. Big trees along the trails were particularly vulnerable. Kangas was quite adept at knowing where to find the best saw-logs in the surrounding forests. He and Esa each fashioned themselves a pair of cross-country skis. As cross-country skiing was another Finnish passion, they made long forays into the forest through deep snow in search of choice timber. They also used them to travel to their Saturday night outings at River Bend.

Clarence marvelled at the skis and wished for a pair of his own. One day he asked Esa, in English, as he almost always spoke English these days, "Mr. Kekkonin could you make me a pair of skis?"

"Sure ting Clarence, I sure you vill enjoy dem," Esa replied, in his broken English.

"I can use them to ski to school."

"Dat would be good idea, I make pair for your sister too. But don't tell anyvone. I try have dem bote done by Christmas."

So Esa fashioned skis from specially cut and planed birch boards for both Clarence and Astrid. Although Clarence knew about the skis, and held his tongue, Esa wouldn't let him see them until the proper time came to present them.

On Christmas Eve Alfred shut the mill down at noon and gave everyone the next two days off. The actual sawing would be stopped until March to give him time to accumulate a new stock of logs. The homesteaders who had worked on the sawing crew would be laid-off, although some of those having draught horses, were offered jobs skidding logs.

The Erlander family were all in the proper Christmas spirit; even

INGRID

Ingrid was excited about celebrating their first Christmas in Canada. They decorated two trees, one for the house and one for the dining hall, using homemade decorations. In the Canadian tradition, Agnes cooked a turkey for the noon meal for the crew. She also had goose cooking in the oven in the house for the family supper later. When the hungry crew came in for their midday meal they were pleasantly surprised to find the dining hall all decorated with streamers and the savoury aroma of roast turkey filling the air. The rough tables were covered with sheets and dishes of homemade candy adorned them. A punch made from a mixture of raspberry juice and Kangas's moonshine was provided and the men all eagerly partook while Alfred carved the turkey. Agnes grumbled that mixing moonshine with the fruit was a waste of her preserves.

As Agnes and Ingrid were about to distribute platters of turkey to the hungry men, Esa stood up with punch glass in hand. He spoke in English:

"I like to make toast for boss. He good boss to tink of his men."

The men raised their glasses in loud agreement while Alfred blushed from the flattery.

"Vell it is Christmas and ve should tink of each udder at Christmas. You have been a good crew and good vork deserves to be recognized. So let's eat and be merry."

The men consumed their turkey dinner in lighthearted spirits. When the main course was over, Swedish pastry and fruitcake was brought out. It was fervently devoured by the men as they sipped their coffee. After Alfred ladled another round of punch for his crew, Kangas stood up with his glass in hand and said; "Don't forget da cooks, dat vas good meal. To da cooks."

The others eagerly responded while Agnes and Ingrid blushed modestly.

"Very good meal Ingrid," Lars added, in Swedish, looking at her with those longing eyes.

"Thank you Lars," Ingrid said with a tight smile. "Mom did most of the cooking."

By mid-afternoon, after Alfred had paid all his men wages due, the crew had dispersed to go to their own homes save Esa and Kangas, their cabin in the yard was their only home. When the others left, Alfred told the two Finns to stay behind for a moment.

Speaking in Swedish, he said. "Why don't both of you come over for supper this evening and celebrate Christmas Eve with us?"

Agnes, who was till cleaning up, stopped in mid-pace. This was the first she had heard of the invitation.

"Thank you Mr. Erlander," Esa said. "Are you sure your wife won't mind?"

"You won't mind if Kangas and Esa join us for supper, dear, will you?" Alfred said to Agnes.

"We'll fit them in," she said with a tight-lipped smile.

"Are you sure?" Kangas said. "Your Missis doesn't seem happy about it."

"Not a problem, she's just surprised because I didn't ask her first," Alfred quickly assured him.

"As long as it doesn't cause trouble."

"Come over about seven o'clock," Alfred said.

After Kangas and Esa had left to go to their cabin and Alfred went into the house, Agnes assailed him. "Why did you invite those two Finns to have Christmas Eve dinner with our family?"

"They have nowhere else to go. Their cabin is their only home."

"Esa is a nice guy," Astrid piped in.

"Yes, I would have no trouble having Esa at our dinner table, but that Kangas, he both eats and acts like an animal."

"But it is Christmas," Alfred persisted. "They are both good men and they have no family. The least we could do is show them a little kindness."

"I suppose," Agnes sighed. "But don't make a habit of inviting Kangas in here."

"Yes dear," Alfred sighed.

At the dinner table that evening, Ingrid had a demonstration as to why she privately called Kangas, *Kangas the Barbarian*. Although he used a knife and fork it seemed he would be more comfortable eating with his hands. Attempting to grapple with basic table etiquette seemed a great struggle for him. He ate noisily, barely suppressed the urge to belch several times and when he talked his voice was loud and his laughter was coarse. At one point he picked up a whole drumstick and gnawed it clean to the bone. It looked for a moment as if he was going to toss the bone away, but he caught himself and put it on the plate.

Esa, on the other hand, seemed to have the table manners born of gentry. Except, that is, whenever his eyes and those of Astrid met. He would grin and wink at her. This caused her to squirm and giggle.

After dinner, the gifts were opened and everyone spoke in Swedish. In addition to those from family members, each member of the Erlander family had received a gift from the McDonald family. Alfred recieved a bottle of expensive whiskey. Kangas looked wistfully at the bottle when Alfred set it on the table. Agnes received a large box of assorted sweets, which the children eyed Clarence received an astronomy book, and Astrid a dress. When Ingrid unwrapped hers, she was breathless when she discovered a fine brass locket and chain. She was moved to tears when Astrid read the attached note to her:

Dear Ingrid.
May you have a very Merry Christmas and thanks once again for that wonderful act of kindness you and your family showed me on the train. It shall never be forgotten.

Love
Flora

Alfred rewarded each of his helpers with a small bonus. To everyone's surprise Agnes presented a small package to each of the Finns. Each package contained a pair of socks.

Alfred looked at Agnes curiously as he thought, '*First you scold me for bringing my two main helpers to dinner then you give each of them a present.*'

Agnes, who seemed to read his mind, smiled as she thought, '*Well, since you invited them to dinner, the least I could do was offer a present, even though the socks were originally intended for you and Clarence as additional footwear.*'

"I am touched," Kangas said with his rumbling voice. "I never expected to be invited to your house for dinner and now your wife knits me a pair of socks. I don't know what to say, I never brought any presents."

"We didn't expect any," Alfred said. "We are just rewarding you for all the fine work you have done for us."

"Well, they say Christmas is for children," Kangas said evenly after a long moment. He reached into his pocket and flipped out a silver dollar for both Clarence and Astrid. "I am not good at presents, so buy something you like," he said modestly.

"Thank you, Mr. Kangas," They gasped, using English.

"But for you Ingrid," he grinned. "You are a beautiful young lady. You deserve something special." Kangas handed her a small wrapped present. Ingrid was too astonished to react. She never thought this ruffian was capable of tenderness.

"Thank you," she said almost inaudibly.

"I hope you like that scent," Kangas continued as Ingrid unwrapped a small bottle of perfume.

"Thank you Kangas," she smiled, as she took the bottle through to her bedroom.

"I have something for the lady of the house" Esa said. He handed Agnes a box wrapped in colourful paper.

"Oh thank you Esa," Agnes gasped as she unwrapped the paper to find a large box of chocolates.

"And now for the two younger ones," Esa stepped into the dining hall and returned with a pair of skis. "For you Clarence."

"Thank you Mr. Kekkonin," Clarence gasped, speaking English, Clarence took the skis and examined them lovingly.

"And pair for you Astrid," as Esa brought in a second pair of skis for her.

"A pair of skis for me!" Astrid exclaimed, also speaking English. She had secretly longed for a pair of skis after seeing the ease with which Esa glided about with them. "Thank you Esa!" She ran over and hugged him.

"I would like to thank both of you for thinking of the children," Alfred said in Swedish.

"Well, like Kangas said, Christmas is for children and your Missis deserves something for her fine cooking."

"This calls for a toast," Alfred said, rising. He opened the bottle of whiskey on the table and fetched three glasses from the cupboard.

Agnes frowned, as she didn't really approve of drinking. However she tolerated a limited amount of it. As Alfred poured the drinks, Clarence announced that he was going to try his skis out.

"In the dark!" Agnes exclaimed.

"There's a full moon out tonight," Clarence said as he started for the door with his skis in hand.

"Don't go too far," Esa warned, He spoke in English as he nearly always did when speaking to Clarence and Astrid. "and take off parka and carry it vit you so you von't get chill. He turned to Astrid and said, "Are you going to try skis?"

"I don't know if I can stand up on them."

"Come outside wit dem and I help you. We need to keep eye on Clarence anyhow."

"First the toast," Alfred said as he gave a small glass to each of the Finns.

"*Skol*," Kangas said raising his glass. The other two repeated the Scandinavian toast.

Both Finns swallowed the contents of glass in one gulp. Kangas set his glass down indicating he wanted more. Esa set his down and turned to Astrid.

"We try out skis now?"

When they went outside, Kangas said to Ingrid. "Would you like a pair too?"

"Me. What would I do with skis? Ski out to the barn?"

"You could take treks through the forest, see the beauty of winter. Think of all the fresh air. I could ski along to keep you company if you like."

"No thanks, I get plenty of fresh air doing my work around here," Ingrid said bluntly. Although she was flattered that Kangas had given her a Christmas present, she did not want to give him any notions of courting her.

Esa carefully fastened the bindings on Astrid's boots and handed her the poles. She wobbled uncertainly and cried, "I going to fall."

"Just keep steady and take small strides,' Esa laughed. "I get skis and come back."

Clarence came back from the mill area in long strides exclaiming how easy it was, then abruptly slipped and fell right in front of Astrid. Both Esa and Astrid laughed.

As Astrid cautiously crept around the yard on her skis, Esa would slide effortlessly by her and literally skied circles around her. Clarence complained about being too hot and pulled off his parka.

After a time, they came back inside. Their cheeks were rosy and they were exhausted.

"Skiing is fun," Astrid beamed. "I'm going to ski to school with Clarence when school starts in January."

"You will need lots of practice first," Esa cautioned. He spoke in Swedish to be clear. "The school is over two miles away and you have to make sure you wear the right clothes so you don't get overheated, then chilled."

Later that Christmas night, Ingrid began a letter to Sigrud in regards to her first Christmas in Canada.

Dear Sigrud,

Well, we had our first Christmas in Canada. It was quite a different experience. We put up a tree and decorations in both the main house and the dining hall. Papa provided a Christmas Eve feast for all the people who work here before sending them home for Christmas. That evening we had our family dinner and the two Finns were invited though Mom was none too pleased. Papa said it was because they had nowhere else to go. While Esa is a nice person and Astrid seems to have a powerful little girl's crush on him, Kangas still remains Kangas the Barbarian. I was surprised when he gave both Clarence and Astrid a silver dollar, then he gave me a bottle of perfume. Esa made skis for both Astrid and Clarence and Kangas offered to make a pair for me. I think Kangas has courting on his mind, but that will be the day. I would be afraid to spend a moment alone with him, let alone let him court me. While my life is lonely at times and I miss you, it certainly isn't uneventful. I will write more in a few days time. Then there was the gift from the McDonalds because I helped Flora on the train that time. It seems she never forgot me and makes it sound so much like I did something wonderful, when I really only did what any compassionate person would do.

When school had reopened in the new year, both Clarence and Astrid were sufficiently trained for their new mode of transportation. They used the skis until the spring thaws made the snow too heavy and sticky, and were the envy of their classmates.

Chapter Ten

One day, early in the New Year, a group of angry homesteaders including both Gunner and Lars Elofson came to Alfred's place and held a meeting in the dining hall. They were concerned about the timber forays of the two Finns, who were beginning to trespass onto their homesteads. Kangas sensed trouble and joined the meeting although Esa took a gang of loggers out for their usual foray.

Ingrid supplied coffee and jelly rolls to the participants and quietly tended other chores in the hall. Since most of the concerned homesteaders were fellow Swedes, the meeting was conducted mainly in Swedish. This allowed her to understand what was going on.

"We have a concern," Gunner began. "We all know you need timber to keep your mill going, but your man here, the Finn, has been trespassing."

"Trespassing where?" Kangas demanded.

"Twice I chased two of your men off my place. They almost got away with a large spruce," Gunner stated.

"I am sorry for that," Alfred said. "I will have to tell them to be more careful."

"This one, you call the Finn," another homesteader named Rollo Engstrom said, nodding at Kangas, "cut and drug away two large spruce from the back of my property. And there are ski trails all over my land."

"Whose land," Kangas retorted. "I never crossed any fences to take timber."

"It wasn't fenced."

"Then how can I know if it's your land?" Kangas shouted as he stood up. Standing with his broad shoulders squared and huge forearms exposed by rolled-up sleeves he looked very formidable. Alfred motioned for him to sit down and Kangas obeyed.

"Kangas always asked permission to come on my land," Lars added. He glanced over at Ingrid.

She sensed that Lars was appearing to side with them only to win her favour.

"There you go," Kangas sneered. "I always ask permission before I go on anyone's land.

"Maybe you should fence your land so Kangas will know when he is trespassing," Alfred suggested.

"My land should be safe, whether it's fenced or not," Rollo declared. "Also if you cut down all the timber, nobody else will get any."

"If you want timber, then cut it down," Kangas said. "Don't leave the big trees to rot or get struck by lightning."

"If I cut the trees down or leave them standing it is none of your business Mr. Kangas the Finn." Rollo added.

Kangas glowered at him.

"I have a suggestion," Alfred said. "I will tell my men not to cut down trees within a mile of any homestead. We will cut to the northwest where there are no homesteads at present. In another month we will have enough logs to start the saw up anyway. On the other hand, if any of you want us to take timber to help clear your land we will do it and give you a percentage of the lumber back. The same applies if you cut your own timber and bring logs here to be sawn."

There was a murmur among the others and Gunner said it sounded like a reasonable offer.

"So, Kangas," Alfred said to his lead hand. "No cutting near any homesteads. I don't want enemies for neighbours."

"No cutting near homesteads," Kangas repeated.

"I told you Alfred was a reasonable man," Lars added. Again his eyes drifted toward Ingrid.

"I would like to add," Alfred said. "My slab pile is bigger than I know what to do with, so you're free to help yourselves to slabs free of charge, the same applies for any shavings or sawdust you might want. Now let's have a coffee and discuss how we can help each other."

There was another murmur of approval, but Kangas still faced a lot of hostile eyes as he was perceived to be the main culprit. He excused himself from the meeting.

After Kangas had left, Ingrid heard Lars say to her father, "You should get rid of the Finn, he's nothing but trouble."

"He's the best logger and mill hand I've ever seen both here and in Sweden," Alfred smiled. "From now on I'll keep him home."

"Some of the stories I heard about him in River Bend weren't very good," Lars said cautiously.

"Such as. . ?"

"Well, the son of the last fellow Kangas worked for landed in the hospital because he and Kangas got into a fight."

"Is that so?" Alfred replied. Then with a shrug added, "I'll have to watch him."

"Ask him about the incident someday," Lars suggested.

"I'll think about it," Alfred replied. Then turning to the others he said, "Well, does my offer sound reasonable?"

Conversation among the homesteaders turned to how they could either bring logs to the mill for sawing or arrange for Alfred's crew to take timber from their properties on a percentage basis. Alfred offered to set up lots where each homesteader could deposit his logs and not get them confused with his neighbours. Nearly all of his neighbours said they would come for sleigh loads of slabs. Many also said they would take shavings and sawdust also, as these two by-products made excellent litter for the floors of chicken coops and pigsties. In the weeks that followed, the slab pile went down so fast that Alfred had to reserve some for his own use. Kangas was kept at home preparing logs and later running the saw.

One morning, about a month after the meeting with the homesteaders, Agnes and Ingrid were cleaning up after breakfast. Agnes felt a twinge of pain. "It is time," she gasped.

"Time for what?" Ingrid asked

"The baby, it's coming." Agnes winced.

"Go lie down Mother, I'll get Papa," Ingrid said anxiously. "He can take you to the doctor."

"The baby will come before I get there."

"I'll tell him anyway," Ingrid said as she headed for the door. Agnes went to her bed and began to calmly prepare herself for the birth that she felt was imminent.

Alfred and Ingrid came hurriedly back into the house. Alfred called for her and Agnes answered in a calm voice from the bedroom.

"I'll hitch up a team and sleigh and drive you to River Bend," Alfred said anxiously.

"No," Agnes replied. "I feel the baby will come at any time and I don't want to bear it on the sleigh in the middle of winter."

"What are you going to do then?" Alfred wondered.

"I'll have it here. Ingrid can help me."

"Me!" Ingrid said incredulously.

"You are old and responsible enough. I'll tell you what to do."

"I'm still going to send for the doctor," Alfred said.

"Send for him if you like, but the baby probably won't wait for him to come," Agnes said as she winced from another labour pang. "I just broke water."

"I'll send Esa to get the doctor," Alfred said as he left the room.

He caught up to Esa by the mill and said hurriedly, "I've got to send you River Bend for the doctor. Agnes is going to have a baby."

"Jehoshaphat, I go right away," Esa replied as he turned and headed for his cabin.

"Aren't you going to take the horse?" Alfred called after him.

"No, I'll use the skis; they're just as fast," Esa said over his shoulder.

It took only moments for Esa to strap on his skis and a few long strides later he vanished down the trail to River Bend.

Meanwhile Agnes calmly instructed Ingrid to have some towels and warm water ready and had Ingrid cushion her in the right position on the bed. Agnes winced again and said, "Remember, if the baby don't cry when it comes out, make it cry. The lungs have to be cleared right away."

"Yes Mother," Ingrid replied. After her initial reluctance, Ingrid calmly braced for the task ahead.

Agnes let out a cry and arched her back, then through gritted teeth demanded, "Ingrid get me a broom."

"A broom?" Ingrid asked incredulously. "Whatever for.?"

"Just get it," Agnes cried in a groaning voice.

Reluctantly Ingrid complied with the strange request. Agnes snatched the broom from her and put her mouth over a spot about halfway along the handle. She bit hard into the broomstick and clutched it with both hands in white-knuckle firmness. There was a mighty groan and heave, then the cry of childbirth. Agnes thrust the broom aside and lay back panting. Ingrid reacted instinctively to the natural miracle she had just witnessed. She turned the baby over so that the crying would expel the fluid from its lungs, pulled off the remaining placenta and washed the baby clean.

"Give me the baby," Agnes gasped.

Agnes had exposed one of her breasts and took the baby to nurse it. Ingrid cleaned up the mess with due diligence. When she had finished Agnes said calmly to her. "You've done a wonderful job dear, now go tell your father he has another son."

99

The doctor arrived a while later only to find Agnes calmly sitting up in bed with a sleeping infant at her side. Upon a brief examination he said, "Well, both you and the child seem to be fine. Your daughter is an excellent midwife."

"Sorry to vaste your time," Agnes laughed as she spoke to the doctor. "I told dem ve could manage."

"It's not waste," the doctor assured her. "If there had been complications, my services would have been most certainly needed."

That evening Alfred and Agnes discussed naming their son.

"I have a brother named Anker," Agnes said, "We could name him Anker."

"I was thinking of something more Canadian," Alfred said. "I know what. We can call him James."

"Yes James or Jim is more Canadian. That's a good idea my dear," Agnes smiled. "Let's call him Jim. It also honours Jim McDonald who has been so kind to us."

One evening in late spring, Lars appeared at the Erlander house. He was all neatly dressed and groomed. Ingrid, who was out in the yard, saw him ride up on horseback. She slipped into the garden behind the house. Her mother had started a vegetable garden that spring behind the house in a small area enclosed with a picket fence.

'I hope Lars didn't see me,' she thought. *'I don't wish to see him. I know he wants to court me but I can't stand him.'*

When Lars came to the door Astrid answered it. "Hello Mr. Elofson," she said pleasantly.

"Hello Astrid," Lars smiled. "Is your father in?"

"Come in Lars," Alfred called from within the house.

"Could I speak to you privately, Mr. Erlander?" Lars said nervously.

"Sure, " Alfred grunted as he came to the door.

"Vy are you so formal?" Alfred laughed, as they stepped into the dining hall.

"Well, you see Mr. Erlander, it is a delicate matter." Lars began speaking in Swedish

"Whatever the delicate matter, you can call me Alfred as you usually do." he replied in Swedish.

"Well, as you know Mr. Erlander. I have my own homestead and have been working very hard to make it a farm. The inspector was out the other day and told me it was proved so I now own it."

"Congratulations, Lars." Alfred smiled.

"Now that I have a farm and future, I. . . uh. . . . come to ask your permission."

"Permission, what permission?"

"We. . . uh. . . Mr. Erlander. . . Alfred, you have a daughter who is nearly sixteen. She is a very beautiful young lady who deserves a good husband."

"And you think *you* should be her husband?"

"Yes, I would take very good care of her and treat her well."

"I see. What does Ingrid think of all this?"

"I haven't asked her yet."

"Don't you think that you should? It is her you wish to marry, not me," Alfred laughed.

"I just thought that I. . .uh. . .should ask you first."

"Well, if Ingrid loves you and wants to marry you, I won't stop her. As long as it is after she turns sixteen."

Lars smiled broadly. "We will set a date in summer after her birthday."

"Don't forget to ask her first," Alfred chuckled.

"Where is Ingrid?"

"She is outside somewhere."

"I will find her," Lars said happily as he turned and stepped out the door.

"What was that all about?" Agnes asked as she stepped into the dining hall upon Lars' departure. They heard Lars call out to Ingrid.

"Lars," Alfred chuckled. "Just asked my permission if he could marry Ingrid."

"Marry her," Agnes snorted. "She'll only be sixteen on June twenty-first."

"Sixteen is an acceptable marrying age," Alfred said. "If she waits too long she'll be an old maid."

"Well, she doesn't need to marry the first bachelor who wants her," Agnes said defensively. "A little over a year ago you worried about that young Irishman on the ship because she was too young. Now you are ready to pawn her off."

"She's a year older now and I told Lars he couldn't marry her until she turns sixteen."

"She doesn't like Lars you know."

"Then I think he'll be quite disappointed. It is too bad in a way, he proved up his homestead just for her."

When Ingrid heard Lars calling, and coming around the side of the house, she stepped out of the garden and started walking toward the mill from the opposite side of the house. She was already past Kangas and Esa's cabin and beside the bunkhouse when he spotted her.

"Ingrid, oh Ingrid, could I talk to you?" Lars called.

Ingrid kept walking toward the mill, but it seemed there was no avoiding Lars as he was coming relentlessly toward her. She would have to deal with him.

He called again, pleading with her to stop. When Ingrid was beside the mill, she turned to face the inevitable as Lars caught up to her in long strides.

"What is it you wish to talk to me about, Lars Elofson?" Ingrid said coldly.

"Ingrid, I . . . uh. . . . Well I just got my homestead approved. I own it now."

"I'm happy for you Lars," Ingrid said without expression.

"Now that I have a home and future it is time. . ."

"Time, Lars? Time for what?"

"Time I found a wife. To make my life complete."

"You are asking *me* to be your wife?" Ingrid said with an astonished look. While she fully expected a courtship request, she was astonished with the outright proposal.

"Yes, uh. . . I would like that very much. I would be a good husband. I would care for you and protect you."

"And I would cook for you and wash your clothes and keep your house," Ingrid mocked.

"That's part of it."

"What about love?"

"I love you Ingrid. I always have. I need you."

"I am sorry Lars, I don't love you. You are a nice hard-working man who deserves a nice wife, but not me. Because I don't love you I can't marry you."

"You could learn to love me."

"No, I can't marry you, and then hope to love you. I must love the man I marry before I marry him."

Lars's face dropped and tears welled in his eyes. It had never occurred to him that Ingrid might turn him down.

"I am sorry Lars, go and find yourself a woman who loves you. I am not ready to marry anyone yet anyway. I am not even sixteen."

"I could wait until you are a little older." Lars pleaded. "We could court for a while first."

"No, Lars," Ingrid said firmly. "I don't love you and I never will." She turned her back on him and Lars stood glumly for a long moment with hat in hand before turning to go back to his horse.

"You could learn to love *me*," said a laughing voice behind her, as Ingrid watched Lars walk away.

Ingrid turned and there stood Kangas. He held a wrench in his hand, suggesting he must have been out repairing the mill.

"Kangas the Finn, how dare you listen in on our conversation." Ingrid flashed angrily. "I would never learn to love *you*."

"Don't be angry my pretty girl with the golden braids. You came down here and let him follow you."

"You could have said you were here!"

"I was here first. It's a shame you broke Lars's heart like that. He really likes you. But then so do I."

"Well I don't like you," Ingrid snapped. "You are a crude and inconsiderate animal."

As Ingrid turned and quickly walked away from him she could hear uproarious laughter behind her.

"Well, what's the verdict?" Alfred asked, when Ingrid returned to the house. "We know why Lars was here."

"He discussed this with you?" Ingrid demanded.

"He asked for my permission to marry you," Alfred replied.

"He asked you?" Ingrid said with astonishment. "What did you tell him?"

"I said it was up to you. But you know that you are nearly old enough to start looking for a man."

"Well that man won't be Lars Elofson," Ingrid said sharply. Then she added abruptly. "Or that Kangas the Finn either."

"Kangas, what's he got to do with this?" Alfred demanded.

"Nothing, he just annoys me."

That night in her room, Ingrid sat at the table in the light of a wick lamp and commented in an ongoing letter to Sigrud:

INGRID

Quite a day today, Lars Elofson proposed to me, after he proposed to father. He means well but he is so dull and unromantic, I turned him down. Then there is Kangas the Finn. Although he has not said so directly, I am sure he has designs on me also. While he has more charm than Lars, he is so crude with his long hair, beard, and rough manner. I guess I was spoiled by Michael. I could have married him right there on the boat. Maybe one day I'll have another beau, but it will take a lot to top Michael.

On the day of Ingrid's sixteenth birthday a stranger came to the door asking for her father. He spoke in Swedish. He was a middle-aged man with a thick moustache and nearly white hair. When Alfred received him in the dining hall, Ingrid heard him introduce himself.

"I am a neighbour from over near Morning Glory and my name is Oscar Lindstrom."

"My men haven't been logging on your land?" Alfred said, with a concerned look.

"No," he laughed. "My sons and I have been felling lots of trees. We would like to bring them over to your sawmill and make some lumber."

"You know that I take a percentage to cover my costs. If your boys come here and work while we saw your wood, my percentage goes down."

"It sounds like a good deal," Oscar said evenly. "We will bring logs over during the summer, when we are not busy, and you can cut them in the winter. My oldest boy, Carl, will come over and help."

"Well, you can start bringing logs over any time. I'll set up a lot where you can keep them. Come in the house and have a cup of coffee. It is always good to meet a new neighbour."

One morning shortly after the first snowfall the following autumn when Ingrid was busy picking up the dishes from the breakfast crew, the door opened and a tall, hugely-built man stepped through.

"Are you Ingrid Erlander?" he said in English

Ingrid straightened up and looked directly up at him. He wore a friendly smile and pulled off his toque exposing a mop of flaxen-coloured hair. They looked at each other for a long moment as if frozen in time then finally she asked him if he could speak Swedish. He replied in Swedish, "My name is Carl Lindstrom. I was told by your father to tell you that I will be eating here from now on."

Chapter Eleven

When the men came in for their midday meal of venison stew, Ingrid looked for the big man who had said that he was Carl Lindstrom. When he took his coat and toque off and rolled up his sleeves to wash his hands, she again thought, '*He is huge, but he is very handsome.*' Carl was taller than Kangas and his arms were every bit as thick, but he was clean-shaven and thus in Ingrid's eyes a lot more civilized. During the course of the meal Carl noticed those bright eyes looking at him and he smiled a warm smile. Ingrid smiled and blushed, then quickly turned the away.

"Could I get a cup of coffee?" Kangas called to Ingrid in Swedish.

Kangas was sitting next to Carl and when she reached over to pour his coffee she brushed against Carl. Then turning to him she said also in Swedish," Would you like some coffee too, Mr. Lindstrom?"

"Yes, I would, and you may call me Carl," he smiled, then replied in Swedish. As this was Carl's first close-up view of Ingrid he suddenly realized that she was extraordinarily beautiful. He added, "Did anyone ever tell you that you have very beautiful eyes?"

Ingrid blushed and replied, "I've heard that remark before."

Kangas scowled and said, "Lars Elofson used to tell her that all the time."

Ingrid turned and walked back to the serving table. Kangas's intrusion with reference to Lars had ruined everything.

As Carl watched her walk away, Kangas rumbled in his ear, "She is too beautiful for you Lindstrom. Alfred doesn't like mill hands flirting with his daughter."

When the lunch break was over, Carl couldn't resist looking toward Ingrid who met his gaze with a warm smile.

"Come on Lindstrom, let's get back to work," Kangas said gruffly.

During the afternoon when Carl worked at getting logs ready to be fed into the mill, Esa, who was helping him, gave him a warning. He spoke in Swedish.

"You should be careful around Ingrid. Kangas is very fond of her."

"Is she fond of him?" Carl asked bluntly.

"What does it matter?" Esa said gravely. "Kangas likes her, and nobody crosses Kangas."

"Is he that mean?"

"Ya, he took on three guys in River Bend one night in a fight over a woman and won. One of them was his former boss's son so you better watch your step. Kangas picked him up and threw him through the barroom window. If he ever hits you with that right hook it will be lights out."

"I still say it is Ingrid who has the final say in anything."

"Don't say I didn't warn you."

Nonetheless Carl was a trifle more guarded when he came in for supper. He made a point not to sit next to Kangas or stand in line next to him when getting his plate full of beans and potatoes.

"Would you like another scoopful, Mr. Lindstrom?" Ingrid smiled as she ladled a large scoop of beans on his plate.

"Dat vould be plenty," Carl replied in English. "I will yust have a slice of bread and a slice of meat."

Ingrid looked perplexed. This was the first time Carl tried to speak to her in English.

Later when Ingrid brought the coffee pot around and asked Carl if he wanted some, he replied again in English. "No tanks, I am too full from dose delicious beans."

"Why don't you talk to me in Swedish?" Ingrid said. "I don't speak English very well."

"You should learn how," Carl said in Swedish. "You will get along better over here."

"I don't need to know how, everyone here speaks Swedish." Ingrid smiled.

Carl smiled too. "Some day I will teach you how."

"Could I have some coffee?" Kangas called from his place at the table. He shot Carl a dark look as Ingrid turned to serve him.

When Carl got up to leave the room Kangas followed him outside. Some of the mill hands such as Esa thought a fight was about to ensue.

When outside, Kangas said to Carl in English, "Vould you like to come over to cabin for drink?"

"I don't usually drink when I am vorking," Carl replied.

"Yust come over I vish to talk vit you in private," Kangas said with a forced smile.

"Oh, all right, I vill come for a minute or two," Carl replied guardedly. He sensed Kangas wanted to talk about Ingrid.

The others followed them outside expecting to find a brawl in progress, and fearing for the well-being of the big handsome Swede. They were surprised to see Carl and Kangas heading for Kangas's cabin.

"Maybe dey are going to fight it out in sauna," Esa laughed.

Once inside the cabin, Kangas lit his wick lamp. Carl could see that it was a well-built neatly-kept cabin with two cots, a small homemade table and a set of chairs. Off to one side was the sauna room.

"Have you ever had sauna, Lindstrom?" Kangas said, as he took an armful of spruce slabs to the stone fire pit that provided the heat for the sauna.

"No, I have never tried it," Carl said uncertainly. He was expecting the wrath of Kangas to descend on him at any moment for daring to be friendly with Ingrid.

"It good for you," Kangas said as he tested a large tub of water on his stove. "Dat is vy ve Finns are so tough." He laughed but his eyes were still and narrow. Kangas carried the heavy tub into the sauna room and deliberately slopped some of the tepid water on the hot stones. "Yust about ready," he muttered as a hiss of steam evaporating from the stones could be heard.

Kangas came back through and drew a gallon jug of moonshine from under his bed and took a swallow. "Sure you don't vant swallow?"

"No tanks," Carl said nervously. He was still waiting for the shoe to drop.

"Vell den, Mr. Swede," Kangas began as he took another swallow. "I told you dat Ingrid is too good for you."

Carl swallowed and replied, "Don't you tink she should decide dat?"

"Suppose I told you I plan to marry Ingrid," Kangas said gravely. "Vhat vould you say to dat?"

"Vell, if she vants to marry you, den dere is notting to say."

"I haven't convinced her yet, but I vill." Kangas continued. He stood up close to Carl, his bearded face sour and his breath tainted with alcohol, "I don't vant you in dere messing tings up."

"It is up to Ingrid to decide," Carl said, as he took a step backwards.

"She is yust voman," Kangas scoffed. Then in a hard voice he said.

"I am varning you Lindstrom, stay avay from Ingrid. I could tell Alfred dat I don't vant you around da mill and he vould send you avay. Or I could use more drastic vay." Kangas slammed his fist against the open palm of the other hand.

"I get your point," Carl swallowed, backing away. Although he had no desire to fight with the formidable Finn, he also thought of beautiful Ingrid with her large flashing eyes. However, now was not the time to settle the issue.

"Vell I tink I vill be leaving now," Carl said as he opened the door.

"Yust you mind what I said," Kangas rumbled as he took another swallow from the jug.

The other mill hands were watching from across the yard, listening for any telltale signs of struggle within the cabin. They were disappointed when Carl walked calmly out of the cabin unscathed and headed for his horse. Kangas glowered out at them with jug in hand and growled. "Vhat are you all staring at?"

The crowd quickly dispersed. Kangas had another drink or two then stepped into his sauna to relax, taking the jug with him. A short while later there was a commotion as Kangas came out of his cabin stark naked and dove into a nearby snowbank. There was a loud exclamation from the shock to his body as he rolled in the snow. After a few brief moments he scrambled up and went back inside, presumably back to his sauna.

Ingrid, who was still working in the dining hall with her mother cleaning up, heard the commotion and looked outside. In the moonlight she could see that the massive hairy body of Kangas was naked. She quickly looked away.

"What is that crazy Finn up to?" Agnes said as she looked also. "Oh my God, he is rolling around in the snowbank, stark naked."

"I told you he was an animal, Mother," Ingrid said.

"You don't have to convince me," Agnes snorted.

Some of the non-Finnish hands also shook their heads at Kangas's behaviour. Esa, who had been over at the bunkhouse visiting them, explained that cooling it in a snowbank was part of the sauna experience. He also remarked, "Dat is vhy ve are so tough."

Alfred was playing his fiddle to a familiar waltz with Astrid accompanying him with the guitar. When she had earlier expressed strong interest in wanting to learn how to play, Alfred bought her a guitar and was now giving her lessons on how to chord.

After a few bars, Alfred said, "Your timing is getting good."

"Thank you Papa. What is the name of that tune again?"

"*Life in the Finland Woods*," Alfred replied as they continued playing.

Their music was interrupted by a pounding on the door with a hoarse voice calling for Ingrid. Kangas had come to main house in an advanced state of intoxication with thoughts of courting Ingrid. Ingrid shrank away into her bedroom, saying, "Please, Papa, I don't want to see that animal."

"Don't let that drunken Finn in here," Agnes reiterated.

"Ingrid!" Kangas cried again as he beat on the door.

Alfred opened it just enough to speak to Kangas.

"What do you want?" he demanded.

"I want to see Ingrid," Kangas replied.

"She is in bed," Alfred said curtly. "It is very late. Go back to your cabin."

"I just wanna see her a minute."

"Goodnight Kangas," Alfred said sharply as he shut the door in his face.

Goodnight Ingrid, beautiful Ingrid," he cried, and as he turned away he began to sing the tune Alfred was playing earlier.

"Why do we keep that crazy Finn around?" Agnes asked.

"He's the best sawyer I've ever had and he gets a lot of work done."

"Surely you can train someone else to run the saw! We can't have him coming to our house at night in a drunken state, terrifying Ingrid."

"No we can't. I'll speak to him in the morning," Alfred assured her.

"Is he an example of life in the Finland woods?" Agnes said sardonically.

Alfred grinned crookedly at her.

When breakfast was served the following morning Ingrid did her best to stay as far away from Kangas as possible. Alfred gave him a hard look so as to suggest he was displeased with Kangas's behaviour the previous night. Finally at the end of the breakfast Kangas brought his empty plate to the wash basin at the head table rather than leave it for Ingrid or Agnes to pick up. He walked directly up to Ingrid and she shrank away from him. Agnes had her hand firmly on a large ladle, ready to brain Kangas if need be, while Alfred stood close by.

Kangas smiled and said in Swedish with a soft voice, "I would like to apologize for my behaviour last night. One should never drink moonshine and have a sauna at the same time. It does crazy things."

"Apology accepted, Mr. Kangas," Ingrid replied in a cold flat voice. She was astonished with his apparent change in mannerisms.

Agnes nodded but said nothing. Her hand, clutching the ladle, was trembling.

"I am sorry Alfred," Kangas said facing him. "I promise I won't bother your family at night again."

"You must know that my house is a private place where my family must feel safe. "You're a good hand Kangas, I'd hate to lose you, but. . ."

"I uh. . ."

"Go back to work Kangas. We will forget it for now."

For the next while Kangas was pleasant, especially to Ingrid. To improve his appearance, he even trimmed his beard and hair somewhat. This worried Ingrid, she was used to Kangas the Barbarian, this new facade that Kangas put forward was unsettling. She knew that Kangas the Barbarian was still lurking under the surface, and that he had designs upon her bothered Ingrid even more.

On the other hand she saw less and less of Carl. He came in only for his midday meals and while at the table avoided eye contact with Ingrid. When she came by with coffee, often deliberately, he would politely accept another cup but there was no more sparkle in his voice. This worried Ingrid because she felt that if ever there was a man who could make her forget about Michael it would be Carl.

Two weeks had passed, and Carl had not come in for any meals, Ingrid was worried that she might never see the big handsome Swede again.

One day Ingrid asked her father. "Why doesn't Carl Lindstrom come here any more?"

"All of the Lindstrom wood has been sawn. They are hauling it home now." Alfred replied.

"Does Carl come for the wood or. . ?"

"Sometimes. Sometimes his father or brother comes. Why the sudden interest in Carl Lindstrom?"

Alfred observed that Ingrid blushed and smiled shyly, avoiding eye contact.

"You like him don't you?"

"Yes. I mean he seems like a nice young man," Ingrid fumbled.

"He *is* a nice young man," Alfred added. "I understand that he, his brother and his father have established a prosperous farm near Morning Glory."

"Well, I hope he stops by for coffee next time he comes for his lumber," Ingrid said nonchalantly.

"I will invite him in," Alfred replied with a knowing grin.

The following day when Carl came for a sleigh load of lumber, the last of the lumber owing to the Lindstroms, Alfred invited him into the little office he had built near the mill.

"Sit down, Carl," he said in English. "I vould like to sit and chat vit you."

"Vhats on your mind Mr. Erlander?" Carl said modestly as he sat on one of the wooden chairs in front of Alfred's desk.

"Ingrid has vondered vhy you don't come to da house for coffee or lunch any more."

"Dere is no need for me to go dere, Mr. Erlander. I yust come for our lumber den go home again,"Carl said nervously.

"You may call me Alfred," Alfred said. He noticed that Carl bore an uncomfortable look with the mention of Ingrid. Then he carefully continued. "How is your farm coming along?"

"Quite vell actually," Carl replied. "Ve are buying anudder quarter of land dis year."

"You vill be bringing me more logs next vinter."

"Ya, quite likely."

"So Carl, now dat you are getting set up, have you ever tought of getting a vife?"

Carl studied Alfred's words and continued. "Ya, I have tought of it. Da girl I vant is spoken for."

"Oh is dat so?" Alfred replied evenly. "Did you ever tink to court my daughter?"

"Ya, dat's who I mean," Carl said nervously.

"Ingrid is not spoken for."

"Kangas da Finn vants to marry her."

"Kangas da Finn," Alfred spat. "I know he vants her but he'll never get her. She doesn't like him and ve vould never allow it."

Carl smiled guardedly.

"He is a good vorker and sawyer, but I don't vant him as part of my family."

"Is dat vhy you are pushing Ingrid on to me?" Carl laughed.

"Ya, partly. But I know she likes you and I like you. If you have a mind to court her, I von't stand in your vay."

"Tank you Mr. Erlander, you have given me someting to tink about. Vell, I should be going now."

The weeks had passed and winter had turned into spring as the warm April sunshine melted the snow away. Carl had not called even though both Ingrid and Alfred had hoped he would. Kangas was satisfied that Carl had been warned away. He was convinced that his new soft approach was working as Ingrid seemed less hostile lately. He was sitting in his cabin one evening after work sipping on his jug, when he saw Ingrid head to the barn to milk the solitary milk cow that Alfred kept. When he was sober, Kangas could contain his feelings for Ingrid, however liquor fuelled his desire for her. He took one last hearty swallow and headed for the barn also. He was going to press the issue with Ingrid and convince her to be his bride.

Ingrid was just about to start milking the cow when Kangas came through the doorway.

"Kangas," she gasped in fear, dropping the milk bucket. She could see that his bloodshot eyes were glazed with alcohol and filled with desire.

"I would like to talk to you Ingrid Erlander," he said in Swedish.

"Yes Kangas,' Ingrid trembled as she began to back toward the wall.

"I would like to talk about us."

"U-us,?' Ingrid quivered.

"We should stop beating around the bush you know. It is time we thought about marriage," Kangas continued, as he advanced toward her.

"M-marriage to you," Ingrid stuttered as she was now against the wall. She could feel the handle of a pitchfork behind her and she clutched it firmly.

"I would make you a good strong husband and give you many children."

"M-marry you? No Kangas, I don't love you, now please leave. You are scaring me."

"What has love got to do with it?" Kangas continued, as he moved toward her. "I love you and in time you will learn to love me. You are a woman and I am a man."

Suddenly Ingrid swung the pitchfork around pointing the tines at Kangas, "Don't come any closer Kangas or I'll stick this in your belly."

"Oh, a woman with spirit," he laughed heartily, undeterred by the pitchfork waving in his face. "You would make a fine wife for Kangas the Finn."

"Marry you? Never!" Ingrid exclaimed. She felt more confident now that she was armed. "I despise you Kangas the Finn, you're drunk and you're an animal."

"Maybe you want that big Swede who was here last winter," Kangas sneered as he moved closer.

"Don't come any nearer!" Ingrid cried, waiving the pitchfork in his face. "I'll stick it in you."

"You'll what," Kangas laughed as he snatched the pitchfork from her and flung it aside.

"Don't come near me!" Ingrid cried in desperation as Kangas moved closer.

Just then the door burst open and in walked Carl Lindstrom.

"Carl Lindstrom!" Ingrid exclaimed with great relief.

Kangas whirled around and said with a growl. "What are you doing here Lindstrom? There is no more lumber for you."

"I came to see Ingrid," Carl replied evenly. Then to Ingrid, he said,"I am sorry I didn't call on you sooner, but I finally got up my courage tonight."

"Came to see Ingrid?" Kangas snarled. "I told you to stay away from Ingrid. She's mine!"

"I'm not yours!" Ingrid screamed. "I hate you!"

"Well then, I guess she's not yours," Carl challenged.

Kangas' huge fist sprang out at Carl but Carl caught it in mid-air as if it were a baseball

Kangas's other fist also shot out and Carl caught it as well. The two of them locked hands and began a titanic struggle of trying to arm wrestle each other down.

"Nobody can beat Kangas the Finn at arm wrestling," Kangas gasped as beads of sweat stood out on his forehead.

"There is always a first time," Carl gasped. Ingrid could see his face beginning to turn purple from the powerful struggle.

Ingrid watched with awe and anxiety as the two powerful men grappled for physical and psychological supremacy. They grunted and groaned, pushing each other back and forth. "Come on Carl," she cried.

As Carl was taller than Kangas, with longer arms, he was given a slight advantage as both men were of about equal strength. Slowly, but surely he was bending Kangas down. Suddenly with one mighty groan of defeat, Kangas collapsed to his knees with his hand bent over the back of his head. Carl released him and collapsed against a centre post in the barn to catch his breath. Kangas remained on his knees putting his sore, red hands on his thighs.

He looked up and smiled, then in a gasping voice, he said, "You know something Swede. You are the first person to ever beat Kangas the Finn at arm wrestling." He looked at both Ingrid and Carl then added. "I guess she's yours."

"She's not mine," Carl replied. "But she has the right to let me court her if she wants. Without any interference from you."

"Well Ingrid," Kangas said with a smile while still remaining on his knees. "Do you want this big Swede to court you?"

"Yes, I would like that very much." Ingrid gave Carl her most beautiful smile.

Kangas crawled to his feet and looked at both of them. "I am sorry for all the foolishness. I'll be leaving in the morning."

"You don't have to," Ingrid said. She was now feeling sorry for the big Finn whose personality seemed to fluctuate from being a villain to a gentleman. "If you promise to leave me alone and accept the fact that Carl and I are courting, I won't tell Papa about tonight."

"You're a fine lady, Ingrid Erlander," Kangas smiled. "I hope this big dumb Swede appreciates this."

"Oh I do, I do," Carl laughed. "I care for her so much that I was even willing to face Kangas the Finn."

"You beat Kangas the Finn," Kangas replied. "Things will never be the same."

"I'll tell no one of this if you leave Ingrid and I alone," Carl offered.

"No you won, I'll be leaving in the morning. Esa or the old man can do the sawing."

Kangas turned and walked out the door. Ingrid let out a sigh of relief and threw herself into Carl's arms. He held her for a long moment until the cow bawled, telling them that it needed to be milked. Carl volunteered to do the job for her.

When they headed back to the house with the bucket of milk, they could see smoke curling from the chimney of the sauna room of Kangas's cabin. They laughed as Carl said. "Poor Kangas he must be sweating his troubles away."

"I am surprised how easily he gave in," Ingrid said. "I would have thought that a man of his reputation woul have challenged you to an outright fight to the finish."

"Yes, I expected that," Carl said gravely. "But I think that under that rough exterior is a man of honour. In his heart he knew you would never accept him as a beau or husband, no matter what he did to me. He knew also that if he had beaten me to a pulp you would have hated him even more. This way he could walk away and hope that you might one day respect him."

"Yes that's true," Ingrid sighed. "He's a very unpredictable person. But I think he is, as you say, a man of honour."

"He'll probably be true to his word and leave in the morning," Carl said. "He was, as the saying goes, defeated in both love and war."

"Let's not say anything about the confrontation in the barn," Ingrid said. "No harm came of it."

"It is yours to tell or not to tell. I will stand by your decision." Carl smiled at her. "You are truly a remarkable woman."

Ingrid smiled radiantly at him and slipped her hand in his.

Chapter Twelve

The following day, which was Sunday, Carl arrived just after lunch with a single seat, one-horse carriage. Alfred was all smiles when he let Carl into the house.

"Vould you like a cup of coffee?" Agnes offered warmly in English as she pulled a chair away from the table for him to sit on.

"Dat sounds like a good idea, by yiminy," Carl replied, as he sat down.

"I will be ready in a minute," Ingrid called from the bedroom in Swedish.

"You're going to have to learn to speak English like everybody else," Clarence added in clear English.

"It's okay," Carl laughed. "She vill learn to speak English in her own good time."

"Did you hear dat Kangas da Finn quit dis morning?" Alfred said.

"No. I tought he vas your right-hand man."

"He vas. He didn't give any reason. He yust said he had to move on."

Ingrid emerged from the bedroom wearing a fine Sunday dress and bonnet. Carl smiled broadly at her radiant beauty. "Yiminy, yehoshaphat, you look beautiful," he gasped.

"Tank you, Carl Lindstrom," Ingrid replied in faltering English.

She drew up a chair and sat down beside him and Carl said to Alfred. "So vat are you going to do vit da sauna?"

"Esa is still here," Alfred said. "He likes it yust as much as Kangas."

"I'll use it too," Clarence piped in. "I love sitting in a sauna."

"Tings von't be da same around here vitout Kangas," Carl said evenly.

"There was a certain animal magnetism about him," Ingrid added in Swedish. She had a sort of oblique attraction to this crude man whom she had faced-down with a pitchfork.

"You're right about the animal part," Agnes added, also in Swedish.

"Ya, yust as well he is gone," Alfred added in English.

Carl turned to Ingrid and said in Swedish, "Well, seeing that you are all dressed-up are you ready for a buggy ride?"

He stood up and offered his arm and Ingrid laughed and slipped her hand through it. He put his huge hand lightly over the back of hers and said to the others in English, "Ve vill be back later on in da afternoon."

"Have a good time, both Alfred and Agnes said. Then she added,"Ve vill have coffee and yelly rolls for you."

"We are going in style," Ingrid gasped as she saw the fine, roofed one-horse carriage with a single leather seat.

"A beautiful lady deserves a fine carriage," Carl grinned as he helped her into the carriage. "Actually, it is Mom and Dad's carriage, they use for special outings."

"Where are we going?" Ingrid asked as they set off on a trail in a direction she had never travelled previously.

"To Morning Glory where I will buy you a soda pop."

"A soda pop?" Ingrid had heard of this North American beverage but had never tasted one.

"There is a new drink called Coca-Cola that is very tasty. Have you never drunk soda pop?"

"No, but I have heard of it."

"Have you ever been to Morning Glory?"

"No, except when the train stopped there when we came out here, but Papa deals there all the time. He says he gets better prices for supplies there than in River Bend. It is a little closer too."

"The storekeeper there, Alistair McLeod, is a fine man. He treats his customers very well and is a friend of mine." Carl said.

"Are there many houses at Morning Glory?"

"Just a few. The store and the people who work for the railroad live there."

The trail was similar to the one that led to River Bend as it also snaked from one ridge to another to avoid sloughs and muskegs. The journey however, was much smoother as the carriage had a soft seat and springs.. Even when they inevitably splashed through a mud hole it seemed like fun. She and Carl would laugh together. Finally they crossed the railway tracks and turned up a trail toward an odd-shaped building with the mismatched gables on the roof. The large sign out front said, MORNING GLORY GENERAL STORE Carl tied the horse to the hitching post out front and helped Ingrid out of the carriage. She still held on to his huge hand as they walked up the broad steps to the store entrance.

A bell tinkled from above the door, and a burly-faced man with kind eyes came through from the back.

"Good afternoon, Alistair," Carl said pleasantly.

"Afternoon, Carl," Alistair replied. Then with a twinkle in his eye added. "I see ye brought some company wi ye."

Carl blushed and said, "Alistair, I vould like you to meet Ingrid Erlander."

"Tis a pleasure ma'am," Alistair smiled as he extended his hand. "Are ye from the same Erlander thah has thae mill?"

"Her fadder owns da mill," Carl said.

Ingrid smiled uncertainly at all this conversation which she only half understood.

"Excuse us," Carl said. "Ingrid does not speak English."

He turned to Ingrid and explained in Swedish what Alistair had said.

Ingrid took his hand and said awkwardly in English, "How do you do?"

"Tis a pleasure." Then to Carl he said, " By jings Carl, ye sure know how tae pick a bonny lass tae be courtin'"

"Alistair says you are very beautiful," Carl translated.

"Tank you," Ingrid blushed.

"A few more comments, Alistair, and ve vill have her speaking English, by yiminy."

Both men laughed and Ingrid looked perplexed.

"Say Alistair, do you have any bottles of Coca-Cola here?"

"Aye, thah I do." He went to a large icebox at the end of the counter and brought two bottles, then popped off the lids.

"Um, good," Ingrid said as she savoured the dark-coloured drink.

"I told you, you would like it," Carl laughed. Then turning to Alistair he said in English. "Dis is da first time Ingrid has tasted soda pop."

Presently a woman came out from the living-quarters. She and Ingrid glanced at each other in instant recognition.

"Yer thae lassie on thae train." the woman exclaimed. "I couldna forget thae bright eyes ae yours."

"You Scotch voman," Ingrid faltered. "Come here, get married."

"Aye, I'm Effie, Alistair sent fer me," she put her arm around Alistair, and Ingrid smiled. "Whah was yer name again?"

"Ingrid."

"Aye Ingrid, ae beautiful name fer ae bonny lass," she said.

"Pity she doesna speak English yet, tae be hearin'a thae compliments," Alistair added.

"Ye don't speak English?" Effie said, looking at Ingrid.

"No English, not well."

"Thah's alright, Carl will have tae teach ye."

Carl turned to Ingrid and explained, "They say I will have to teach you to speak English."

"Maybe sometime," Ingrid laughed and replied in Swedish. "But don't ever expect me to learn how to read it."

They all chatted for a while with Carl serving as an interpreter. He could sense Ingrid's discomfort at being in the midst of conversations she couldn't understand, so they continued on their outing. They doubled back over the same trail for awhile then took another trail that led to a well-appointed farmstead composed of log buildings and rail fences. There was a grove of planted spruce trees along the laneway. A small flock of sheep were in the field beyond the fence. Their bleating could be heard rippling through the flock.

"Who lives here?" Ingrid gasped.

"We do," Carl laughed. "This is the Lindstrom farm."

"It is very beautiful," Ingrid said as she looked all around.

They drew up in front of a well-built log house that was about the size of her father's house minus the dining hall. As Carl helped Ingrid down from the carriage a middle-aged woman with graying hair done up in a bun, came to the door and smiled at Ingrid.

Carl introduced Ingrid to his mother, Alva.

"Come right in," Alva beckoned in Swedish. "We will put the coffee on, and I have some freshly-baked cookies." The Lindstrom house was a three-roomed house like her father's with a loft above the bedrooms, but the loft was small due to a lower pitch to the roof and appeared to be used exclusively for storage. There was a stone fireplace to one side and in front of it was a large spinning-wheel and a quantity of raw wool, in a wicker basket. There were photographs and tapestries on the walls, and shelves full of books. Ingrid was offered a choice of one of two rocking chairs near the fireplace and spinning-wheel. Carl sat on a regular chair beside Ingrid.

"What a beautiful home you have here, Mrs. Lindstrom," Ingrid gasped, as she looked around the well-appointed room.

"Thank you. We try to live as comfortable as possible out here on the frontier," Alva laughed.

Presently the door opened and in walked Oscar, and a young man in his mid-youth with copper-coloured hair. Ingrid smiled at her recognition of Oscar from the times he was at their place.

Oscar smiled and said, "You are Alfred Erlander's daughter. What was your name?"

"Ingrid," Carl and Ingrid said together.

"Ingrid, yes that's it," Oscar laughed.

"Since you already know my father," Carl said I would like to introduce you to my brother, Ole."

"It's a pleasure to meet you, Ole," Ingrid smiled warmly.

"Pleased to meet you," Ole smiled shyly.

Oscar sat in the other rocking chair. After Alva brought the coffee and cookies, she sat at a stool by the spinning-wheel and spun wool while she visited. Ole sat quietly back beside the kitchen table.

"So when did you come from the Old Country?" Ingrid asked Oscar.

"We came at the turn of the century, first to the American state of Minnesota, a lot of Swedes went there, and after a few years we came here. Minnesota was too well-settled, I wanted something new and fresh, then I heard that there was still plenty of land in Alberta."

"You sound like Papa," Ingrid laughed.

"Anyhow, Carl and I came to Morning Glory in the spring of 1905, before the railroad came. We liked what we saw and there were already some Swedish families here such as Gunner Elofson. So, I filed a homestead and here we are."

"Interesting," Ingrid replied sipping on her coffee. "Do you have other children beside Carl and Ole?"

"We have a married daughter, Clara, back in Minnesota" and with a twinge of sadness in his eye added. "There are two more buried there. One died of pneumonia at age four and the other was killed in an accident at age six."

Ingrid noticed tears in the corners of Alva's eyes at the mention of the two children.

Oscar added, "That is the main reason we moved on. Too many memories."

"I am sorry to hear that," Ingrid said sympathetically.

"So, how many in your family?" Alva asked.

"Just Astrid, Clarence, little Jamie and myself," Ingrid replied. "I am the oldest, little Jamie was born last year and Papa says he's our true Canadian son. We were going to call him 'Jim' after Mr. Mcdonald, but Mom said 'Jim' was an older person's name so we called him 'Jamie'."

"So, do you know how to speak English yet?" Oscar laughed.

"Not very much," Ingrid blushed. "I know I should learn, but everyone I know can speak Swedish."

"We are the same," Alva laughed. "I don't think I know more than ten words of English."

"I might learn how to speak it someday," Ingrid said, "But I doubt if I can ever learn how to read it."

"Reading it is easy," Carl laughed. "The spelling of some words is kind of odd, but basically it is similar to Swedish."

"That's what Clarence says," Ingrid replied. "Since they started school, both he and Astrid can speak and read English fluently."

Alva turned her attention to the spinning and Alfred packed a pipe full of tobacco. The conversation turned to talk about the mill and the Erlander family.

After a while Carl took Ingrid home. As he helped her from the carriage in front of her father's house she smiled and said. "Thank you for the wonderful day Carl. Thank you for the soda pop and thank you for introducing me to your parents. They are wonderful people and I hope to see them again."

Carl smiled and said, "Does this mean we are officially courting?"

"Officially, I would have to say *yes*," Ingrid smiled shyly.

"Then I will come calling again next Sunday," Carl grinned, squeezing her hand.

Ingrid stood on her tiptoes and kissed him briefly on the lips. "Bye Carl, see you soon."

As she turned and went into the house Carl watched her go; his stomach seemed full of butterflies.

As the courtship grew, Ingrid wrote about it in a letter to Sigrud.

June 23, 1912
Dear Sigrud,
I think I am in love. As you know, the big handsome Swede, Carl Lindstrom, has been courting me since spring. The other night, both to celebrate my seventeenth birthday and the passing of the solstice, we had a Midsummer Festival at the Lindstrom farm. Both our family and the Elofsons attended, except poor Lars. We had a big bonfire and watched the sun go down. It gets darker here at midnight than back home, but there is still a glow in the north. Carl gave me a gold necklace, but I can't imagine where he got the money to buy it. We sat up nearly all night and talked. I felt so warm and secure with his great, huge arm around me. Papa says that if he has a good summer with the mill he may have enough to send me back to Sweden for a visit in the Fall.
I am looking forward to the Dominion Day picnic on July 1st. That is a special day in Canada honouring its nationhood. This will be the first official celebration that Morning Glory will host. Of course Carl will be escorting me and this makes it all the more special. I will stop for now and finish this letter after Dominion Day.

Carl came for Ingrid mid-morning on Dominion Day. He brought the one-horse carriage. Normally his parents would have used it for such an important outing, but since Carl was courting a special lady of whom they were very fond, they conceded to go to the picnic in the wagon with Ole.

The celebration was held in a clearing near the store that had been designated as a community area, where they later hoped to build a community hall. Two booths, built from slabs and culls donated by Alfred, had been set up previously. One served as a concession where soda pop, homemade popcorn and candy were sold. The other was a bazaar where some of the women displayed or sold their handiwork. On the shady side of the concession booth a Crown and Anchor game-of-chance was set up. Here many of the men bet pennies and nickels on the squares where they hoped the clicking wheel would stop. The proceeds from both, the Crown and Anchor and the two booths were to go toward the building of the planned Community Hall.

INGRID

A flagpole had been erected near the main booth and a flag-raising ceremony was held at noon. Alistair did the honours. When the ceremony got underway, he declared in his clear but Scottish inflected voice:

"Today is a grand day for thae community ae Mornin' Glory as we host our first celebration ae Canada's birthday. Forty-five years ago this day Canada became ae proud dominion in thae British Empire. And seven years ago, Alberta became ae province."

There was a loud outburst of applause and cheering.

"Now if ye will all stand at attention please."

Everyone stood still and erect as he hoisted the Union Jack to the top of the flagpole.

Effie began to sing *O Canada* and she was soon joined by the schoolchildren and those adults who knew the words. Although Ingrid did not understand most of Alistair's speech she felt a great feeling of pride and emotion with the flag raising and song that honoured her new land.

In the early afternoon races were held for the children. The three races held were, the standard race, the three legged race and the sack race. The winner of any given race was given a candy from the booth. While children ran the races, the women visited, some knitted or crocheted while they talked, many neighbours met each other for the first time. The men alternated from the Crown and Anchor wheel to the area where the horses and wagons were tethered. Here, out of sight of their wives, they could enjoy a snort of moonshine or a sip of home-made wine.

As Ingrid walked across the grounds in search of Carl she spotted a young woman, leading a toddler by the hand. She was dressed in that head covering she had seen on ship, worn by the Bokovinian women. Suddenly she recognized the woman and cried out, "You are Olga."

The woman smiled a broad smile and said, "*Tak[1]*, you Ingrid."

"How are you?" Ingrid smiled in faltering English as she embraced Olga. "You live here?"

"I live dere," Olga pointed to the road leading north out of Morning Glory. "Vhat doing you here?"

"I live here too," Ingrid pointed to the south. "Papa saw wood."

[1]*Tak* - yes

Presently a dark-haired man with a broad face and pleasant disposition, came up along side the woman and spoke to her in Ukrainian.

"Dis your husband?" Ingrid asked.

"*Tak*, husband man," Olga replied.

"You know my Missis?" the man asked.

Olga informed him, in Ukrainian, that they had met on the ship that brought them both to Canada.

"You little boy?" Ingrid smiled, looking at the toddler by her side.

"Ya, Peter he born last year already," the man said.

"Hello Myron," Carl said as he came upon the scene.

"Carl Lindstrom, *yak samayete*[2]," Myron smiled in turn. "Dis your voman?"

"Not yet, but maybe soon," Carl laughed, as he took Ingrid's hand in his.

"Maybe soon we have big wedding yet," Myron laughed.

"Ya, maybe soon," Carl smiled in turn. Ingrid wore a perplexed smile as she sensed that she was the centre of conversation.

Olga spoke to Myron in Ukrainian and they excused themselves.

"What were you talking about?" Ingrid asked.

"We were talking about you. He wanted to know if you were my wife." Carl grinned.

"What did you tell him?" Ingrid probed.

"I said, no."

"Carl Lindstrom, is that all you said?" Ingrid demanded.

"Yes, it is a little early to tell him anything else," Carl teased.

"Humph!" Ingrid exclaimed.

They walked along in silence still holding hands. Finally Ingrid asked. "Is her husband Bokovinian, too?"

"Boko. . what?" Carl asked with a puzzled look. "Her husband's name is Myron Kostiuk, I think they are called Ukrainians."

"I met her on the ship," Ingrid said. "Although we didn't understand one another, I was able to find out that her name is Olga and she came from Bokovinia which Clarence says is part of Austria-Hungary."

"The Austro-Hungarian Empire rules a lot of different people and probably includes some Ukrainians." Carl replied.

Clarence came running up to them excitedly and asked in English, "Hey, Mr. Lindstrom, do you want to play baseball?"

[2]*yak samayete* - How are you?

"Baseball?" Carl replied with a knitted brow. He had heard of this popular American game that was the rage of the schoolchildren. He had also heard that there were supposedly two adult teams in River Bend. "I don't know how to play baseball."

"Most of you adults don't, but we'll teach you. We are trying to get enough players for two teams," Clarence said breathlessly. "So will you play Mr. Lindstrom?"

"Vell if da udder adults are playing I vill give it a try," Carl sighed.

"Thanks a lot Mr. Lindstrom. Come over to where the races were held. We are going to set up a diamond there." Clarence turned and ran to recruit some more players.

"What did he want?" Ingrid asked with a puzzled look.

"He wants me to play baseball."

"Baseball?"

"Yes, it's an American game. All the schoolchildren are crazy about it."

"So are you going to play?"

"I think it might be fun. That is, if you don't mind."

"I think it would be fun to watch you play a game," Ingrid laughed.

Chapter Thirteen

A crowd of young men gathered, all eager to learn how to play baseball. The teacher of the Aspen Ridge school, a one-roomed school located halfway between Morning Glory and River Bend, and the same one that Astrid and Clarence attended, took charge of the situation. He declared that each team needed a captain and since the massively-built Carl towered above most of the others he was chosen for one team.

"Me!" Carl blushed. "I don't even know how to play."

"None of us do," the teacher assured him.

"I'll help you if you pick me to be on your team, Mr. Lindstrom," Clarence offered.

"Yes Clarence, you are on my team," Carl said quickly.

"And for the captain of the second team I pick you," the teacher said Carl turned to find that Kangas the Finn had just joined them. Kangas's hair was shorn to a respectable length and his beard was neatly-trimmed. Carl also noticed that Signe Elofson was clutching his hand. Kangas looked at Carl and laughed, "So we are in competition again, Lindstrom."

"So it seems," Carl replied. "I see you have a lady friend."

"Ya, Signe," Kangas said, as he squeezed her hand causing her to giggle. "After I left mill I start vorking for Gunner Elofson."

"Let's get on with the team selection," the teacher said.

Dag Elofson offered to coach Kangas in the same way Clarence had offered Carl.

Meanwhile, Carl chose his brother Ole, Esa and Myron Kostiuk among his players

Kangas chose Elfin and Lars Elofson among his.

Each team ended up with twelve players but the teacher explained that only nine of them could play at a time and the others could be rotated in during the game. Clarence was pitcher of one team and Dag the other. Even though most of the players on each team were full-grown men and Clarence and Dag were each only fourteen-years-old, they made up for their youth with more knowledge and practice with the game. Ole and Lars were catchers for their respective teams. Carl played first base on his team and Kangas played shortstop on his. The school supplied the bats and balls, along with a catchers mitt, to be shared. Only the school students had ball gloves and most of those were makeshift or in disrepair. Others were left to try to catch the ball barehanded.

The bases of the diamond were roughly paced out and marked and since there was no backstop, the spectators were advised not to sit directly behind the catcher. As the game got underway, the teacher, who served as umpire, had to employ younger boys to chase after the balls that the catcher missed as they bounced into the bush. After a few errant balls nearly struck some of the bystanders, the growing crowd of spectators heeded the teacher's advice about not sitting behind the catcher. The players, most of whom only had heavy boots for footwear, found them too cumbersome and soon resorted to playing barefoot. Curses could be heard from time-to-time when someone stubbed a toe. The players soon learned that playing without a catching glove was a painful experience especially if the fly ball was driven by a bat wielded by either Carl or Kangas. Conversely, these two were the only ones with tough enough hands to repeatedly catch fly balls barehanded. Soon, whenever Carl or Kangas hit the ball, no one tried to catch it. In any event they usually hit the ball so far that they were assured a home run.

The spectators soon got caught up in the game and were cheering wildly for their favourite team. Ingrid found herself jumping up and down and screaming whenever Carl hit the ball or caught a fly. The players were also caught up with the emotion of the game as many arguments erupted in disputes as to whether a player was declared either *safe on base* or *out*.

As the game wore on, some of the players showed special skills. Carl and Kangas were heavy hitters, Clarence was a skilled pitcher, and the adroit Esa was an expert at stealing bases.

At one point, halfway through the game, with Kangas's team lagging behind, Esa sprinted for third-base on a steal. Kangas, from his shortstop position, stepped in his way and Esa collided with this massive bulky man and found himself sprawled on the ground. The third baseman caught the ball and Esa was declared out.

Esa jumped up in anger. "Vhat you knock me down for?" he demanded.

"You always steal bases," Kangas roared back.

"You cheating," Esa argued.

"Says who," Kangas roared.

The game stopped as the two Finns argued ferociously. When they started cursing each other they switched to speaking in Finnish. Finally Kangas gave Esa a shove with both hands nearly knocking him over. The other players and spectators watched in amazement as Esa sprang into the air as if his legs were springs, turned a somersault and drop kicked Kangus in the face with both his bare feet. Kangas was knocked over onto his buttocks, while Esa landed with the agility of a cat. He danced around Kangas ready for his next move. In a moment Kangas was on his feet and charging at Esa like an enraged bull. He swung out with a huge haymaker punch with a force that would have shattered Esa's jaw if it had made contact, but the ever agile Esa easily side-stepped him and kneed him in the solar plexus. His knee however, bounced off Kangas's hardened stomach muscles as if they were made of rubber. Kangas grabbed Esa and was about to embrace him with a crushing bearhug, but Esa wiggled free. In a moment he was behind Kangas whereupon he drop kicked him again, between the shoulder blades. Kangas was knocked flat on his face, but was soon on his feet charging and growling like a wounded bear.

The men in the crowd were cheering wildly, mostly for Esa. They were glad to see that the formidable Kangas might not be so invincible after all. The women were generally disgusted. Agnes remarked to Alva who was sitting beside her, "Those crazy Finns, all they ever do is drink and fight."

Finally the teacher tried to restore order and several players gathered around to break up the fight. Carl grabbed Kangas from behind, putting his arms up under Kangas' shoulders and locking his fingers behind Kangas's head in a Full Nelson. This effectively immobilized Kangas though he cursed and swore, and demanded to be let go. Ole and one of the mill-hands grabbed Esa and held him fast.

The teacher came into the fray and glaring at both Finns he said, "The next lesson in baseball is, fighting on the field is absolutely not allowed. I want both of you to cool off and go sit on the benches for a couple of innings."

"But I got team to run," Kangas protested.

"So, run it from the bench," the teacher said firmly.

"Did you hear da teacher?" Carl said in English as he momentarily applied more pressure to Kangas's neck.

"I heard," Kangas gasped.

Both belligerents were released and went to their respective benches, that being an area at the sides of the diamond where they sat in the grass. They glowered at each other across the home plate for a time. They may well have got into a second fight had it not been for the intimidating presence of Carl Lindstrom who kept a watchful eye on both of them. Ingrid was very proud of the fact that her beau was the only man around who could handle Kangas the Finn.

The game carried on and after a couple of innings, Kangas and Esa were both back in the game. They carried on as if the altercation between them had never taken place. Then came the bottom of the ninth inning with two out. Kangas's team was three points ahead, but Carl's team was up-to-bat. The bases were loaded and Carl took his place at bat. Dag was nervous as he knew that if Carl hit the ball, the game would turn around. Twice the ball went by Carl and twice Carl swung and missed. Dag wound up and threw his best overhand pitch as hard and fast as he could, hoping that Carl would miss again.

Crack!! The bat connected and the ball shot far over the heads of both the shortstop and left fielder at bullet speed to land in the forest at the edge of the clearing. The left fielder, who had no glove, ran after it. Even if he had caught up to the ball he had no intention of trying to catch it until it bounced off the ground at least once. Carl ran the bases and seemed to literally chase the players ahead of him as four successive runs including Carl's home run were tallied. Wild cheers erupted everywhere and Ingrid was ecstatic. Even as the other players hugged and clasped Carl on the back Ingrid rushed in and hugged him tightly. Since his team did not have another turn at batting and thus no hope of reversing the score, Kangas conceded defeat. There were chants of "Hip, hip hurrah" for the winner and then the losers. The players from the opposing teams shook hands, including Kangas and Esa.

When Kangas shook hands with Carl he said, "You von lucky Swede, Lindstrom. You beat me at bot love and baseball." He slapped Carl on the back so hard that Carl coughed and winced.

"It looks like you didn't lose at love after all," Carl gasped as he indicated Signe on the sidelines anxiously waiting for Kangas..

"Ya, vell I guess I have to vork on baseball part," Kangas laughed.

"If you got time, vhy don't you come to my vagon for some good drink. You not vorking today."

"I yust might do dat," Carl laughed.

Most of the adult players congregated near the wagons of Kangas and Myron where they sipped moonshine and rehashed the pros and cons of the game. Many of them needed the drink to ease the smarting pain of their swollen hands. All agreed that they would have to get together in the future to play ball again, after they had a chance to purchase proper ball gloves.

When Carl joined the others over at the wagon, Ingrid lingered by the booth. Signe came alongside her and struck up a conversation in Swedish.

"Is Kangas the Finn courting you?" Ingrid asked, still unable to believe any woman would be brave enough to allow herself to be courted by him.

"Oh yes," Signe giggled. "Kang is a lot of fun. He's so big and strong."

"He is that," Ingrid sighed.

"You're beau is a big muscle man too, I see," Signe giggled again.

"Uh Carl, yes he is a real gentleman, too."

"Where did you meet him?" Signe asked enviously.

"He worked for Papa last winter. He lives near here."

"Well, I'm going to have to meet him myself."

"Carl and I are officially courting," Ingrid added sharply as she sensed that the flirtatious Signe might have an eye on the big Swede.

"Oh, I'm sure you are, but he is such a big handsome man."

"You're better off with Kangas the Finn, I can see he is more your type," Ingrid said tersely as she walked away.

That evening a dance was to be held at the ball diamond. Since there was no hall they decided to have an open-air dance on the grounds. Some of the homesteaders went home to milk their cows first, as Ole and Oscar did, but Carl and Ingrid stayed and were invited to supper with Alistair and Effie. Others like Kangas and some of the mill hands stayed around the wagons and drank moonshine while waiting for the dance. Some of the more daring young women like Signe stayed with them. Signe enjoyed sipping on the dandelion wine that was on hand.

Boris Tymchuk, one of the players on Kangas' team, and his teenage son, Steve, were walking by the boisterous party beside Kangas's wagon. They were each carrying a musical instrument, Boris a fiddle and Steve a mandolin.

"Hey dere, Boris, is it?" Kangas called. "Play tune for us."

"We get ready to play for dance," Boris said.

"So have some practice, and I give you drink."

"Okay, a deal."

Boris took a swallow of the moonshine and proclaimed, "*doche dobre*.[1]"

"You like gypsy music?" Boris asked as he and his son readied their instruments..

They played a rousing round of gypsy music that got everyone's spirits going. Kangas grabbed Signe and began to dance around. Signe broke free and began to twirl to the beat of the music almost as if it was natural for her. Kangas began to clap and grin lustfully. He grabbed Signe and kissed her passionately while he held a bottle of dandelion wine in the other. He tipped the wine bottle so the wine ran down their faces. Signe sprang away sputtering trying to wipe the sticky liquid off her face. Kangas laughed lustily and took another swallow of wine. Boris laughed so hard he quit playing.

"You act like couple of *Roshyns*," he laughed.

"Russians!" Kangas said in a sober tone. "Don't talk to me about Russians, dey are oppressors of Finland. "You Russian, Tymchuk?"

"I not *Roshyn*," Boris said quickly. "I fight *Roshyns*, I *Ukransky*."

"You play Russian music."

"It gypsy music. You asked for gypsy music so I play."

"Oh, so I did," Kangas said in a low tone. "Vell play some more."

As some of the homesteaders returned from chores to continue the festivities, one of the wagons was brought down to the ball diamond and placed over home plate. This was to be for the musicians. Among the musicians to join that night were Alfred and Astrid. Alfred had learned several popular North American tunes since coming to Canada. Astrid who could chord with the guitar and was considered quite good for someone who wasn't quite twelve years old.

The sun was still above the horizon when the dance started. Some of the younger boys were sent to gather wood for a bonfire for later. The Tymchuks played several Ukrainian polkas to get everyone in the

[1]*doche dobre* - very good

right spirit and soon the infield of the diamond was full of people hopping around. Kangas and Signe danced at a dizzying speed and frequently collided with others as Kangas whooped and hollered. Signe squealed with delight as he often swung her off her feet. Esa, when not dancing with someone, did cartwheels and somersaults through the dancing crowd, bringing more comments about wild and crazy Finns. Astrid however, laughed at Esa's antics', she thought everything he said and did was funny. When he popped up in front of her like a jack-in-the-box and asked for a dance, she giggled and accepted. Another of Boris's sons took a couple of sticks and played them on the wagon wheel spokes to the beat of the music. Carl and Ingrid did the polka to a much more civilized pace though he would often lift her out of the way to avoid collision with either Kangas or Esa. While everyone else was having a joyous time dancing, Lars Elofson stood soberly on the sidelines watching Ingrid longingly.

When everyone was exhausted from the polka the Tymchuks stepped aside to let Alfred and Astrid play a while. They played a series of waltzes including *After the Ball is Over*. As Carl and Ingrid danced to this delightful tune, they seemed as in a world of their own, eyes fastened on each other as they danced out of the crowd toward the outfield in the gathering dusk.

The spell was shattered when Clarence and Dag came along. "Wanna help us light the fire, Mr. Lindstrom?" Clarence asked in English..

"What do you boys want?" Ingrid asked sharply in Swedish.

"We need Mr. Lindstrom to help us with the big logs," Clarence replied in Swedish.

"I will help them," Carl said to Ingrid. "Go back to the others. It will be just a few minutes." He squeezed Ingrid's hand

"Oh, alright," Ingrid sighed.

She headed back to the crowd while Carl went with the youths to get the bonfire properly going.

Lars Elofson took another swallow of moonshine as he stood beside the booth watching Ingrid come from the outfield alone. As it was now starting to grow dark, the tipplers had moved their drinks to the now-closed concession booth. Lars had never been able to accept the fact that Ingrid had actually rejected him when he felt he had so much to offer her. How could she reject him when he had known her since she came to Morning Glory? How could Ingrid so quickly take up with Carl Lindstrom after such a short time of knowing the big man? In his muddled mind, Lars felt he should make one last pitch for her before she ended up marrying Carl.

As Ingrid came near the booth he called out in Swedish, "Hey, Ingrid, could I talk to you?"

Ingrid stopped and said, "Hello Lars," in a flat tone. "What can I do for you?"

"I - we need to talk." His voice was slurred from the alcohol.

"Talk, talk about what, Lars?"

"Talk about us," he stumbled.

"There's nothing to talk about for us," she said uncomfortably. "Now if you'll excuse me." She turned to walk away.

"Wait," he said as he touched her shoulder.

"What?" she demanded, as she turned around and stepped away from him.

"What has Carl got that I don't have?" His voice had a pathetic whine to it.

"I love him, that's what," she blurted. "Now I've got to go."

"Please, Ingrid," he whined, and again clutched at her.

"Leave her alone," said a rumbling voice behind him, in Swedish.

Lars turned and come face-to-face with Kangas the Finn. Ingrid turned to watch also.

"What is this to you?" Lars demanded. He was too drunk to be afraid of the fearsome Finn.

"She doesn't want you," Kangas growled. "Carl Lindstrom is courting her."

"But. . .but."

"No buts, now get out of here. Carl Lindstrom is the only man who ever beat me in arm wrestling. Think what he might do to you if he catches you bothering his woman."

"You want her yourself," Lars whined.

"I can see why she don't want you, you snivelling. . ."

Lars made a clumsy attempt to throw a punch at Kangas. However, Kangas' huge fist sprang out and Lars was laid out unconscious on the ground at the end of the booth.

"Thank you Kangas," Ingrid smiled.

"Better you go find your man," Kangas grinned.

"I am here, " Carl said as he walked briskly to the scene.

"What is going on?" he asked.

"I, . uh . . it was Lars." Ingrid faltered.

"I rescued your woman for you," Kangas laughed. "Lars doesn't understand why she rejected him."

"Lars used to court you?" Carl asked incredulously.

"No," Ingrid scoffed. "He wanted to marry me but he proposed to Father first."

"She rejected me too," Kangas laughed. "So you are one lucky Swede."

"Yes, I feel pretty lucky,' Carl said as he put a huge arm around Ingrid. She put an arm around his waist and smiled.

"You take care of her now," Kangas called after them as Carl and Ingrid walked away arm-in-arm. "Next time I won't let you beat me at arm wrestling."

"I don't know what to make of Kangas," Ingrid laughed. "He's an animal one minute and a gentleman the next. He reminds me of one of those South American lizards."

"A chameleon," Carl laughed.

The dance carried on well into the night. The roaring bonfire kept constantly fed by youthful boys, and the full moon above, provided the only light for this warm summer evening. At one point when Kangas was off having a drink, Signe decided it was time to meet Carl Lindstrom. Carl and Ingrid were standing hand-in-hand at the side of the dancing area.

Signe grabbed Carl by the free hand and said, "Come on big man, let's dance."

Carl looked at Ingrid reluctantly and she gave a forced smile suggesting it was all right to dance with Signe. She was uncomfortable with the idea of Signe dancing with Carl but was too polite to make a public issue of it. Instead, she glared at Signe every time their eyes met.

"So how come I haven't seen you around, handsome?" Signe said in clear English.

"I spend most of my time vorking on da farm." Carl blushed uncomfortably at her seductive tone.

"You found enough time for Ingrid Erlander."

"I met her vhen I vas vorking at da mill."

"Do you like her a lot?" Signe said huskily as she rubbed against Carl.

"Ya, she is wery a beautiful voman."

"Am I beautiful?"

"You are wery pretty. Kangas is lucky to be courting you."

"Kangas, all he does is drink and act up," she scoffed.

"Dat's because he is a Finn. He has his good side, too."

Meanwhile Kangas appeared and noticed Carl dancing with Signe. He glowered jealously at them and began muttering how that big Swede was stealing every woman he ever liked. He was slapping a clenched fist against the open palm of the other hand.

Ingrid noticed him and feared a confrontation. She moved quickly and asked Kangas to dance with her. He accepted but kept watching the other two.

"Don't mind them," she said. "Your girlfriend is a flirt."

"Is that so?" Then with a grin, he said. " You are pretty bold to ask to dance with Kangas the Finn."

"I don't fear you any more because I've seen the good side of you," Ingrid smiled.

Kangas grinned, "That is good and you may be sure you will never have to fear me again."

They passed near to Carl and Signe and a silent communication passed between Ingrid and Carl. They each let go of their respective partners and joined together in dance. While they danced, gazing into each other's eyes, Kangas severely berated Signe as everyone danced around them. Carl and Ingrid never let go of each other for the remainder of the evening and there were no more incidents. When Lars recovered from the effects of Kangas's fist, he slunk home and was seldom seen either in public or at the mill again.

Chapter Fourteen

"Hey you two, wake up," called a voice, as Carl felt his boot being shaken. Slowly both Carl and Ingrid came awake. They were so tired from the Dominion Day celebration that they had fallen asleep in the carriage on the way home and the horse dutifully carried them to the Lindstrom farm. The horse stood patiently, harnessed and hitched to the carriage, for the remainder of the night. Through the following sunrise it had moved only slightly as it sought to graze in front of the house. They were so comfortable in each other's arms that neither Carl nor Ingrid cared to stir or take note of their surroundings.

"Wh-wh-at," Carl said with surprise at finding himself still in the carriage with Ingrid in his arms. The sun was well above the horizon.

"I guess the party was too much and you fell asleep," Oscar laughed.

"Oh, my God!" Ingrid exclaimed, upon realizing where she was. "Mamma and Papa will wonder what has become of me, or will think that we are up to no good."

"What time is it?' Carl asked

"It was six o'clock when I last looked."

"Six o'clock!" Carl exclaimed. "I had better get Ingrid home. Her parents will be angry."

"You might as well come in. Alva will have breakfast on. Then we can decide what to tell your parents."

"We have nothing to lose," Ingrid laughed nervously, although she knew they would likely be upset when she finally got home.

During breakfast, Alva offered to write Alfred and Agnes a note. "I will tell your parents you were both tired and spent the night here. I will tell them you have done nothing dishonourable." She gave them a quizzing look.

"Absolutely not," Ingrid said quickly. "We just fell asleep."

"I believe you," Alva laughed.

After breakfast Carl took Ingrid, hand-in-hand, to a large cleared and levelled spot a little ways away from the Lindstrom house.

"Do you think this would be a good spot to build a house?" Carl asked with a glint in his eye.

"Is your father building a bigger house?" Ingrid asked nonchalantly.

"No. . . Our house."

"Our house? Carl Lindstrom do you mean. . ?"

Carl looked directly into her large beautiful eyes and said, "I love you Ingrid and want you to be my wife."

"Yes, Carl, yes!" Ingrid exclaimed ecstatically.

She threw herself into his arms and he lifted her up and they kissed for a long moment.

"We will build a big house with two storeys," Carl said between kisses.

"And we will have lots of children to fill it up," Ingrid replied bubbling with joy. "Oh Carl, I love you so much."

They walked back to the house arm-in-arm with dreamy smiles on their faces. When Oscar and Alva came out to meet them, Carl said casually. "I guess we will have to build another house"

"For. . ?" Alva smiled, giving them a curious look..

"We're going to get married," Ingrid blurted, unable to contain herself any longer.

"Well, congratulations." Oscar said as both he and Alva broke into broad smiles. He shook hands with his son and hugged Ingrid. Alva hugged them both.

When they arrived at the Erlander place, Alfred and Agnes met them in the dining hall. Both wore serious concerned looks on their faces.

"Is this how you treat my daughter, Lindstrom, keep her out all night?" Alfred said gruffly.

"Read this note Mr. and Mrs. Erlander," Carl said quickly, handing over the note his mother had written.

As their faces grew less serious after reading the note Ingrid said, "I can't hide the truth Mamma and Papa. Carl and I fell asleep in the carriage and woke up at six o'clock in front of the Lindstrom house."

"You slept all night in the carriage?"

"It was so late when we left the dance, daylight was already breaking," Carl said. "We dozed off and the horse went home to my place."

"Well, that's quite a story," Alfred grunted.

"And there's more," Ingrid beamed.

"I asked Ingrid to be my wife," Carl said calmly. "She has agreed and I hope you don't object."

"Object!" Agnes said. "We had you two matched up all along."

"Well then, I guess we'll have a celebration this summer," Alfred grinned.

"What's going on?" Astrid asked in English as she entered the room.

"Vould you like me for a brudder-in-law?" Carl answered in English.

"You mean you and Ingrid. . ," Astrid beamed. "Gol-ly!"

Little Jamie toddled over to his mother's side. He looked up at Carl grinned and spoke in baby gibberish.

"It looks like even Jamie approves," Alfred laughed.

That night Ingrid finished her letter to Sigrud. After describing in detail the incredible Dominion Day celebration, and the marriage plans, she concluded the letter:

I guess I won't be going back to Sweden this fall or probably any time soon. Carl proposed to me and I accepted. The money Papa set aside for the trip will be given to us as a wedding present to help us start our new home. So you will have to save up your money and come over here for a visit, or to stay. I wish you could come over here in time for our wedding. I will write and tell you all about it.

Your Dear Friend
Ingrid

The twenty-fifth of August in that year of 1912, was the day of the wedding. As the time for the ceremony approached, Ingrid fussed with her wedding dress. Agnes helped her adjust it. Then she turned to help Astrid with hers as Astrid was maid-of-honour.

"You look like a princess," Astrid said to her sister in English. Ingrid was dressed in white and her long blonde hair was combed out and held in place with a flowered hoop rather than being done-up with the usual braids.

"What did you say?" Ingrid asked in Swedish.

Astrid repeated her statement in Swedish and continued, "Why don't you learn to speak English like Carl?"

"I swear I am never going to learn how to speak English if everyone keeps nagging me about it," Ingrid snapped.

"It is your sister's wedding day," Agnes said to Astrid in Swedish. "Now is not the time to argue and we will all speak Swedish for her sake."

There were voices outside as people were beginning to arrive for the wedding. It was being held outside the Erlander home beside a small flower garden Agnes had started. The guests were to be seated on wooden benches that Alfred had the mill hands put together for the occasion. Esa was traffic coordinator as he instructed the guests where to tie their horses and wagons for the day. Clarence served as usher, escorting the various guests to their seats, as well as relaying messages to his family who were still in the house.

As the Erlander women fussed around the final stages of preparation, Alfred came into the house. He was already dressed for the celebration wearing the same suit he had used on his voyage to Canada. He looked at both of his daughters and said, "I never knew I had such beautiful daughters. And, of course, I have a beautiful wife, also."

The Erlander women all smiled warmly at him and Agnes said, "Yes, our little Astrid is starting to be quite a lady since she turned twelve last month."

Astrid smiled and asked, "How old is Ole?"

"I believe he's seventeen," Ingrid replied.

"He is so handsome with that red hair," Astrid said dreamily. "I'm glad he will be standing up with me at the wedding."

"He is a little old for you," Ingrid laughed. "You're barely twelve years old."

"I know," she sighed. "I wish I was old enough for either Ole or Esa to notice me."

"You have a crush on both of them don't you?" Ingrid teased.

"Yes." Astrid sighed. She was particularly fond of Esa

"I was just talking to the preacher. He brought the organ and organist with him." Alfred said lightly. " Now all we need is the groom."

Clarence burst into the house saying, "The Lindstroms have just arrived."

"Don't look out the windows, Ingrid," Agnes said. "It is bad luck to see your groom before you come down the aisle."

Ingrid dutifully retreated into her bedroom and Alfred told Clarence to go back outside and continue his duties as usher. Agnes checked the many pots cooking on the stove as she was also the provider for the reception. Oscar and Alva Lindstrom came into the house each carrying some pots of food.

"Thank you," Agnes said. "You didn't need to bring food."

"Well, you shouldn't have to do all the cooking," Alva replied. "After all, it is our son who is getting married as well."

"You had best get outside so the wedding can start," Alfred said.

"Are you ready Ingrid," Alfred called, after the others had left.

Astrid and Ingrid emerged from their bedroom both smiling with nervous anticipation. Just then they heard the sound of something go past the house that sounded like a motor.

"Was that an automobile?' A wide-eyed Astrid asked.

"Sounds like it. There are getting to be a few of them around since the Ford Model-T went on the market last year," Alfred said quickly.

"My wedding is really in style, if I have guests arriving in an automobile," Ingrid beamed.

"I'd better check and see who our recently arrived guests are," Alfred said as he stepped outside. "Come through to the dining hall and wait for me."

Ingrid and Astrid went through the dining hall where tables had already been set up for the reception, and waited. Agnes, leading little Jamie by the hand, went outside and Clarence escorted them to their seat in the front row. After a few minutes Alfred came to the door and offered his arm to Ingrid. The organist, who was set up with a small pedal organ just outside the door, began to play the *wedding march*. Alfred took Ingrid in his arm and Astrid started down the aisle a few steps ahead of them. Coming down the aisle consisted of going around the corner of the house and up between two rows of benches where the guests were seated. Ingrid's heart trembled at the sight of the massive flaxen-haired man, dressed in a suit, standing in front of the altar with his back to her. Beside him stood his copper-haired brother. Carl turned slightly and smiled as Alfred delivered her to him at the altar.

After the ceremony, guests filed by the bride and groom offering congratulations. Among them were Kangas and Signe. He smiled and clasped Carl's hand with an iron grip. Carl countered with an iron grip of his own and it looked for a moment like they might become embroiled in another arm wrestle Finally Kangas smiled and said in Swedish, "Well you finally did it. May you both find happiness."

Ingrid smiled radiantly and daring to do something she thought she would never do, she turned a cheek toward Kangas and he kissed it lightly. Then he said, "You look even more beautiful in your wedding dress."

"Thank you, Kangas," Ingrid beamed.

"You know Signe and I are getting married in the Fall," he added with pride.

"That's wonderful, Kangas," Ingrid smiled. "I'm very happy for both of you."

As Kangas and Signe moved away from them, Alistair and Effie gave their congratulations. Then came the big surprise for Ingrid. Jim and Flora McDonald stepped forward to give their best.

"You, Flora and Jim you come," Ingrid gasped, as she reached to hug Flora.

"I wouldn't miss it for the world," Flora said, kissing her. "Your parents sent a note in the invitation to keep our planned attendance secret. Jim recently purchased a Model-T and we drove it all the way out from Edmonton."

"All da vay from Edmonton?" Carl said with astonishment. "Dat's over sixty miles."

"It took about three hours," Jim said. Then looking Carl in the eye, he said, as he clasped his hand. "You must be the lucky man,"

"Ya, I vould say dat," Carl smiled.

"My husband man, Carl," Ingrid beamed.

"Didn't you teach her to speak English yet?" Flora laughed.

"She's a stubborn voman," Carl laughed.

"What are you saying?" Ingrid demanded.

"They were surprised that you haven't learned to speak English yet." Carl translated.

Ingrid flushed with embarrassment. This was one of the few occasions when she really wished she had learned to speak English fluently. "Ask them about their baby."

Carl translated and they informed him that Edward was now two years old and starting to talk.

Before the reception had started, the Editor and Publisher of the tiny River Bend newspaper was on hand to take photographs of the wedding party. Since he was one of the few people in the area to own a camera, Alfred employed him for the job. While the photographing was going on, the other men partook in sipping the moonshine and home-made wine that was kept on the shady side of the house. Most of them also went over to marvel at Jim McDonald's shiny black Model-T. Few people of this area had ever been close to an automobile.

After the photographing Jim and Flora took Carl and Ingrid for a ride and they had a joyful time driving over to the Lindstrom farm, and back. The women, meanwhile, helped Agnes lay out the food for the reception in true Scandinavian *smorgasbord* style. When all was ready, the wedding party beginning with the bride and groom filed in to fill their plates from the sumptuous side table loaded with ham, venison, veg-etables, cheeses, boiled eggs and Swedish meatballs. Homemade wine was available on each table.

From her place at the head table, Ingrid noted the guests at the reception, among them were Alistair and Effie, the McDonalds and all of the Elofson family except Lars. He had stayed at his homestead and agonized that Ingrid was lost to him forever.

Alfred and Oscar each made a brief speech welcoming the new member to their respective families. Then, unexpectedly, Kangas the Finn stood up with glass in hand. An uneasy silence fell over the group as no one could be certain as to what this raucous unpredictable man might say or do. Carl and Ingrid smiled though, convinced Kangas would do no harm.

"I would like to propose a toast," he slurred in Swedish, obviously under the influence of strong drink, as he wobbled slightly. "You know, Carl Lindstrom is one lucky Swede to have wooed and won such a beautiful bride as Ingrid. You know, there was a time. . ," he slurred and stumbled. "There was a time when I hoped to win the hand of this beautiful woman myself. But she's a smart lady." He bumped against the table nearly spilling several glasses. Then looking at Carl he smiled and said, "but he had to arm wrestle me down to get her. He's the only man who ever beat Kangas the Finn. Right Lindstrom?"

"How much longer are we going to put up with this," Agnes grumbled. "Somebody should throw that drunken Finn out."

"The only person capable of doing that is Carl and he seems to be enjoying Kangas," Alfred replied.

While most of the guests were showing obvious disgust at Kangas's drunken prattle, Carl and Ingrid were genuinely amused. They realized that Kangas was paying proper respect in his own way.

"Kangas, you are making a spectacle of yourself," Signe chided.

"Sit down Kangas, you are drunk," Esa reiterated in Finnish.

Finally, Kangas becoming aware of the growing annoyance of the guests, concluded his speech. "Here's to Carl and Ingrid, may they live long and have lots of children." Raising the glass he said, "*Skol*."

Carl smiled and raised his glass repeating the Scandinavian toast. Reluctantly the others all raised their glasses. Kangas then sat down.

With the reception over, the dining hall was cleared by the women while the men again partook in the refreshments outside. A couple of musicians Alfred knew in River Bend provided the music for the dance to follow. For the opening waltz however, Alfred took out his own violin and played *Over the Waves* as Carl and Ingrid whirled around the floor with eyes fixed on each other. In their eyes, the crowd around them seemed an insignificant blur.

As Alistair and Effie watched the opening number Effie began softly singing the words.

When you are in love, it's the loveliest night of the year,
Stars twinkle above, and you almost can touch them from here.

"I can't believe this is really happening," Ingrid gasped as she gazed up into Carl's eyes.

"It is like a fairy tale," Carl smiled. "I feel like the prince who has just won Snow White."

"You will always be my Prince Charming, darling Carl," Ingrid smiled up at him.

With the opening waltz over, Alfred put down his violin and joined his wife in a dance with the rest of the wedding party consisting of Oscar and Alva, and Ole and Astrid. Ole danced the whole circuit with Astrid and never spoke a word. He wore a shy uncomfortable look on his face.

"Don't Carl and Ingrid make a beautiful couple?" Astrid said trying to start a conversation.

"Ya," Ole replied. He felt nervous and awkward dancing with twelve-year-old Astrid.

During the next waltz, Esa asked Astrid for a dance. It was sheer delight for Astrid to waltz with someone as dexterous and light on his feet as Esa. When she looked up into his dark eyes, he smiled and winked. Finally, he said in English, as he looked down at the attractive girl with her auburn locks done up in ringlets, "You turning into beautiful young lady."

"Thank you Esa," Astrid smiled. "I just wish that I was older than twelve."

"Don't be in hurry to grow up," Esa smiled. "Stay young and beautiful. Vhy you vant to grow up?"

"I see all the handsome young men like you or Ole, but I am so young nobody will look at me."

"Men vill look at you plenty, pretty soon. You don't vant old man like me."

"How old are you Esa?"

"I be twenty-two in Fall."

"That's not old."

"Too old for beautiful young girl like you."

"Yeah," Astrid sighed.

During this same dance set, Kangas approached Carl and Ingrid. "I would like to have a dance with the beautiful bride," he said to Ingrid with a lopsided grin. "That is, if I don't have to arm wrestle Carl for permission."

Ingrid and Carl both laughed as Carl held up his hands suggesting that he was offering challenge.

"I don't want to get your suit dirty." Kangas laughed.

"I'd better dance with you, before you two cause a spectacle," Ingrid laughed as she grabbed Kangas's arm.

As they waltzed around the floor, Ingrid looked up at this massive, hairy man who held her so gently. With his suit coat and tie, along with his trimmed hair and beard, she decided that Kangas looked handsome in his own way.

"So have you and Signe set a date?" she asked.

"We are still deciding, but she better decide soon."

"Why? Are you that impatient to be wed?"

"I could wait for a long time, but we have a baby coming."

Ingrid gave Kangas a shocked look at the revelation. Then finally she said with a wry look, "I guess you'd better get married soon to protect her honour."

"Does this surprise you?" Kangas grinned.

"Nothing that Kangas the Finn does surprises me," Ingrid laughed. Then looking directly at Kangas, she added with a crooked grin on her face. "Did she conceive it in the barn?"

An uncomfortable look swept across Kangas's face at this oblique reference to that unpleasant incident with Ingrid. "No," he replied in a small voice.

They danced silently for a few moments then Kangas said. "I never did apologise for that foolish incident in your father's barn. To think that I might have hurt you. You should have stuck that pitchfork in my belly."

"Would you have hurt me?"

"I like to think I wouldn't have but uh . . . if you can forgive me I'd like to forget that time."

"You are forgiven," she smiled. "When I saw how easily you admitted defeat that time, I knew in my heart that you would never have hurt me. Until that time that Carl forced you down on to your knees, I thought you were an animal and I privately called you Kangas the Barbarian. Then I saw that there was, after all, a human being behind that beard of yours."

"You are a very beautiful person, Ingrid Er. . I mean Lindstrom. Carl is a very lucky man," Ingrid noticed tears in the corners of Kangas's eyes as he spoke. "May you have a long and happy life together."

"Thank you Kangas, I feel I'm a very lucky woman. You know, I never did learn your first name."

Kangas laughed and said, "You probably couldn't pronounce it. It's Yrjo"

Ingrid struggled to say Kangas's first name but then resigned herself to saying, "I'll stick with Kangas."

The dance set ended and Kangas returned Ingrid to the anxiously waiting Carl. Looking at Carl, he said in his usual hoarse voice, "You take care of her eh! She is a very special lady."

"You don't have to tell me," Carl laughed.

The wedding festivities last until about midnight and Carl and Ingrid again used his father's carriage to drive over to their new home for their wedding night. Carl had finished enough of it to be habitable for summer living by the time of the wedding. It was a two-storey log house with a large kitchen, and a stone fireplace in the living room. It had room for three bedrooms upstairs in addition to the master bedroom located downstairs near the bottom of the staircase. The big house was in preparation for the large family they planned to have. Upon arrival, Carl scooped Ingrid into his powerful arms and carried her over the threshold of their new home and on through to their wedding bed without lighting any lights.

When Ingrid awoke the following morning, her head was resting on Carl's massive hairy chest. The morning light was streaming through their bedroom window. The sound of his heartbeat was so close it was almost as if they were one. When she stirred she felt his hand caress her long flowing blonde hair.

"Awake darling?" he said softly.

"Yes, dearest Carl," she replied dreamily as she turned her head and kissed him. "I can't believe something this wonderful could happen to me."

"Nor to me," Carl replied. Then as he continued to stroke her hair he said, "I love your hair like this. Why do you braid it up all the time?"

"The braids keep it out of the way." Ingrid replied. "But for you darling I will let it down every night before we go to bed."

"Promise?"

"I promise." After a time of dreamy silence she said, "It's so peaceful here. No crew of hungry men to feed, no sound of a sawmill running all day with its puffing steam engine."

Just then a cow lowed in a pasture nearby, followed by the sounds of Ole herding it. In the background they heard a round of bleating from the flock of sheep.

"Maybe it's not so silent here after all," Carl laughed.

"I'll take the sounds of a cow bawling over a sawmill any day," Ingrid replied. Then after a moment, she added, "Don't you have to help with the chores?"

"Not today. This day belongs to us. So we can just lie here all day if we wish."

"We might get awfully hungry," Ingrid laughed. "I should get up and make you breakfast."

"Um, a cup of coffee would be nice about now," Carl smiled.

Ingrid kissed him briefly and swung out of bed. When she turned to face him Carl stared after her beautifully sculpted body which seemed to be outlined in a halo from the sunlight streaming in behind her. "My God you're beautiful," he gasped.

As if suddenly realizing that she was naked, Ingrid blushed and grabbed for her clothing. "Men, is that all they think of?"

As she turned to scurry from the room Carl scrambled up out of the bed after her. With a giggle Ingrid grabbed the blanket and threw it over him then went out into the living room to dress. Although she was alone with the man that she dearly loved, Ingrid was shy about being naked in front of him in the full light of day.

Carl bounded in after Ingrid and threw his arms around her from behind just as she was trying to button up her dress.

"Carl Lindstrom, behave yourself," she cried as he nuzzled her neck.

"But I love you," he murmured as his lips sought hers.

"I love you too," she said through a kiss. "I thought you wanted a cup of coffee."

"Coffee can wait."

With a giggle she wiggled free and said, "Make yourself decent and I get your coffee started."

Carl made a step toward her.

"Go on, you're as naked as a jay bird." Ingrid turned and started for the kitchen.

"I love you," Carl called after her. She turned and smiled radiantly from the kitchen doorway.

Carl and Ingrid spent most of that day setting up their new home. In the afternoon, after they had walked arm-in-arm through the pasture looking at the various livestock that included horses, cattle and sheep, they went over to his parents' house for coffee. That evening Carl helped with chores as Ingrid prepared to cook him supper.

After finishing what Ingrid considered to be an ordinary supper Carl said, as he wiped his face with a napkin, "Well darling, that was an excellent meal. You know, your cooking alone would be reason enough to marry you."

"I hope it is not the only reason," Ingrid smiled as she came over to his chair.

"No, it is not," Carl grinned as he pulled her down on his knee. "I would still love you if you burned everything on the stove."

Ingrid laughed and kissed him, then she said, "It is quite a change, from cooking for a mob of men who just gobble down everything put in front of them, to cooking for just one man who appreciates and savours every mouthful."

"Yes, well those mill hands don't know what they are missing," Carl said kissing her again. "Or maybe they do now."

A year and a day after Carl and Ingrid's first anniversary their first child was born. It was a daughter successfully delivered by Alva, who was a skilled midwife.

Carl looked down at the tiny baby suckling its mother's breast and said empathically, "Let's call her Karen Ingrid Lindstrom."

"Karen is a Danish name," Ingrid remarked.

"Nonetheless it is a beautiful name." Carl declared. Then as an afterthought added, " That is, if you don't object."

"No, Karen is fine. I have to agree, Karen is a beautiful name."

Chapter Fifteen

The new year of 1914 offered bright new prospects for Ingrid. She was sitting in the living room one spring morning watching Karen crawling around on the rag mat. She had been feeling nauseous all morning. Thinking about her nausea and watching Karen triggered a suspicion. She thought of the last time she had her monthly cycle and was struck with the realization. *'I'm expecting another child.'*

Just then Carl came in with an boxful of groceries. He had just returned from the Morning Glory store.

"A letter for you," he grinned, as he handed Ingrid a letter from Sigrud. She opened it and read:

April 20, 1914

Dear Ingrid,
I have been saving my money diligently, and by autumn I should have enough money saved up to book steerage to Canada and coach fare to Morning Glory. I have decided to come to Canada for an extended stay, perhaps a permanent one as I feel there is nothing left in Sweden. Since you now speak so well of Canada, and I will be living in a mainly Swedish community, I will be right at home. Even the winter there sounds much like those in Sweden so I will fit right in. See you in nine months time.

Your Dearest Friend
Sigrud

"Wonderful news Carl!" Ingrid cried ecstatically. "Sigrud is coming over in the Fall, maybe permanently." She grabbed Carl and hugged him fiercely for a moment and Carl smiled as he kissed her.

"And that is not the end of the good news, dearest," Ingrid beamed. "I'm expecting another baby."

"Are you sure?"

"As sure as an expectant mother can be. I think it will be born in October just in time for Sigrud's arrival. Oh Carl, maybe you'll have your son."

"A son, yes a son," Carl beamed. Karen made some baby sounds from her place on the mat and Carl reached down and picked her up. "However, I best not forget my beautiful daughter." He briefly kissed the infant. Although he dearly loved his daughter, Carl longed for a son.

Ingrid was in a joyous mood for the rest of the Spring. She wrote Sigrud a return letter to convey all the good news:

May 3, 1914

Dear Sigrud,

I am overjoyed that you are coming to Canada, we have plenty of room in our big house to keep you indefinitely. It will be so wonderful having you here. I have just discovered that I am again with child and should give birth sometime in October, hopefully after you arrive. We are hoping for a boy this time so Carl can have the son he desires so much. We will have a grand time together in Canada, perhaps we can teach each other how to speak English. I'm afraid I have been lazy about learning the language thus far. So let us hope October comes quickly.

Your Dear Friend
Ingrid

As spring moved into summer it would seem that fate had other plans in regards to Ingrid and Sigrud. Carl came home from the store one day in June and said solemnly. "It doesn't look good in Europe. An Austrian prince has been assassinated at Sarajevo and there is talk of war."

"Sweden won't be in that war if there is one?" Ingrid asked anxiously.

"I don't think so. The Scandinavian countries are too sensible to go to war."

"Then Sigrud should still be able to get over here in the Fall?"

"I should think so," Carl assured her.

INGRID

By August full-scale war had broken out. The British Empire, France and Russia were aligned against Germany and Austria-Hungary. Canada, as part of the British Empire, was automatically involved. A call went out from Ottawa for volunteers to fill the ranks of the army and there to answer was Lars Elofson. Tired of living his lonely existence on the homestead and brooding about the woman who rejected him, Lars joined the army within a month of the outbreak.

Shortly after the outbreak of war, people began complaining that mail from Sweden was irregular and often tampered with. It was getting close to October and Ingrid had not heard from Sigrud since July.

Alistair, who was the most informed of the people of the area in world events explained to the concerned homesteaders what had happened, one day at the store when Carl, Alfred and Gunner were all present.

"Thae British have blockaded the North Sea tae prevent ships from either leavin' or reachin' German ports. They have been so concerned about war material reachin' Germany via thae neutral countries, thah commerce wi Scandinavia has been nearly cutoff."

"Dey have no right," Gunner said firmly. "Da Scandinavian countries are minding dere own business."

"It is always da neutral countries dat suffer," Alfred added. "Look at Belgium, da Yermans ran right over top a dem."

"Thah's noh all," Alistair continued. "Thae German submarines are sinkin' any ship thah gets close to thae British Isles or France."

"Oh my God!" Carl exclaimed. "Ve vere expecting Ingrid's friend, Sigrud, to be coming over dis Fall."

"Ye can ferget that idea," Alistair said. "It woldna be safe tae travel on a ship anywhere around thae North Sea."

"I yust hope she had enough sense to stay home."

"Aye."

When Carl explained the situation to Ingrid she shuddered with the thought that Sigrud might have been on a ship that could have been torpedoed by a submarine.

'Oh dear God, I hope you have enough sense to stay in Sweden, Sigrud.' she thought. *'I guess I will have to have the baby without you.'*

October had come and Ingrid gave birth to their second child. As Carl waited anxiously outside the bedroom, he heard the cry of birth and a few moments later his mother came out of the bedroom and calmly announced, "Carl, you have a son."

"A son," he beamed. "A real son. May I see Ingrid now?"

"Yes, son, she and the baby are doing quite well."

"Well dear, your dream has come true," Ingrid smiled from the bed where she held the tiny infant to her breast.

"Yes, I now have my son," he said joyously, looking down at the infant. "What shall we name him? I chose the name for our daughter, you choose it for our son."

"How about Carl Everett?" Ingrid suggested.

"Carl Everett," Carl repeated. "If we use the name Carl it might be confusing in the long run. Just think in a few years time, when you call out for Carl, we'll both come running, neither knowing which one you wanted."

"What do you suggest dear?" Ingrid laughed.

"We could still register him as Carl Everett, but let's call him Everett."

"Alright we'll call him Everett," Ingrid agreed. "I will have to write Sigrud a letter and tell her about it, and hope she gets it. I wish I could hear from her to know if she's is all right."

"Yeah," Carl sighed.

Finally in the spring of 1915, Ingrid got a letter from Singrud written six months earlier

.

October 12, 1914
Dear Ingrid,
As you probably know, there is a war on in Europe. Although Sweden isn't involved we are victimised by it. The British have blockaded the North Sea, and the German submarines are sinking every ship they can, so travel is not advised.

I guess I will have to stick it out in Sweden until this crazy war is over. Maybe I will have saved enough money by that time to go first-class rather than steerage, ha, ha. So cheer up Ingrid, you are far from the war and don't have to worry about a blockade.

Your Loving Friend
Sigrud

Ingrid was relieved that Sigrud had not set out after the war broke out, but was disappointed that their long cherished reunion was postponed indefinitely. Ingrid was pleased to discover however, that she was once again with child and was expecting it to be born in early winter. She laughed as she thought of Sigrud, *'By the time she gets here I might well have a house full of children. If my next child is a girl I am definitely going to call her Sigrud.'*

Alistair, who got regular newspapers and updates from the telegraph office at the station, continued to inform everyone in the community about the progress of the war, a war that seemed to make no progress as the combatants were locked in deadly stalemate.

One day when Carl was at the store, Alistair told him of the latest news from the war. "Thae bloody Germans are usin' poison gas. They say this chlorine gas eats thae lungs so ye canna breathe. Trust thae Hun for commin' up wi ae weapon like thah." He continued. "It says in thae paper, thae poison gas caused ae breach in thae French lines at Ypres. But get this, thae Canadians came tae the rescue and drove thae Germans back."

"It sounds like Canada has a good army, by yimminy," Carl replied.

"Aye, ae bloody good army."

"I vonder how Lars is doing? Gunner says he is over at, how you say it, Eeps."

"Aye, I bet he's givin' thae Hun ae good run for their money."

The answer to Lars' fate came a few days later when the Elofson family got a telegram. Lars was killed in action at Ypres. A Memorial Service was held in the Lutheran Church at River Bend for Lars a few days after the family had received the telegram. Ingrid sobbed her way through the service along with the Elofson family, as she thought of the slow-moving clumsy man who tried so hard in his own way to win her heart.

"I didn't know that Lars's death would bother you so much," Carl remarked after the service.

"I know, I didn't think much of him when he was alive, but I couldn't help think of that evening when I turned down his marriage proposal. His heart was crushed. He meant so well but it was just that. . ."

"I know dear," Carl said. "We may dislike a person in life, but when he dies we suddenly see the good in him."

"There was nothing really bad about Lars," Ingrid sniffled. "If I had married him he might not have joined the army and got killed."

"Would you have been happy marrying him?"

"No," Ingrid sniffled. "But. . ."

"I know, there is always guilt associated with death. I'll miss him too. I never really had a quarrel with Lars. However, death is part of life, and we the living must go on."

"I hope this horrible war ends soon."

"So do I Ingrid, so do I." Carl said as he placed an arm around her.

On the way home they stopped at Ingrid's parents' place as Astrid was babysitting the younger children. When they came through the door, Everett, who was standing hanging on to a chair, grinned up at Carl and cried,"Daddy, Daddy!"

He let go of the chair and took his first steps towards his father's arms. Carl caught him just as Everett was about to fall.

"My little boy has just taken his first steps," Carl cried joyfully as he hoisted the infant high above his head. Little Everett squealed with delight. Carl placed Everett on his shoulders and bounced him around even as Everett place his hands over Carl's eyes.

"Carl just loves his little boy," Ingrid said to the others. "Everett is his whole world."

Karen ran up and hugged her father's leg. "I love my daughter too," Carl replied as he tussled her hair. Karen then returned to play with Jamie. Carl sat down on one of the chairs and lowered Everett onto his knee.

"Now that he can walk, I'll soon take him out to learn how to farm," Carl laughed as he bounced Everett on his knee

"How's the coffee coming,?" Alfred asked Astrid. Astrid had started the coffee when she saw them all arrive home from the funeral.

"It should be ready soon," she replied as the pleasant aroma of boiling coffee began to fill the room.

As they sat at the table, Everett attempted to crawl on to it

"Carl, don't let him crawl onto the table," Ingrid said.

"Aw he just curious," Carl said as he gently pulled Everett away.

"I swear you're going to spoil him rotten," Ingrid said.

As Everett grew restless on Carl's knee, Alfred gave him a beckoning look and said, "Come see grandpa."

Reluctantly, Carl let go of the child as Alfred picked him up, although his eyes still followed his cherished son.

Later when they were all sitting at the table enjoying a cup of coffee, there was a knock at the door. Astrid opened the door and smiled," Come in Esa, we are all having coffee."

"Vell maybe I shouldn't," Esa said humbly. "I yust come to say goodbye. Mr.and Mrs. Erlander, it has been real pleasure vorking for you," he said In English.

"Vhat are you saying?" Alfred asked. "Are you quitting?"

"Vell our country is fighting, and if poor Lars got killed, den I yoin army in his place."

Astrid's face fell. She was very fond of Esa even though she was still much too young for him to return the affection.

"Vhen are you leaving?" Alfred asked.

"I make sure you have good man for saw and planer tomorrow, den I go to Edmonton and see army office," Esa replied. "So excuse me, I make tings ready."

"Ve are going to miss him around here," Alfred said to the others when Esa had left.

"What is going on?" Ingrid asked, as the conversation with Esa had been in English.

"Esa is going to join the Army," Carl explained to her.

"Well, I must say I liked him a lot better than Kangas," Agnes said.

"Kangas has changed a lot since he got married," Ingrid said.

"If you say so dear," Agnes sighed.

The following morning as Esa was about to head out, Astrid ran out to say goodbye.
Esa stopped and smiled at the girl with the auburn locks who came running up to him.

"I will miss you when you are gone," Astrid said with tears in her eyes.

"I vill miss your smiling face too," Esa replied.

"Would you like me to write to you?" Astrid offered.

"Ya, dat might be good idea," Esa said. "I don't know anybody else who write to me."

"Be sure to write right away so I will have an address," Astrid said anxiously.

"You might not understand letters," Esa laughed. "I write vorse den talk."

"I'll understand them, maybe it will help you learn to speak and write English more clearly."

"Oh, Astrid you are such beautiful girl," Esa smiled with tears in the corners of his eyes. "I hope you find nice young man someday."

"I already have," she replied in a low voice.

"Vell goodbye Astrid, may life do you vell."

"Goodbye Esa," Astrid sniffled.

Esa leaned over, kissed Astrid lightly on the cheek, then turned to go on his way.

As autumn wore on Ingrid grew increasingly heavy and uncomfortable with child. She felt very weary, and struggled to get her daily work done. Often she would doze off while sitting in the living room with Carl during their quiet time in the evening.

"You are going to have to slow down darling," Carl said one evening as they sat in the living room. "You are wearing yourself out."

"I think I am having too many children too quickly," Ingrid said. "Karen and Everett are walking and getting to be a handful Having to chase after them all day is chore enough, let alone do all the extra washing of diapers and such."

"Everett, he is getting to be a handful," Carl chuckled. "I'll start taking him with me some of the time."

Everett toddled over to Carl and he took the child on his knee. "Daddy, give me horsey-back ride." Everett gurgled.

Carl got down on his hands and knees and Everett climbed onto his back and Carl began to crawl around the living room

Ingrid smiled, "He sure is the apple of your eye, isn't he?"

"Yes, he is my little boy," Carl smiled with pride, rearing up and causing Everett to giggle. "But I haven't forgotten my darling little Karen either," he added, as Karen came over and also climbed on his back. "I know she's going to grow into a beautiful woman like her mother one day."

"I wonder what this one will be?" Ingrid said, putting her hand on her swollen abdomen.

"Have you thought of any names?"

"Well, if it's a girl, I'm definitely going to call her Sigrud. If I never see my dear friend again, her name will live on in my child. If it is another son, I'll let you pick the name."

"Another son," Carl mused. Then he added soberly, "So is this one dragging you down more? You seem so tired."

"Yes, this one feels more like a dead weight than a child. It seldom moves. I just hope it will be all right when it's born."

"I'm sure it will dearest, I'm sure it will," Carl assured her. He crawled up on the chair to kiss Ingrid with his children still clinging to his back and laughing.

Finally on the first of December, Ingrid felt the first pangs of labour while getting dressed. Carl ran to fetch his mother then hurried back to take care of the other children, while Alva prepared to deliver the baby. The delivery came easy and Ingrid felt the expulsion of the child from her body but there was silence. Alva hoisted the infant up by the heels and slapped it on the bottom to revive it, but to no avail.

"My baby! What is wrong with my baby?" Ingrid cried.

"Sh, shh," Alva cautioned. She had the baby down on her lap trying to massage it and still no sound. Then she looked up sadly.

"My baby, oh no, my baby!" Ingrid cried in desperation.

Alva shook her sadly then she wrapped the infant in a blanket completely covering it. Ingrid began crying out loud. This brought Carl into the room.

"My baby, I've lost my baby!" Ingrid cried.

Carl cradled Ingrid in his arms as she cried out loud. He looked to his mother for an explanation, also noticing something wrapped in a blanket.

"It was dead at birth," Alva said gravely. "I couldn't save it."

"Was it a boy or girl?" Ingrid sobbed.

"A girl," Alva replied.

"Oh no! I was going to call her Sigrud." Ingrid cried with her head buried in Carl's chest.

"I will take it over to my house," Alva said picking up the bundle. "We will have to give her a burial."

"That would be best," Carl said gravely. "After that, take the children too. I'll need to sit with Ingrid for a while."

After remaining cradled in Carl's huge arms for a time, Ingrid said through sniffles. "How can I conceive another child? How can I carry a child around inside me for nine months, wondering if it will dead when it is born? How?"

"We will not worry about that for now," Carl replied in a gentle voice. "We have two other children to take care of. We must give them all our love, and if fate decides we will have more children, we shall have more children. Maybe you will have another daughter."

"If I do, I could never call her Sigrud. This one was meant to be Sigrud."

"Should we register her as Sigrud and mark her grave that way?"

"No!" Ingrid cried. "I don't want to equate Sigrud with death. It will simply be baby Lindstrom."

"As you wish my dear."

As there was no cemetery in Morning Glory at this time the unnamed infant was buried in the cemetery at River Bend. There was a simple service in the Lutheran Church with just the Lindstrom and Erlander families attending. Ingrid resolved to carry on. If she was meant to bear more children so be it.

Chapter Sixteen

Two days after Everett's second birthday he became ill, developing a raging fever. Alva, who was both a master at home remedies and at utilizing locally-grown herbs, could do nothing for him. After a day or so, they bundled little Everett up and took him to the doctor at River Bend. The cold, ten mile journey in a carriage during October served only to aggravate his condition.

Upon examination, and above the wailing of the child, the doctor then told them. "Mr. and Mrs. Lindstrom I am sorry to say that your son appears to have contracted meningitis."

"Can you cure him?" Carl asked gravely.

Ingrid spoke in Swedish demanding to know what the doctor had said and Carl translated.

"He has had it for a day or two has he not?" the doctor asked.

"Ya," Carl replied.

"Meningitis is an infection of the spinal column and membrane enclosing the brain. There is no medication available to cure the infection."

"Den he vill. . ." Carl trembled, not wanting to say the word.

"It does not look good," the doctor said gravely.

"Vould it do any good to take him to da hospital?" Carl asked desperately.

"In Edmonton? How would you get him there?"

"Tomorrow's train."

"It would be worth a try," the doctor replied. "The hospital is the best chance for him."

Carl turned to Ingrid and explained in Swedish what was just discussed.

"Where would we stay?" Ingrid wondered. They could not afford a hotel room for more than a day or two.

"I could take him in and sleep in the hospital waiting room if need be," Carl said.

"I'll go with you," Ingrid insisted. "Everett will need his mother."

"What about Karen?"

"Your mother can look after her."

"Okay, when we leave today I'll stop at the station and get two tickets from Morning Glory to Edmonton."

Turning back to the doctor, Carl said in English, "Ve have decided to take him to da hospital togedder on tomorrow's train."

"Smart idea," the doctor said. He did not expect the child to survive long enough to get to a hospital but to give them hope he said, "They've just installed a telephone line to River Bend so I'll phone the General Hospital ahead of time."

"Tank you doctor," Carl said. "Is dere anyting ve can give him to help da fever and make him sleep?"

"I'll prescribe some quinine, and a new drug called aspirin," the doctor replied. "It should help some."

During the buggy ride home, Everett alternated between crying and fitful sleep as the fever raged on. Everett was put straight to bed in his upstairs bedroom when they got home and Carl and Ingrid each took turns at keeping a vigilant eye on him through the night, neither daring to think the worst. Carl kept the fires in the house blazing almost to the point to where it was intolerably hot for the rest of the family.

Carl took the late shift. He sat on the chair by the bed while the room was illuminated by a wick lamp. Carl periodically applied a wet cloth to Everett's forehead to try and stem the fever, or would lie beside him draping an arm across little Everett when he cried out, trying to soothe his son into going back to sleep. During one session of cuddling Everett through the blankets, Carl dozed off. He was awakened by Ingrid calling him to breakfast from the foot of the stairs. When Carl awakened the room was dark, the wick of the lamp had burned down and extinguished itself. Everett seemed quite calm and his forehead felt cool.

"I think his fever broke," Carl cried excitedly as he made his way to the stairs.

"Why do you say that?" Ingrid said from the bottom of the stairs as Carl came down.

"He's sleeping peacefully and feels a lot cooler. Maybe we won't have to take him to the hospital," Carl said hopefully.

"Well, we probably should, just to be safe," Ingrid insisted.

"I'll have Mother look in on him before we leave," Carl said. "The train won't be by Morning Glory before eleven o'clock, so we have a few hours yet. We'll see how things are after chores."

While Carl was at chores with Ole and Oscar, daylight broke over the October skies. Ingrid went upstairs to check on Everett. She drew back the curtain of his window to let the morning light in. Everett was lying in his cot on his back, quiet and still. *'How tiny he looks in the bed,'* Ingrid thought. *'He seems so peaceful.'*

She went to the bedside and listened for his breathing, but could hear nothing. She put her hand on his forehead hopefully but he did not stir and his forehead felt cold

"Everett!" she cried as she reached under the covers to try to pick him up. Everett's whole body was stiff and cold.

"Everett, please wake up!" Ingrid cried

Karen, awakened by the commotion, came in. "What's the matter with Everett, Mommy?"

"Karen, go back to your room!" Ingrid said harshly.

"Why, Mommy?"

"Just go."

Karen went back to her room wondering why her mother was so harsh with her.

"No, no, no," Ingrid cried as she came to the horrific conclusion about Everett. She dropped him back into his bed and fled from the room and back downstairs. She ran for the door to go tell Carl, but as she opened it Alva was about to enter.

"He's dead, he's died!" Ingrid cried hysterically as Alva caught her in her arms. Ingrid cried copiously on Alva's shoulder. Alva guided her back inside.

"You're sure now," she said softly.

"I went to pick him up, and he is so cold and stiff," Ingrid sobbed.

Alva's own heart was pounding. She had lost two children of her own and could empathize with Ingrid. Now, she apparently had lost a grandchild as well. Alva guided Ingrid to the couch and sat her down. "I will go up and check myself." she said quietly.

"Yes, please do," Ingrid choked, clinging desperately to a straw.

Ingrid resumed crying as Alva went up to Everett's bed. She quickly drew the same conclusion as Ingrid. She sobbed and wiped away a tear as she drew the blanket over Everett's head.

"Why are you covering up Everett, Grandma?" Karen asked from the doorway. In light of all the commotion, Karen could no longer obey her mother's order.

Alva sniffled then regained her composure. She then took Karen by the hand and as they left the room she closed the door. Alva sat down on the top stair and drew an arm around Karen.

"Everett has gone to Heaven now," she said quietly. "He won't be sick any more."

"Will we go to Heaven someday and see him?" Karen asked.

"Someday, perhaps, someday," Alva assured her. "Let's go down and see your mother, she will need all our love now."

When Alva and Karen entered the living room holding each other's hand, Ingrid looked up, red-eyed with desperate hope. Alva shook her head sadly and Ingrid began to cry again. Karen ran to her mother and Ingrid hugged her as she cried.

"How am I going to tell Carl?" she sobbed. "Everett was his whole world."

Alva looked out the kitchen window and saw the men returning from chores. She opened the door and called for them all to come over.

"How's Everett?" Carl asked hopefully as he entered the house. Then he saw the sad look in his mother's eyes. Ingrid came through and he could tell from her red eyes that she had been crying a lot. "He. . . he's. . . not. . .?"

"We lost him," Alva said sadly.

Carl's lips began to quiver and he continued, "But he was so quiet and peaceful this morning."

"He was probably dead," Ingrid said in a sobbing voice.

She ran to Carl and they hugged while Ingrid wept uncontrollably. Tears were running down Carl's face also. Karen hugged her grandmother desperately. Oscar turned to Ole and said, "You had better ride over to the Erlanders and tell them about their grandson."

With the passing of Everett a cleared area near the Morning Glory town site was declared a cemetery and little Everett was laid to rest there as the first occupant. He was buried in a pine wood coffin built by his grandfather, Alfred. Everett's two uncles, Clarence and Ole, served as pallbearers. A simple service was held right at the grave side as the first winter snow began to gently fall. Devastated, Carl and Ingrid clung to each other sobbing. They were so lost in their grief that they scarcely acknowledged Karen. Karen, in turn clung to her grand-parents for solace. A few days later Ingrid received a sympathy card and letter from the McDonalds. Carl tried to read it to her but broke down in tears, so later she had Astrid read it to her. Ingrid kept the card and letter tucked away as a keepsake, lest she one day learn how to read English.

Ingrid adjusted to life without her son as best a mother who has lost a child could, but her grief lessened as she began to worry about Carl. The loss of his son was a crushing blow to Carl. He became listless and indifferent, and spent long periods of time staring into space. Oscar and Ole also noticed this when Carl went about his chores and farmwork. He became locked in a state of grief. He kept hearing his young son's voice and seeing him running across the house to meet him crying, "Daddy, Daddy. Daddy give me horsey-back ride."

One morning he woke from a dream about Everett, and he began crying upon realizing it was only a dream.

"Oh Carl darling," Ingrid soothed as she held him. "You have to let go, Everett is gone."

"I can't let go," Carl sobbed. "I see him in my dreams. I hear his voice when I pause during the day. It is driving me mad."

"I know dear," Ingrid soothed, "I cannot think of him without pain either. But we must go on. Remember how you told me to look to the future when we lost that child at birth. Life must go on, perhaps one day we'll have another son."

"I don't want another son." Carl cried as he swung out of bed. "What good is another son. Everett is dead. Another son might die just like him, how do we know if Karen will even survive?"

"We don't, but we must live with hope."

"Hope," Carl snorted, as he finished pulling on his clothes. "People are killing each other by the thousands in France, our son is taken from us, you can't even get a letter from Sweden, and you talk about hope. It's a hopeless world out there."

Carl lit the lamps and stoked the morning fires in silence before going out to chores. He usually had breakfast first, but he needed to be busy to contain his grief, so he started milking well ahead of Ole and his father.

When Carl returned to the house, he found Karen sitting on Ingrid's lap crying.

"What's wrong with her?" he said indifferently.

"She had a dream about Everett too," Ingrid said gravely. "She thought she could hear him crying in his room."

"Daddy, I don't wanna sleep upstairs any more. It's too scary."

"So where else are you going to sleep?" Carl said harshly.

"Take it easy Carl, she's frightened," Ingrid said.

"Maybe I should rip the staircase out and make your room in the little alcove where the stairs are now," Carl said somewhat more gently. "We'll probably never use the upstairs again anyway. Maybe I should rip the whole second storey off this house."

Ingrid looked at him in anguish. "Maybe we could move Karen's bed downstairs for a while."

Carl sat and picked at his breakfast, the dream about his son was still vivid in his mind. He took a swallow of coffee and got up. He looked over the area by the staircase and surmised that if the staircase was removed a small room could be built for Karen on the main floor. He went up the stairs to appraise the situation from above. Then he saw the closed door to Everett's room. He suddenly recalled the morning of Everett's birthday just before he took sick. Carl had gone upstairs that morning just as Everett was awakening.

"Daddy, Daddy," Everett cried as he raced across the foyer to Carl.

"How's my birthday boy?"

"I two today," Everett said.

"Yes you are," Carl said. "You are getting to be a real big boy."

"I help farm soon?"

"Yes very soon," Carl placed Everett on his shoulders and went downstairs.

It had been a joyful day celebrating Everett's birthday. The Erlander family had all come over to join the party. All joked about how Carl would soon have a new helper on the farm.

Carl winced and sobbed with the realization that all was lost. He thought he heard Everett call to him again. He turned and quickly came back downstairs.

"Karen is right, there are too many ghosts up there," Carl sobbed. "I've got to get out of here."

Ingrid could only watch helplessly as Carl put on his outerwear and walked out the door.

Carl did not return for lunch and the afternoon passed without any sign of him. Finally when he failed to show for supper, Ingrid inquired of Ole about Carl's whereabouts. Ole said he had seen Carl walking along the trail to River Bend early in the day. He was surprised Carl hadn't returned. Ingrid had passed a sleepless night, with Karen curled up beside her, waiting for Carl to return.

In the morning Ole volunteered to go looking for him. "I'll ride over to River Bend as see what has become of him."

"A good idea," Oscar replied.

"I hope nothing has happened to him," Ingrid said fearfully. The thought of losing her husband, as well as a son, was too much to bear.

When Ole rode into River Bend on horseback, he stopped first at the beer parlour to make enquiries. The bartender informed him that a person matching Carl's description was in there last night drinking until closing time. Ole tried the Immigrant Hall, wondering if Carl had flopped there during the night

"Yeah, he was here," the proprietor said. "He crashed in here about midnight and slept in the lobby. If he had been a smaller man, and if I didn't know who he was, I'd a thrown him out."

"Vhen did he leave?" Ole demanded.

"About an hour ago. He looked in pretty rough shape."

"He is. I must find him."

Ole rode around town looking for Carl. He saw a man on the railway trestle that crossed the river. It was Carl. He was standing on the trestle looking down at the river some four hundred feet below. Ice was already forming along the shores but open water was still running in the middle.

"Carl!" Ole cried from the near end in English. "Carl vhat are you doing?"

Carl turned and looked at him indifferently. The depression caused by a night of heavy drinking compounded his grief and had pushed Carl to the edge of despair. Ole scrambled from his horse and started walking on the trestle toward Carl.

"Don't come closer or I'll yump," Carl replied.

"Carl don't do dis. Ingrid is vorried about you."

"Go avay," Carl shouted as he started walking toward the far end of the trestle.

The two men shouting on the trestle was beginning attract several other people from River Bend, among them Kangas the Finn. Kangas and Signe resided in River Bend near the river bank by the railway tracks.

"Vhat is going on?" he demanded as he came to the end of the trestle.

"There's a man out there trying to commit suicide," someone said.

Kangas looked again.

"Carl Lindstrom?" he said incredulously. "Who is dat going out after him?"

"His brother Ole."

"Carl Lindstrom, you come back here!" Kangas hollered as he started to walk briskly down the trestle jumping from tie to tie.

"Go back!" Carl cried.

"Don't you dare yump off dat bridge, Carl Lindstrom," Kangas shouted as he caught up to Ole.

Carl stopped and stood on the edge as if he was about to jump.

"Vhy is he doing dis?" Kangas demanded of Ole.

"He has not been da same since he lost his son."

"Oh ya, I heard about dat,' Kangas replied. "Vhere is Ingrid?"

"She is at home vorried sick."

"Carl Lindstrom you come back here," Kangas yelled again. "You can't leave Ingrid like dis. Tink about her and your little girl. Vhat her name?"

"Karen," Carl replied. He started quivering and sobbing. As he thought about Ingrid and his little girl, the suicidal impulse started to leave him.

Just then, a train whistle sounded indicating a train was coming toward them from Carl's side.

"Carl, a train is coming!" Ole cried, as he started for his brother.

Kangas caught Ole and held him fast, saying, "Train vill be here before you reach him and ve all be killed."

"But Carl. . ." Ole struggled frantically.

Carl started running toward them hopping from tie to tie, trying to outrun the oncoming train with the hope of getting off the bridge before the train reached him. The whistle blew again and they could clearly hear the chugging of the locomotive and the plume of smoke from its chimney. It rounded a curve and came on to the trestle.

167

"Let's get off here," Kangas said tugging at Ole. Ole reluctantly followed him to safety at the end of the trestle.

Carl was near the end of the trestle as the train bore down on him.

"Yump, Carl, Yump!" Ole cried desperately.

Carl sprang for the river bank beside him just as the train gave a deafening blast from its whistle. He landed at the top of the river bank as the train went thundering past him. The bank was a sheer cliff for about sixty feet straight down before changing to a steep slope the rest of the way down the river. As Carl landed against the face of the cliff rather than on the level ground at the top, he clawed desperately for a handhold getting momentary reprieve with some rock and bush, but these soon gave way and he slid down the sheer face of the cliff triggering a minor landslide. His descent continued on down the steep slope below the cliff carrying him into the edge of the icy river. As he slid down the bank he cried out, "Ingrid I love you!" The mass of earth and rock that came down with him nearly buried Carl in the mud at the edge of the river. Only his head and one arm was showing above the mud.

"How do ve get down to him?" Ole asked desperately.

"Dere is trail on udder side of bridge," Kangas said. "You vill be able to vork your way down to him. I get rope from store and tell Signe to fire up sauna. He need to be varmed up vhen we get him out of dere. I yoin you in few minutes."

Ole worked his way down a steep path that led down the face of the cliff and to the river. His actions caused a minor slide of their own. Carl was struggling weakly to get out of the mud and freezing water. Ole waded into the mud to help his struggling brother, but Carl was weak, and his teeth were chattering intensely from the onset of hypothermia. By the time Ole got Carl to shore he was also feeling the effects of the cold water but the need to save his brother kept him going.

Kangas ran to the nearby general store where he barged through the door and grabbed a spool of rope.

"What are you doing?" the storekeeper demanded.

"Go to rescue man. Don't vorry I bring back," Kangas said breathlessly.

Ole had managed to drag Carl out of the mud, but wondered how he was going to get his brother back up the steep trail, He was clearly too big and bulky to carry.

"C-c-cold," Carl said through chattering teeth. He was starting to lose consciousness.

"Vatch out below," a voice cried from above.

Ole looked up and Kangas threw the spool over the cliff while hanging on to one end of the rope. The spool played out with the lower end of the rope only a few yards above them.

"Tie rope on to him, and you push vhile I pull," Kangas called.

Carl moaned weakly as Ole drug him up the steep bank far enough to reach the rope. He tied the rope around Carl's shoulders and signalled Kangas. Kangas began pulling on the rope as Ole climbed up behind Carl pushing as best he could. Carl seemed only vaguely aware as to what was going on. Soon a few other men joined Kangas in pulling. One even came part way down the steep trail to help.

Soon they had Carl up top. Kangas looked at him and grinned, "Now you big dumb Swede, vhat you tink you are doing?"

Carl groaned again but didn't answer. He was fading in and out of consciousness.

"I better get him varmed up," Kangas said as he picked Carl up. The others watched in awe as the brawny Finn slung Carl across his shoulders and started for his house "You better come too, " he said to Ole, gasping under the heavy load. "Your teeth are chattering."

The effects of the cold wet clothing were beginning to catch up to Ole as well.

"I have yust ting for bote of you," Kangas said as they approached his house. "Sauna vill varm you up.

Kangas generally kept a low fire in the sauna, built on the side of his house, most of the time as he used it often when he came in from work. When they reached the house, he and Ole carried Carl across their shoulders through the house to the sauna room. Along the way, he instructed Signe to get a couple of blankets. Inside the sauna, Ole stripped off Carl's wet clothing and his own while Kangas stoked up the fire. It was not long before the intense heat and steam of the sauna reversed Carl's hypothermia. Kangas switched him on the back with a small birch sapling he kept in the sauna. It was used for flagellation purposes while in the sauna to stimulate circulation.

"Ouch, vhat are you doing to me?" Carl complained. "Giving me a beating?"

"I should be," Kangas laughed. "Anybody stupid enough to yump off bridge and leave beautiful vife and daughter behind should be vhipped.

Hitting your back vit svitch help make blood flow and varm you up faster." He switched Carl again.

"Give me dat svitch," Ole said with a wicked grin.

He took it from Kangas and swatted Carl heavily across the back. "Dere for all da trouble you cause." He switched Carl again and added. "Dat von for Ingrid who is vorried sick about you."

"I guess I deserve dat," Carl said glumly.

When the Lindstrom brothers were thoroughly warmed up, they wrapped themselves in the blankets Signe had provided and went through to the main part of the house and sat by the fire while their clothing dried out.

"Vhat made you vant to yump off bridge anyhow?" Kangas asked.

"I, uh vas feeling so bad, I lost my son you know. He vas only a little over two years old," Carl said with watery eyes. "Life vasn't vort living."

"I sorry about dat," Kangas replied. "But you are very selfish man. Remember Ingrid lost son too and she grieves for him as much as you do. If you killed yourself, she would have you to grieve over too. Den dere is little girl, she vouldn't have fadder, because he yump off bridge and kill himself. I should have vhipped you harder in sauna."

"Vhy do you care so much about me?" Carl asked. "I didn't tink Kangas da Finn cared about anybody."

"Look, you sawdust brain," Kangas said sharply. "Who said any-body care about you? It is Ingrid I care about. If you lucky I von't tell her you tried to yump off bridge."

"Please don't," Carl said looking at both Ole and Kangas.

"Only if you go straight home to Ingrid and be husband you sup-posed to be," Kangas laughed. "Right Ole?"

"Right," Ole replied.

Carl borrowed a horse from the livery stable to ride home with, and when he and Ole rode into the yard Ingrid ran out to meet them. She cried as Carl dismounted, "Oh Carl I was so worried about you."

Carl scooped Ingrid up into his arms lifting her off the ground and kissing her. He said in Swedish, "Oh Ingrid I love you so much. I'll promise I'll never leave again."

"It's alright Carl darling," she said wiping a tear from her eye. "You are so tortured by the loss of Everett, but remember your grief is my grief and we still have a daughter."

"Where is Karen?" Carl asked

Before Ingrid could answer she came out of the house and ran to her father. Carl scooped up his daughter into his arms and together they hugged Ingrid again.

Chapter Seventeen

It was now mid-year 1917 and it was nearly two years since Ingrid had heard from Sigrud. Since the letters they wrote to each other after the war had started took a long time to get through and were often tampered with by censors, they postponed writing regularly until the war was over. Though Ingrid was beginning to doubt as to whether she would ever hear from Sigrud again, it was, in general, a year of great optimism. On the world front, the newspapers spoke of great victories by the Canadian army at Passchendaele and Vimy Ridge. Most importantly, Ingrid had news for Carl when he came in for his lunch.

"Carl dearest," she said with a smile. "I've been sick this morning."

"You seem pretty chipper now," Carl grunted.

"Not really sick, you big lunk," Ingrid scoffed. "I think I'm with child again."

"You're expecting another child?" Carl said with eyes lighting up. "Are you sure?"

"Your mother thinks so, but why don't you drive me over to River Bend this afternoon to the doctor. I haven't been away from here for a long time."

"Sure we could make an outing of it," Carl said. "We'll leave Karen either with Mom or your parents. After what we've been through, maybe a real doctor should look at you."

Ingrid was glad that Carl took the news on a positive note as he was so bitter about having more children after Everett's death.

Turning to Karen, Carl said, "Which grandparents do you want to stay with this afternoon, while Mom and Dad go to River Bend?"

"I'd like to stay with Grandma Erlander," Karen said. "And see Aunty Astrid, and play with Uncle Jamie."

The doctor at River Bend assured Ingrid that her pregnancy appeared to be normal and he had no real concerns. After leaving the doctor's office, Carl and Ingrid poked around in various shops walking hand-in-hand.

"Are you glad we are having another baby?" Ingrid asked as they walked along.

"Yes, a new life is always a good thing. It helps you forget about the old."

"Maybe you'll have another son," Ingrid ventured.

"Son or daughter, it does not matter," Carl replied with a sigh. "If the child grows up healthy and happy it is all that matters."

Ingrid looked up at Carl and smiled. "I love you Carl," she said softly.

"I love you too," Carl replied, squeezing her hand. "As long as we have each other, we can face anything."

Later, as they started on their way home they stopped at the railway crossing near the station to wait for the passenger train which had stopped, blocking the roadway. They saw a familiar figure get off. He had a duffle bag slung over his shoulder and walked with a painful limp. He was using a cane.

"That's Esa!" Ingrid cried.

"So it is," Carl said, as he drove the buckboard they were travelling in a little closer to the station.

"Esa!" he cried.

Esa looked up and grinned. "Carl Lindstrom, Carl and Ingrid Lindstrom."

' "Hello Esa," Ingrid smiled.

"Do you speak English yet, Ingrid?" he laughed.

"No English yet," Ingrid replied, feeling somewhat embarrassed by the fact.

"She's a stubborn voman," Carl replied.

Esa laughed.

"Are you out of da army now?" Carl asked.

"Ya, my leg got badly vounded at Vimy. I lost part of it." Esa tapped his lower left leg with his cane. It had a hollow wooden sound. "Dey give to me honourable discharge."

"Oh My God," Carl said. "Did you lose it all?"

"Yust from knee down."

'Dat vas still some battle," Carl said. "Da papers are all talking about da Canadian Army."

"What is going on?" Ingrid demanded in Swedish. She didn't understand the conversation but was aware that something was very wrong with Esa's leg.

"Esa lost the lower half of his left leg at Vimy," Carl explained.

"Oh no," Ingrid said sympathetically. "So where are you going?"

Speaking in Swedish for Ingrid's sake, Esa said in a downcast tone. "Well I hope I can find a job somewhere, if someone will hire a man with a wooden leg,"

"I'm sure Papa can find a job for you," Ingrid said assuredly.

"Well I, uh, don't know," Esa fumbled. "I could only do some things. I could never cruise for timber again."

"Astrid will be glad you are back," Ingrid said. "She has wondered why you didn't write to her this last while."

"Yes, well I was recovering in the hospital," Esa said quickly. "I couldn't bring myself to tell her that I had lost part of my leg."

"I don't think Astrid will mind. She is very worried about you," Ingrid said emphatically.

Esa smiled quietly.

"We have to stop at the Erlander place on the way home so why don't you come along." Carl offered. "You could enquire about a job. I know that Alfred said that he would have a job for you when you came home."

"Yes, I could tag along. I owe it to them to at least call on them," Esa replied. "Is Kangas still around?"

"Yes, he lives here in town. He has five children and works for the mine."

"Maybe we should call on him, I'd like to see him again."

"Why don't you jump on board and we will take you to Kangas's house."

Esa threw his duffle bag into the back of the buckboard and crawled up onto the back letting his legs dangle over the edge.

When they arrived, Esa knocked on the door and Kangas answered. They looked at each other for a moment, exchanged greetings in Finnish, then hugged briefly.

"So what are you doing home anyway? The war is still on." Kangas said in Swedish for the others' sake.

"I got wounded in battle."

"Come in all of you," Kangas said, looking at Carl and Ingrid. "We still might have some tea left."

Carl looked at him curiously, but when they entered the house, they could see packed luggage and boxes of household effects in the middle of the living room floor.

Signe smiled and said "Hello" as the others entered the house. Then turning to her children said, "That will be all the packing for now. Run along outside so we can visit."

The children all obeyed save for one toddler who clung to her side. "Moving out?" Carl asked.

"Yes, I got a chance to go work in a real logging operation in Prince Rupert B. C. That's where the big timber grows. We're leaving on tomorrow's train."

"And if we had not come by you would have left without saying goodbye," Ingrid said with a frown.

"Well, I just got the offer two days ago. A fellow Finn has set up a logging operation and sent word for me to join him." Kangas said. " You wanna come too, Esa?"

"No, I have a wooden leg so I'd be no good at logging any more."

"What are you going to do then?"

"I might get my old job at the Erlander mill. I can still probably run the planer."

"You can probably get the old cabin with the sauna."

"I'd like that. Say, did you hear that Finland is now a free country?"

"No, is that so? How did they get rid of the Russians?"

"Well, Russia is in the middle of a revolution so Finland declared its independence."

"This calls for a drink," Kangas said with elation. He drew out a jug of his special moonshine but only the men accepted a drink.

"To Finland, proud and free," Kangas toasted in Finnish.

"To Finland, neither Russia or Sweden shall rule us again," Esa added in Swedish.

"May the long association and friendship between Finland and Sweden continue," Carl added.

"How about, *To Canada*?" Signe asked, speaking English. "We are all Canadians now."

"To Canada," the men agreed.

Later, while on the way home Ingrid remarked, "You know, I never thought I'd ever say this, but I'm going to miss Kangas."

"Yes, he's quite a character," Carl sighed. "Things will never be the same once he's gone."

"I remember when I first met him," Ingrid reflected. "I thought he looked like a wild animal. Certainly some of his actions seemed to suggest that he was."

"I remember the time you and Kangas got into a fight at the ball game," Carl laughed, looking over at Esa. He was seated on the other side of Ingrid.

Esa laughed too and shrugged, "Those things happen."

"Mother called you a pair of crazy Finns," Ingrid added with a laugh.

"Yes, I suppose we were."

"Talk about the sauna experience," Ingrid laughed. "I remember the night he came out of his sauna drunk out of his mind and rolled in the snowbank, stark naked."

"Or the time in the barn," Carl said

"Oh *that* time, when I thought he was going to rape me and you came to the rescue."

"I thought I got off lucky when all I had to do was beat him at arm wrestling. If he had wanted to fight, he probably would have killed me."

Ingrid laughed, "He is a strange person, an animal one minute and a gentleman the next."

"Kangas is good at heart," Esa added. "He is just a little rough on outside."

"I despised him for a long time, but now I have to agree with you."

The sounds of a sawmill in action heralded the approach to the Erlander place. When they turned in the lane, they could see Astrid, Jamie and Karen coming from the garden.

"Mommy, Daddy," Karen cried as she ran to meet the buggy.

"Watch out for the horses," Astrid cried, running after her.

"Is dat Astrid?" Esa asked.

"She's grown a lot since you left." Ingrid laughed.

"I'll say," Esa said staring after the pretty girl who had transformed into a beautiful young woman during his absence. He slid off the buggy, carefully landing on his good leg, and limped toward Astrid.

"Esa?" she gasped, with mouth agape.

Esa grinned as he surveyed the beautiful young lady with her auburn locks and tumble-down hair style that was combed close around her heart-shaped face. She smiled radiantly at him.

When Ingrid climbed from the buggy she took Karen by the hand as Karen chatted away telling her of all the things that she had enjoyed at Grandma's house. The others all went into the house to leave Esa with Astrid.

"Vhat has happened since I vent avay?" Esa gasped, speaking English. "Little girl has become beautiful voman."

"You never wrote these past months?" Astrid said.

"I vas vounded." Esa said gravely. " I lost leg." He tapped his wooden leg.

A shocked expression came over Astrid's face for a moment then she regained her composure. "Well, you can still walk," she smiled.

"I didn't know if I should come home. Vhat I going to do?"

"Papa or Clarence will find a job for you," Astrid said confidently. "I'm glad you are back."

They looked at each other for a long moment then opened their arms for a big hug. Esa noticed that she radiated a sweet feminine essence. When they released their hugs Astrid still held on to one of his hands and Esa smiled at her.

"You go to school yet?"

"No, I'm out of school. I help Mom with the cooking."

"Still got dining hall eh?"

"Still got it. Come, let's go for coffee."

"You got young man in your life?" Esa asked carefully, still hanging on to her hand but resisting her tug.

"No." Then she asked cautiously, "Have you got a wife or sweetheart?"

"No. Maybe I vait for young voman to grow up," he laughed.

"Do you have to wait much longer?"

"No I tink I vait yust about long enough," he squeezed Astrid's hand and she squeezed back.

They walked hand-in-hand until they reached the door. Once inside, Agnes greeted Esa warmly and poured him coffee. Soon Alfred came in to join them. For Ingrid's sake conversations were conducted in Swedish.

"Welcome back stranger," he said shaking Esa's hand. "Are you out of the Army now?"

"I was wounded, and lost part of my leg, so they discharged me."

"It is well that you are back home, the way they are slaughtering each other over there."

"Do you have any jobs for man with a wooden leg?" Esa asked guardedly.

"Can you still run the planer?"

"I should be able to manage."

"I am sure I can use you. If the planer is too hard, you can sharpen saw and planer blades, and the old cabin with the sauna is still empty."

"Thank you Mr. Erlander, you are a good man to give me back my job. You know one thing I really missed in the army is the sauna."

"I did say I would keep a job for you when you got back. I'll discuss it with Clarence when he gets back. He runs much of the business now."

"Where is Clarence?" Esa asked.

"He went to Morning Glory to do some business." Alfred replied.

Just then, Clarence walked into the house. He greeted everyone and shook hands with Esa but he wore an anxious look.

"Look at this," he said, waving an envelope in his hand. "It's from the government. I've been called up for military service."

A look of horror swept over Agnes's face. Ever since Lars was killed she feared for the day that Clarence might join the army. "Do you have to go?"

"Let me see it," Alfred demanded. Clarence handed him the envelope.

"Do you want to go?" he said.

"Well, our country is at war."

"Can't he stay?" Ingrid said. "Ole was called up, but they deferred him."

"That's because he's a farmer," Carl said. "They won't draft farmers except as a last resort."

"What about a lumberman?" Agnes added. "Making lumber is important for the country too."

"I will look into it," Alfred said.

"Maybe I wanna go," Clarence protested.

"Believe me Clarence, you don't want to go," Esa said. "Even if you are lucky enough to live through it, you will see things that no man should ever see."

"Such as?"

"You will spend your time in a stinking trench up to your knees in mud with rats and lice crawling all over you. You will see your friends and comrades die horribly and the smell of death is always present. I was very lucky that I only lost part of a leg." He again tapped his wooden leg. "No Clarence, you don't want to go to war."

"I think I should go to the Army Recruiting Office and plead that we need Clarence to run the family business." Alfred said gravely. To Clarence he said, "I know it is an honourable thing to go and fight for your country but I need you."

"You are only nineteen," Agnes said. "I think you are too young to join the army."

'We will look into it." Alfred reiterated. "Meanwhile we can put Esa back on the payroll. I'm not happy with the man who runs the planer now anyway."

"Are you able to work with your bad leg?" Clarence asked.

"He can walk quite well," Astrid said sharply in Esa's defence.

"I tink I can still run planer," Esa said, somewhat downcast.

"Okay Esa, you can start on the planer tomorrow morning," Clarence said. "We'll find you a bunk."

"I told him he could have his old cabin with the sauna in it," Alfred said. "After all, he is kind of special around here."

Astrid and Esa exchanged warm smiles.

As Carl and Ingrid headed down the road home, Carl remarked, "It looks like your mother might end up having a Finn in the family after all, if the looks in Esa's and Astrid's eyes mean anything."

"You noticed that too," Ingrid laughed. "Actually, Mom had no quarrel with Esa, it was Kangas that she despised."

Carl was silent for a moment then said in a small voice, "Kangas eh, you know he probably saved my life once."

"Saved your life?"

"Remember just after Everett died and I was losing my mind?" Carl winced, with a tear in his eye. It was still very painful for him to mention his departed son.

"Yes."

"Well that time I wandered away and went to the River Bend beer parlour to drown my sorrows."

"Yes."

"The next morning I was so depressed that I was going to jump off the railway trestle."

"Oh my God," Ingrid gasped.

"First Ole came along and tried to talk me out of it. Then Kangas came out of the blue and started to talk to me. He reminded me about you and Karen. Then I realized what a foolish thing I was going to do. I saw a clear vision of yours and Karen's faces and knew I must get back to you. Then a train started coming with me stuck on the bridge. I didn't quite make it to the bank before I had to jump. So I ended up sliding down the river bank into the icy water below."

"Oh my goodness." Ingrid gasped.

"Ole rescued me but by the time he got me out I was almost dead from exposure from the cold water, and he wasn't much better because he had to wade in it to get to me. Anyway, Kangas pulled me back up to the top and took us to his house and made us go into the sauna, while Signe dried our clothes."

"So what happened next?"

"I tell you, that sauna was a sure way to warm a person up, then Kangas flogged me with a birch sapling."

"Flogged you?"

"He says its part of the sauna experience and is good for the circulation. Finns do it all the time, apparently. I think Kangas gave me a few extra swats for being so stupid. Ole gave me one or two also."

Ingrid laughed, then said soberly. "No one told me you tried to commit suicide."

"It was such a stupid selfish thing. I asked them not to breathe a word. Luckily for me you don't go over to River Bend very much, it was probably the talk of the town. I hope you'll forgive me for keeping this from you."

"I forgive you," Ingrid said nestling beside him. She added. "If I'd known earlier I could have thanked Kangas myself and when we get back I'll definitely have to thank Ole. You big lunkhead."

Carl smiled as he put a huge arm around her.

Chapter Eighteen

The year had passed and still Ingrid had no word from Sigrud. Mail however, seemed to be getting through more regularly now as Alva got a letter from her sister that was only two months old. When her father got a letter from Uncle Nils that was less than a month old, Ingrid wrote to her uncle asking of Sigrud's fate.

The winter of 1918 was awkward for Ingrid as she was very heavy with child. Alva would do most of her heavy work with little Karen helping. Carl doted on her, fearful that she might overdo herself and lose the child she was carrying. Finally on April 12 Ingrid awoke early one morning with a twinge of labour pains.

Carl woke also and Ingrid said, "It is time. Go get your mother."

Carl sprang out of bed and rousted out Alva. When they returned the labour was quite intense. As Carl was pacing about in a fit of anxiety Alva ordered him to go do his chores. Carl tried to contain his excitement and concerns by taking his time at chores. Finally he returned to the house and as he entered he heard a baby crying. Alva was washing some bloodied towels in a tub by the stove. She turned and smiled, saying, "Carl, you have another son."

"Another son," Carl beamed. "Can I see him?"

"Of course."

Carl quickly went through to the bedroom and Ingrid was propped up by pillows with the newborn infant suckling her breast. She smiled at him saying, "Providence has been kind to us and has given you another son."

Carl looked down at the infant and smiled. "Somebody up there gave us a test and we passed by jiminy. We have a second son."

"What will we call him?" Ingrid asked.

"I don't want my name in it. That's bad luck." Then after a moment of thought Carl said abruptly. "Lets call him Svend Oscar"

"Svend Oscar Lindstrom, I like the sound of that," Ingrid smiled. "So Svend Oscar it will be."

"Carl dearest," Ingrid said carefully after a time. "Now that we have another child we will need a bedroom for him."

"Ah yes, a bedroom," Carl looked upward and thought of the abandoned upper storey. He swallowed at the thought, but reality caught hold of him and he said. "I will reinstall the staircase and Karen can move back up there."

"Are you up to putting the stairs back up?" Ingrid asked carefully.

"Yes, I will do it sometime soon and get Ole and Dad to help me," Carl said with resolution.

Later that spring, the Lindstrom men reinstalled the staircase. Ole and Oscar did the required work on the upper part of the stairs as Carl did not want to go upstairs until all was ready. Finally, Ole came down the stairs announcing that all was in order.

"Shall we go up dearest?" Ingrid said, clasping Carl's hand.

"I suppose," he sighed.

"Are you coming Karen?" Ingrid said extending her other hand to her daughter. Karen clasped it with apprehension

"Oscar, Ole and I will be right behind you," Alva assured them.

Slowly they all climbed the stairs. The midday sun streamed through the south window, but the air was musty and there were many cobwebs in the corners.

"It is like a haunted house up here, by jiminy," Ole said unthinkingly.

"Yes," Carl said in a small voice.

"Open some windows. it's stuffy up here," Ingrid said.

"I'll go down and get a broom, and get rid of all these cobwebs." Alva said as Ole opened the south window.

Ingrid was about to open the door of Everett's room but Carl stopped her. "I'm not ready for that yet," he swallowed. "You may go in and tidy it when I'm not around, if you like."

"Okay darling," Ingrid said tenderly. "I'll get your mother to help me."

They went on to Karen's room. Karen went ahead of them and raced around in the empty room. Carl opened the window and the cross-breeze through the upstairs was quite refreshing.

"Do you think you might like your room back now, Karen?" Ingrid said gently to her daughter.

"It will be lonely, so far away from you and Daddy."

"Here, I will clean it out and it will be nice and fresh," Alva said as she went about with the broom sweeping away cobwebs. She went about it in a way that made Karen laugh. "We'll scrub it and make it fresh. Then we'll do Everett's bedroom."

"You can stay downstairs for a few days until you get used to the idea of being up here," Ingrid offered.

"Okay."

"I think I'll leave now," Carl said. "If you are going to clean Everett's room." Carl winced with the mention of his departed son. "Perhaps, once Svend moves into that room, when he is a little older, I will be able to look inside."

"I understand darling," Ingrid said, as she stood on her tiptoes and kissed him.

Although Carl excused himself from the unpleasant task of dealing with Everett's room. Ingrid braced herself as Alva opened the door. They entered with Alva placing an arm on Ingrid, the room was still as it was the day Everett had died, save for the bed sheets. They had been removed, washed and placed in the linen closet after Everett had been taken away. His Teddy Bear was still on the chest-of-drawers and his clothing was in it.

"Open the window Ole," Alva said, as she reached up with the broom to sweep cobwebs from the corners.

"Let's put the bed against the other wall and move the chest-of-drawers," Ingrid said with resolve. "This way when Svend takes over this room it will look different from when Everett had it."

"Good idea," Alva said. "We should check Everett's clothing in the drawers to make sure that the moths haven't eaten them."

This was another difficult task for Ingrid, but as she delved into checking Everett's clothing, while the men rearranged the furniture, she felt the ghosts leaving her mind. *'If I can only convince Carl to come up here now that everything has been changed,'* She thought.

When they were back downstairs again enjoying coffee at the kitchen table and Carl had joined them, Ingrid said. "Carl, would you like to come up to Everett's room with me and see how we've changed it?"

"No," Carl replied in a small voice.

"You would never recognize it as the same room," Alva added. "It will set you free."

"I said No," Carl replied sharply. "I consented to allowing Svend to take that room when he's old enough even though there is room enough up there to build a third bedroom. Is that not enough?"

Ingrid rubbed his shoulder with her hand and said. "The past is very hard to let go of, Carl dearest, but once I faced it, it became easier with every passing moment."

"I'll deal with it in my own time and way," Carl said firmly. "I would appreciate it if everyone would leave me alone."

A few days later, when Ingrid was in the bedroom nursing Svend, she heard Carl come into the house. Apparently he had brought someone with him as she also heard an unfamiliar male voice. Since they were speaking in English she didn't know what they were saying. When she came through to the kitchen she saw that the stranger was a pleasant-looking man with whitish blonde hair. He was smaller than Carl but very robust-looking.

"Hello," he smiled. "I presume you are Carl's wife."

She understood his words but they were pronounced differently, then she realized where he came from. "You're Danish!" she gasped.

"Ingrid, I would like you to meet Marty Polsen. He hopes to be our new neighbour. Marty, this is my wife Ingrid." Carl said in Swedish.

"Pleased to meet you," she smiled.

"The pleasure is mine," Marty smiled in turn.

"So do you have a wife and family, Mr. Polsen?" Ingrid asked.

"No," he laughed. "Maybe if I can successfully start a homestead, I'll look for a wife."

"He is going to look at some land about a mile from here," Carl added. "One of the few places where your father hasn't taken all the timber."

"Well I hope you are successful, Marty Polsen," Ingrid said sincerely.

"I hope so too," he smiled. "I kind of like it out here. It's so far away from everything."

"Yes, like the war," Ingrid said.

"Father was glad I decided to come out here," Marty laughed. "He said that maybe the government won't find me to draft me into the army if I'm a way out in the bush."

"Oh, they know how to find you," Carl said. "Ole was called up, but they let him stay because he is a farmer."

"And my brother Clarence," Ingrid added. "Papa tried to talk them out of taking him, but all he got was a two-year deferral because of his age. We can just hope that the war will be over by then."

"Yeah, I suppose if they catch up to me I'll have to go," Marty said. "I thought of joining up at one point, but Father said he didn't bring me over to Canada to start a new life, just to have me killed in a war."

"Yes, one of the neighbour boys was killed in the war and another came home with a wooden leg," Ingrid said.

"Would you object to us putting Marty up for a while, while he files his homestead and builds himself a cabin?" Carl asked.

"I don't want to put you out, Mrs. Lindstrom," Marty blushed.

"Ingrid if you please. It will be no trouble at all. You can use Everett's old room."

"Everett's old room," Carl said guardedly. Even though Ingrid and Alva had cleaned it and rearranged the furniture the door was closed again. Carl had yet to set foot inside it. He dreaded the day when Svend would be moved up there.

"Carl, it is time we opened the door and let the ghosts out," Ingrid said firmly. "It is the only extra room that has a bed in it."

Marty looked from Carl to Ingrid.

"Everett was our son," Ingrid explained, in a matter of fact way, though her eyes betrayed a painful expression. "He died of meningitis a year and half ago."

"I'm very sorry to hear that," Marty said. "Maybe I shouldn't use that room if it is a sensitive issue. I can sleep in your barn loft just as easily."

"No you should stay in the house. If Ingrid wants to make a bed for you in that room you can use it," Carl said with great effort and determination. As he spoke he had a sense of great relief.

"But. . . " Marty said uncertainly.

"You will sleep up there. It is time to put the past behind us," Carl said firmly. "We were given a second son to make up for the loss of the first one and one day soon he'll be using that room. If you use it first the spell will be broken. Come I'll show it to you."

Ingrid broke out in a beautiful smile.

When Carl and Marty had returned from upstairs, Carl remarked to Ingrid, "You are right, the room looks completely different. Svend will love it."

"So will I," Marty laughed.

"It is a good thing you came along, Marty Polsen. You have set us free of our past sorrows," Ingrid said.

Marty was uncertain as to what he had done to deserve this praise.

Marty Polsen became a regular feature around the Lindstrom house.

He had filed his homestead and Carl, Ole and Oscar helped him build a log cabin. They also loaned him horses to skid logs over to the Erlander mill.

Even after the cabin was built and Marty had moved into it, he was still a frequent visitor. He often came by to help out at the Lindstrom farm as part of repayment for their generosity, usually getting supper in the process. Often he would beg a loaf of bread from Ingrid. Ingrid didn't mind though, as she often told Carl. "Marty is such a good man, I hope he finds himself a nice wife."

One day in late summer a letter came for Ingrid from her Uncle Nils. Oscar, who had been to the post office merely dropped it off and went to his own house. She opened it eagerly but her heart fell when she read:

Dear Ingrid,
It is not a pleasant thing that I have to tell you but bear with me. Sigrud has been very ill this past year. She was diag-nosed with diabetes. She spoke often of you and clung des-perately to the hope of coming to Canada to see you right up to the very end. As you know there is no cure for diabe-tes and she passed away on April 11. I hope things find you well otherwise.

Kindest Regards
Uncle Nils

Ingrid sank down into a chair and began to cry. When Karen saw her mother crying she asked, "What's wrong Mommy?"

"Go away," Ingrid cried harshly in a sobbing voice.

The last time Karen had seen her mother like this was when Everett died. She fled from the house to her grandma's place and Alva came directly over. Ingrid was still sitting at the kitchen table with her head resting on her arms sobbing. Alva picked up the letter and read.

She put a gentle arm on Ingrid's shoulder and said, "Sigrud was very special to you wasn't she?"

"We were as one. We were never apart from the day we were old enough to play with each other, until my family decided to come to Canada," Ingrid sobbed.

Carl came into the house. He had been fencing nearby when Karen came out to him telling him that something had upset her mother. Alva handed Carl the letter and he read it

"Oh my God," he said. Ingrid had told him many times about her special friendship with Sigrud and the great hope she had of Sigrud coming to Canada once the war was over. He lifted the sobbing Ingrid into his arms and she clung desperately to him.

"Damn Father for coming to Canada. If we had stayed in Sweden I would have been with Sigrud in her final days," Ingrid sobbed. "Damn this stupid war that prevented her from coming over here, or even to have meaningful correspondence. If I hadn't met you I would have gone back for a visit."

She turned away from Carl and fled to the bedroom, flung herself across the bed and continued crying out loud.

"What's wrong with Mommy?" Karen asked with sorrowful eyes.

Carl picked his daughter up and looking sadly at her, he said, "Your mother has lost her best friend."

"Did she die like Everett?"

"Yes, like Everett," Carl swallowed. "You will have to be patient with her for the next little while."

"Why don't you come to Grandma's house for a while?" Alva suggested to Karen. Then to Carl she said. "Maybe I should take Svend too."

"Leave him, he is sleeping in his crib," Carl said. "When he wakes up and starts to cry it will help bring Ingrid out of her grief."

The others left and Carl made himself a pot of coffee. He sat at the kitchen table pondering how he was going to cope with Ingrid's sorrow *'She has endured so much,'* he thought, *'Brought to Canada against her will, she endured a stillbirth, a loss of a young child, and now her dear friend is dead.'*

Svend, who was in the crib near the bed, began to cry. Ingrid ignored the crying even as it grew louder and more desperate. Carl came through and picked the infant up out of his crib. He tried rocking Svend in his arms, but the crying would not abate.

Finally he said to Ingrid, "Your son needs you, I think he is hungry."

"Your son," Ingrid snapped.

"*Our* son," Carl said gently as he sat down beside Ingrid. "*Our* son needs both of us as does our daughter."

187

He placed the howling Svend on the bed beside Ingrid. Slowly she turned to Svend, undid the top buttons of her dress, and offered a breast to the hungry infant, then she cuddled little Svend next to her. Carl went back through to the kitchen. The banging of pots could be heard as he made an attempt to organize supper. Ingrid smiled as she heard him.

When Svend was properly fed and changed Ingrid came through to the kitchen to find Carl peeling potatoes. His peeling was clumsy and a lot of potato was being wasted with the peel.

"Here, let me do that," Ingrid said practically taking the potatoes out of his hands. "Go back outside and milk the cows or plough the field. Let me do the cooking."

Carl smiled as he heard her speak. He got up and put a huge arm around her, then kissed her lightly on the forehead before leaving the room.

Later that evening when Carl was relaxing on the living room sofa, Ingrid came and sat close beside him.

"I'm sorry Carl if I was harsh with you," Ingrid said in a flat voice.

Carl put his arm around her and replied softly. "Don't let it bother you Ingrid. Losing a friend is a terrible thing. Your whole life was geared for seeing her again."

"Yes, I suppose in a way it was, but it was so long since I last saw her. She was fourteen then, but when she passed away she was almost twenty-three. It has been two years since I last even had a letter from her, thanks to the war."

"Well, at least that should be over soon," Carl continued. "Alistair was telling me that the last German offensive was reversed."

"Too late for Sigrud though," Ingrid sniffed. "If I only could have got another letter from her."

"I know dear, I know," Carl said as he cradled her in his arms. "We should have postponed our wedding a year so you could have gone back to the old country to visit her."

"That wouldn't have helped," Ingrid replied. "I would only be leaving her again."

"Sometimes, love gets in the way," Carl sighed.

"Oh, Carl I do love you so. I don't regret for a moment having met you when I did or having married you when I did. You have made my life have meaning and purpose."

"I love you too, Ingrid," Carl said with a tear in his eye. The two of them kissed for a long moment.

"We lost a son, and we got another," Carl said speaking into her braided hair as she nestled against him. "You lost a friend and you may gain another."

"Another friend like Sigrud? I haven't met anyone over here that can even approach that friendship." She thought of how Flora McDonald could have become such a friend, but Flora was several years older, lived in the city and had a totally different lifestyle.

Just then the dog started barking. Carl looked out the window and said, "Marty Polsen has just arrived."

"Marty is such a nice man," Ingrid said rising to make ready for their guest.

"Yes, to me he is a real friend," Carl added.

Warm greetings were exchanged as Marty was let into the house.

"So how are things on the Polsen homestead?" Carl laughed, as Marty sat down. He spoke to Marty in Swedish, for Ingrid's sake, even though he and Marty usually talked in English to each other.

"Well, my cabin is finished and I have about ten acres cleared," Marty laughed in turn, he likewise spoke in Danish for Ingrid's sake. "But I am leaving for Toronto in September."

"What is the matter? Is the homestead too much for you?" Carl chuckled.

"No, I'll be back. You won't be rid of me that easy."

"You must have a sweetheart in Toronto," Ingrid grinned. Marty's refreshing presence made her put her grief to the back of her mind.

"No, I'm afraid not. I don't know many people in Toronto but my father wants me to come back and help him with his cabinetmaking business."

"I've heard that excuse before," Carl said. "You'll like the big city and stay there."

"I don't like the big city," Marty insisted. "That's why I came out here. I'm only going back to earn some more money to help develop my homestead. I plan to come back in the Spring"

"Unless you meet a woman that changes your mind."

"No woman will change my mind," Marty said. "If I find a woman, she will have to like homesteading."

"Aren't you afraid they might conscript you for the army if you go back to civilization?" Carl asked.

"Like you said before, if the army wants me they'll find me wherever I am," Marty replied. "Besides I don't think the war will last much longer anyway. The Germans, Austrians and Turks are all in retreat."

"I hope you are right," Ingrid said as she started the coffee.

The dog barked again and this time a one-horse cart with two people on board came into the yard.

"It's Astrid and Esa!" Ingrid exclaimed as she looked out the window.

"Esa, he's that Finnish fellow who works for Alfred, is he not?" Marty said.

"Yes. He's courting Ingrid's younger sister, Astrid."

"Hello, Marty Polsen," Esa said as they entered the house. Everyone noticed that both Esa and Astrid each had a joyful radiance about them and they were holding hands. "Have you ever met my wife-to-be, Astrid Erlander?"

"I have seen you at the dining hall, but I've never met you personally," Marty said gently taking her hand. "But I am very pleased to meet you."

"Wife-to-be?" Carl asked carefully, although he was not surprised.

"Yes, Esa finally proposed to me last night," Astrid bubbled.

"I got a higher paying job now," Esa said modestly. "And I can walk a little better now."

"Clarence made him foreman of the whole crew," Astrid said with great pride as she squeezed Esa's hand. "And he doesn't need a cane any more to get around."

"So when is the big day?" Ingrid asked excitedly.

"In early October. Papa wants to have the wedding at home again. So we can't wait till winter. Actually I can't wait another moment." She and Esa exchanged a kiss.

"Oh I'm so happy for you," Ingrid said excitedly. She hugged both Esa and Astrid.

"Well, congratulations to you," Marty smiled.

"Of course we do expect you at our wedding Marty Polsen," Esa said. "Don't we dear?"

"Oh yes, by all means," Astrid smiled. "We'd be disappointed if you didn't show."

"Thank you very much, but I won't be able to come," Marty said with a twisted brow.

"Oh, why not?" Esa said.

"He's running away to Toronto," Carl laughed.

"You're not going away for good?"

"Oh no, I'll be back in the Spring," Marty smiled. "I have to go help my father and make some more money for the homestead."

"I'm very sorry you can't get to our wedding," Astrid said.

"I'll send you a present from Toronto."

"The coffee is ready," Ingrid said. "Let's go into the living room."

Carl and Ingrid saw Marty to the train on the morning of his departure. As the train started to pull in, Marty turned to his friends.

"Take care of my cabin for me and make sure no animals try to claim it,"

"Will do," Carl assured him.

"I will stop and take your laundry home to wash it," Ingrid assured him.

"Thank you," Marty said. "By the way there are several large trees I knocked down but never had a chance to haul. Take them over to Alfred's mill and you can have the lumber for your effort. Just bring me back some slabs."

"We'll take care of it," Carl said. "Just don't go falling in love while you're back in Toronto."

"I have no intention of falling in love until my homestead is properly established," Marty laughed.

The conductor cried, "All aboard!"

"Well, farewell for now, see you in the Spring," Marty said as he climbed into the train.

When the train pulled away, Ingrid said, "Do you think he'll be back?"

"Unless something big changes his mind, I think he'll be back," Carl replied. "He's quite excited about his homestead."

"We will miss him coming around in time for supper, or asking for a loaf of bread," Ingrid said soberly.

"Yes he's a very fine fellow," Carl replied.

Chapter Nineteen

On a cold grey November day, Ole, who had been at the store, came riding into the yard at full gallop. Carl and Ingrid were having coffee with his parents when Ole burst through the door.

"Great news," he said excitedly. "The war is over. It ended at eleven o'clock, two days ago on the eleventh. A telegram was sent to the post office."

"On the eleventh hour of the eleventh day of the eleventh month," Oscar observed.

"Now maybe we can hear from the old country again," Alva stated.

"A little late for me," Ingrid said glumly.

Carl put an arm around her. "The Elofsons will never see Lars again either."

"Yes, I suppose you're right," Ingrid sighed. "The loss of Lars to them was probably greater than the loss of Sigrud to me."

"Alistair says we should have a celebration in the new hall," Ole said excitedly. "To celebrate our victory and to remember the dead."

"That would be a good idea," Carl said.

A week later, just after the first snow had fallen, the people of the Morning Glory community gathered in the hall to celebrate the end of the war. The women brought food, and people who were musically inclined brought musical instruments. Some men slipped a few bottles of moonshine into a small room by the door where they could sip during the course of the celebration.

The men who were politically inclined talked about vast new changes in the world order.

"So what do you think of the revolution in Russia, Oscar?" Alfred asked.

"It will be very interesting if the revolution survives," Oscar replied enthusiastically as he was a man of strong socialist leanings. "They say this Lenin is going to build a workers' paradise. That is a good idea, because the Tsar was so oppressive."

"Well I don't know if these communists, what do they call them, Bolsheviks, have all the answers either."

192

"I'm glad they kicked the Kaiser off his throne, now maybe the Germans will learn to live in peace," Gunner added.

"The old order is changing all over," Oscar observed. "The Austrian Empire has collapsed and now there are a bunch of small nations in central Europe."

"That old Hapsburg Empire was long past its time anyway," Alfred remarked.

Esa noticed a short man with a prominent nose in the crowd. He seemed like a stranger as he stood on the sidelines with, apparently, his wife and a small child. Esa walked over to him and struck up a conversation.

"You new here?" Esa asked in a friendly manner.

"I've been here since well before the war," the man replied, smiling. "I live down by the lake and don't get out very much."

"I see," Esa continued. "Vell pleasure to meet you, my name Esa Kekkonin."

"Roman Polowski. And this is my wife Lydia and son Adam."

"Pleased to meet all of you," Esa smiled

"Were you in the war?" Roman was curious because of Esa's limp

"Ya, I vas vounded at Vimy."

"Great battle, great day for Canada. Is that where you got the limp?"

"Ya, I lost lower part of left leg. Dis var has made lot of changes," Esa said.

"Yes, my homeland is now free," Roman said.

"Your homeland too?"

"Yes. What was your name again?"

"Esa Kekkonin, I am Finn."

"Ah yes, Finland got away from the Russians too. "My homeland is Poland. Actually the Russians, Germans and Austrians all stole parts of my country."

"Let's go out by door and have toast to celebrate liberation of our countries from Russians."

"I'm for that."

Before too much celebrating got underway, however, Alistair took the podium and called everyone's attention. "Let's begin by singin'

God Save the King." When the anthem was over he continued, "Well, I know thah victory over thae Hun, is cause for a great celebration."

There was an outburst of cheers and Alistair waved them to silence.

"Some have paid dearly for our freedom. I would now like tae ask a moment ae silence for thae Elofson family wi thae loss ae their son Lars."

A silence fell over the hall as everyone stood up.

After the silence, when everyone was again seated, Alistair continued. "I would like tae acknowledge our other son, who survived thae war, more or less intact. Although he paid a price too. Esa Kekkonin please stand up." Esa stood up amid cheers.

"Well I'm nae preacher but, I think we should bow our heads and say thae Lord's Prayer in thanks fer this war comin' tae an end."

All bowed while Alistair recited the Lord's Prayer and all those who knew it in English recited it with him. At the end of the service, Effie led in the singing of *O Canada*.

With the formal part of the celebration over, the food was laid out and this was followed by a dance. Alfred and the Tymchuks supplied the music.

"I sorry darling, I don't dance good any more," Esa said apologetically to Astrid as he struggled to waltz with her. "Hard to dance vit vooden leg."

"It's alright dearest, you are doing fine." Astrid assured him, "and I'd still love you even if you were in a wheelchair." Astrid kissed him lightly on the lips.

"You some voman," Esa smiled through watery eyes. "You vait for man to come home from var yust to have him vit vooden leg."

"You waited for me to grow up," Astrid replied with a teary smile. "And you don't need two good legs to show me what kind of a wonderful loving person you are."

Esa snuggled her tightly to his waist and kissed her again.

"Look at poor Esa," Carl said as he danced with Ingrid. "I remember when he could do handsprings across the dance floor. Now he can hardly dance."

"He's lucky to have Astrid," Ingrid smiled. "She has adored him from the day Papa hired him, back when she was just a little girl."

When the celebration had ended around midnight the people had to drive home through heavy snowfall and were grateful that the horses instinctively knew their way.

Carl and Ingrid were sitting at their fireplace one cold winter night in early January, talking about how the new year of 1919 was the first year without war since 1913, when they heard a knock at the door. When Carl opened the door a figure, nearly hidden under a toque and behind a large scarf, stumbled in.

A familiar muffled voice said, "It's about time you let me in."

"Marty Polsen!" Carl exclaimed as the figure unwound his scarf. "What are you doing at our doorstep in the dead of winter?"

"I thought you weren't coming back until spring," Ingrid chimed in.

"Well, a slight change of plans," Marty said with a curious smile as he unbuttoned his greatcoat.

"Change of plans, what change of plans?" Carl demanded.

"I've got to come back and get the cabin ready," he continued with that mysterious smile.

"Ready for what?" Carl demanded.

"You know what?" Ingrid said with a glint in her eye. "I think Marty has found a sweetheart back in Toronto."

Marty smiled bashfully and his face turned redder than it was from the cold.

"That's it, isn't it?" Carl laughed.

"Yes, at least I hope so," Marty confessed. "But there are a few complications."

"Come sit by the fire, and tell us about them," Carl said.

"I'll put some fresh coffee on," Ingrid added as she stirred the fire in the stove.

Carl put another log in the fireplace while Marty settled in an easy-chair.

"What is her name?" Ingrid called from the stove.

"Ginny."

"Ginny?" Carl remarked.

"Virginia Claire Cunningham, but she goes by Ginny."

"Ginny is a pleasant name, I bet she's pretty," Ingrid said as she came back to the fireside.

"She is beautiful," Marty glowed, "both inside and out."

"No doubt," Carl remarked. "So what is the complication?"

"She is from a rich family," Marty said glumly.

"And her parents want nothing to do with you?" Ingrid said

'Ginny,' the name reverberated in Ingrid's mind. 'Ginny is from Toronto.' this triggered something in the back of Ingrid's mind. She shook her head to be rid of such notions.

"Exactly." Marty replied with a downcast look.

"Are you sure *she* wants you?" Carl asked.

"Positive. She accepted my proposal of marriage at the railway station when I left."

"And she didn't come with you?"

"No, I wanted her to stay and think about this great change in lifestyle that she'll face if she comes out here to be my wife. I hope she doesn't change her mind."

"If she really loves you, she won't," Ingrid assured him as she went to check on the coffee. Its warm aroma was starting to fill the room.

"So you are going to sit out here and fix up your cabin, hoping she won't change her mind," Carl said.

"Yes, what else can I do?" Marty sighed. "By the way, do you know what happened to my bedding and extra clothing? The cabin has been stripped."

"It's all here," Ingrid replied. "I brought it all here so the mice wouldn't get into it." Then with a crooked grin added. "Since you were going to be away so long."

"Thank you, but I guess you'll have to put me up for the night," Marty laughed

"We've put up with you before," Carl laughed.

Once again Marty became a regular feature around the Lindstrom house. Even though he worked hard on his own homestead felling timber and running traps, or working at the Erlander mill. Sometimes he would borrow books from Oscar and Alva's collection to read on long dark nights and other times he would sit and play chess with Carl. As spring approached he became more and more excited about going to fetch his intended bride. Finally one night near the end of March he told the Lindstroms of his plans.

"I'm leaving on tomorrow's train to get Ginny."

"Get Ginny?" Carl laughed. "I trust then that the complications have been worked out."

"Well; er. sort of," Marty said. "We're going to elope. Her parents will never know until we are married and safely on our way back out here."

"Sounds very romantic and adventuresome," Ingrid laughed. "Ginny must be a very brave and remarkable person."

"Oh, she is, she is," Marty laughed. "That is why I love her so much."

"I can hardly wait to meet her," Ingrid said excitedly.

"I promise to bring her over as soon as we get back, so take care of my cabin while I'm gone, but don't remove my bedding and extra clothes." He looked at Ingrid and smiled.

"I will leave your bed but I'll wash your linen," Ingrid laughed. "I am sure you'll want to bring your bride to a clean bed."

"Thank you, that would be much appreciated."

Ingrid was beside herself with the anticipation of meeting Ginny. Marty was such a pleasant person that she couldn't help but believe his wife would be equally pleasant. The name Ginny continued to ring a bell in the depths of her mind, but Ingrid could not fathom why. As the days passed she pestered Carl to watch the railway station for the passenger train so they could meet Marty and Ginny at the station, but Carl said he was uncertain as to how long Marty planned to stay in Toronto or whether there might be other *complications*.

One afternoon in early April, Ole returned from the store on horse-back when Ingrid was out in the yard looking over her garden patch thinking about what to plant. Ole drew up beside her and announced, "I hear Marty Polsen has returned with his wife."

"He has!" Ingrid exclaimed. "Did you see them?"

"No, but Alistair did. They arrived on the train yesterday and he drove them out to their cabin."

"What did he say about Ginny?"

"He said she is very beautiful, or 'bonny' as he calls her, 'and a gem of a person.'"

"Oh, I can't wait to meet her," Ingrid bubbled.

She was nearly tempted to walk over to the Polsen place and introduce herself, but waited for Carl to come in for supper.

"Can we go over to Marty Polsen's place tonight?" Ingrid asked anxiously. "Ole said Marty has returned with Ginny. Alistair met her and said she is very beautiful and nice."

"I am quite sure Marty will bring her here to meet us once he is settled in. He did say he would bring her over as soon as they got back. Besides, you don't want to barge in on a newly-married couple."

"I suppose not, but I am dying to meet her."

"I have never seen you so excited about meeting someone you know nothing about and who probably can't speak a word of Swedish."

Ingrid sobered with the thought of her inadequacy in the English department. " Since Sigrud passed away, I have a great yearning to have a friend and confidant. I don't know why but ever since I heard that her name is Ginny I've had a good feeling about her"

"Well maybe in a day or two, if Marty hasn't brought her over, we could drop in on them," Carl said.

"Yes dear, I suppose you are right," Ingrid sighed as she went about tidying up the supper dishes.

Later as they settled in the living room to relax, Ingrid picked up her knitting. She was making a sweater for Karen. Karen was entertaining Svend on the rag mat in the middle of the room. Ingrid asked Carl as he was about to settle in his chair, "Carl dear, can you light a fire, it feels a little chilly in here."

"Sure thing my love," Carl replied as he went over to the fireplace. He tore a strip of bark from one of the birch logs in front of the hearth and used it to start the fire burning.

"I love the smell of birch-bark burning," Ingrid remarked.

Just then, they heard the dog bark.

"It's them!" Ingrid exclaimed as she looked out the window. Carl put a split log in the fire, rose to his feet and looked out too. There they saw Marty and, apparently, Ginny riding in a wooden-wheeled lumber wagon drawn by a team of draught horses.

Carl went out to greet them while Ingrid scanned around the kitchen to make sure everything was tidy and in order. As Carl had left the door open, she could see what was going on outside. When Marty had helped Ginny from the wagon he introduced her to Carl. Ingrid could already see that Ginny was indeed very beautiful. Little Svend, who was just learning to walk, toddled out through the doorway.

"Karen, go get your brother," Ingrid said quickly. As Karen scrambled to do the task, Ingrid heard Carl introduce Ginny to their children.

When Ginny was brought into the house and she and Ingrid made eye contact, Ingrid had a strange sense of deja vu. Those large hazel-coloured eyes and that ginger-coloured hair, those striking aristocratic features. She swore she had seen Ginny somewhere before.

Carl introduced her in English and Ingrid gave her faltering reply in English. Marty and Ginny were led into the living room where Ingrid told them to sit while she made coffee. While she busied herself in the kitchen she could hear them speaking English and had only the barest understanding of what they were saying. She felt embarrassed by it. At one point Ginny looked at her and gave her a warm smile.

'*That face, I've seen that face,*' Ingrid thought. Then she remembered, '*A little girl's face, I saw her on the ship. There was a little girl and her brother on the ship. She had eyes like that. The girl had sat beside her, curious about the magazine that was written in Swedish. She had said her name was Ginny and that she came from Toronto. She was just a little girl, younger than herself, but that was nine years ago. She could now be old enough to be Marty's wife.*' Ingrid continued to think deeply racking her brain for memory recall. The man who was apparently her father had came down from the upper decks to call them back. She didn't know what he had said but she clearly rememberd the names Paul and Ginny. *Paul, Ginny, the names went back and forth in her mind.. Could this Ginny be the same person? That little girl was, after all, from Toronto. Those eyes, there is no mistaking those eyes. I must now learn to speak English so I can find out whether this Ginny and the other are the same.*'

She brought through the tray containing cups of coffee and some sliced jelly rolls and was pleased to observe that when Ginny sampled one, she liked the taste.

Ginny attempted to talk to Ingrid and Ingrid felt embarrassed that she could understand but a few words. Finally she said "I am sorry. I not speak English well."

"It's alright," Ginny replied warmly. "In time you will learn it. I'll even teach you if you want."

Ingrid looked puzzled as she only partly understood Ginny but guessed it was something about wanting to teach her English. For the first time since she was with Michael, Ingrid was now anxious to learn the language. Then came the ultimate confession. "I vould like to read English. All da labels, I don't know vat dey mean."

Ginny spoke to her and Ingrid looked to Carl for explanation.

"She wants to show you how to read the labels and recipes," he said.

"Perhaps you could teach me some Swedish," Ginny said.

This statement more than any other caused Ingrid to realize that her need to learn English fluently was long overdue. She replied, "Oh, no. Svedish is for da old country, English is for Canada."

Ginny again spoke to her in a warm sincere manner and again Ingrid didn't know what she said. This time Marty explained.

"Ginny says she will teach you English, if you will teach her how to cook and bake bread."

"Tell her I would love to teach her how to bake bread.," Ingrid said enthusiastically.

Ginny spoke again and Marty relayed. "Ginny says that because she is a spoiled rich girl she has much to learn about living out here and she wants you to be her teacher."

Ingrid smiled and took Ginny by the hand. She led Ginny to the kitchen and sat her on one of the chairs. Ingrid then pulled out some product boxes and cans. Pointing to the labels she said, "Vat dey mean?"

Ginny carefully read the labels and the recipes that were often with them. She went over them word by word using hand gestures to try to explain. Ingrid quickly caught on to some of the more basic instructions. She in turn began to teach Ginny how to bake bread. She used elaborate hand gestures to illustrate how to knead the dough and how far it should rise before putting it in the oven. She pulled things out of the cupboard like salt and yeast to show Ginny the ingredients and measurements Soon the two women were laughing and having a most enjoyable time. In the course of their conversation, Ingrid had learned at least a dozen new English words and, better yet, could recognize some of them in printed form.

Ole dropped in for a visit and was introduced to Ginny. He complimented her on her beauty.

"Maybe *you* should go to Toronto and find yourself a woman," Ingrid teased Ole.

Marty translated to Ginny and everyone except Ole laughed. He blushed brightly.

"I'm sure he'll find one," Ginny smiled. "He seems like a nice person and certainly knows how to pay a compliment."

They all laughed again and Ole was relieved when the men went into the living room.

After a few hours of entertaining and enjoyable visiting, the Polsens prepared to go home. As she saw her newfound friend to the door, Ingrid thought of Carl's words. Everett had been taken from them, but they received Svend. So, Sigrud was also taken from her but she was given Ginny, as a dear friend and confidant.

"You come back and teach me more English," Ingrid called as Ginny climbed up into the wagon seat.

"I will if you teach me to cook some more," Ginny replied with a warm smile.

"So you finally want to learn English." Carl laughed as they watched the Polsens go out of sight.

"Oh yes, Ginny will teach me. Who knows? I'll probably even learn how to read it."

Epilogue

Ginny did indeed teach Ingrid how to both speak and read English, and she in turn taught Ginny all about homemaking on the homestead. In teaching Ingrid English, Ginny found it difficult to get Ingrid to speak without a Swedish accent. This was probably due to the fact that Carl spoke with an accent and his parents rarely spoke any English at all. In the end she resigned to letting Ingrid keep her accent as it gave her character and let her keep a little piece of Sweden. When Ingrid became sufficiently fluent in English, she asked Ginny if she was the little girl on the ship. Ginny, who by now also had a feeling of previously meeting Ingrid, quickly recalled the incident, confirming Ingrid's suspicion Both agreed that the chance meeting on the ship was, of special purpose, foreshadowing things to come in regards to a bond between them.

Ingrid had one more child, another son, whom she and Carl named Ivor. His story and the story of her other children Karen and Svend, along with the deep and lifelong friendship between Ingrid and Ginny are told in the saga, *Ginny - A Canadian Story of Love and Friendship*.

About the Author

Eric John Brown was born on August 13, 1947 the youngest son of John and Ruby Brown. He was raised on a farm in the community of Magnolia about one hundred kilometres west of Edmonton, Alberta.

Magnolia was, during his childhood, a hamlet consisting of a store, a church and a community hall. The community was a closely-knit one and his family was a warm loving one. During his early grades, he attended a one-roomed school about a mile from home then completed his remaining grades at Seba Beach School from which he graduated. He has always been a keen student of modern history, geography, and science.

Virtually all of his working life has been spent first with Canadian National Railways Signals Department and later with TransAlta at the local Sundance power generating plant.

While on a trip to Scotland to visit relatives in 1971 he met his future wife, Isabella. They were married in Scotland nearly two years later and have since raised two sons, John and Colin.

The author began writing stories when he was thirteen years old but most of his early writings were of the science-fiction genre. Later, as he became more skilled at character development, he turned to standard fiction. He has also developed a keen interest in the ethnic and linguistic background of the vast mosaic of peoples that make up Canada. He, in particular, has focused on peoples seldom mentioned in mainstream literature such as Finns, Latvians, Ukrainians and Scandinavians.

The saga of *Ginny*, his first publication, was conceived when he was only twenty-three years old. At the time however, he lacked the necessary writing skills to tackle a work of this magnitude. It remained, however, in the back of his mind like bedrock, even as he worked on other writings. The details of *Ginny* slowly filled in over the years. Finally after the acquisition of a home computer in 1994, the author tackled this long overdue novel in earnest. As the author set to writing, what was originally to be the story of a community, a strange thing happened. In the author's own words, "the character, Ginny, leaped out of my imagination and took control of the saga making it her story." Since that time this powerful and warm, loving character has captured the hearts of hundreds of readers of all ages.

The result of his literary labours was the publication of *Ginny* on December 11, 1998. With the highly successful publication of *Ginny* via the route of self-publishing, the author has continued to write novels which have found broad appeal on the marketplace.

Eric J Brown continues to reside today on the old family farmstead. Here with his good wife, Isabella they raised two sons John and Colin and recently they have discovered the rewards of grandchildren. From this rustic setting he hopes to continue writing stories about the people and times of Alberta

Anna
An Odyssey to Freedom

Anna is a bright eighteen-year-old girl, a member of a happy family and has a bright future ahead of her. Then her world is shattered when the Soviet Union forcibly annexes her tiny homeland of Latvia in the summer of 1940. A year later it is conquered again, by the Nazis. Anna's family is destroyed and she is forced to live by her wits. Her only hope is to somehow find her brother, who is abroad, and the young man in her life who is also lost in these brutal crosscurrents of history. Her only dream is to reach the faraway golden land of Canada. Thus, begins Anna's incredible odyssey to freedom.

Ginny
A Canadian **Story of Love & Friendship**

Ginny is a rich girl from Toronto who dares, against her family's wishes, to elope with Danish immigrant named Marty Polsen to his homestead in Alberta. Ginny faces many challenges on the homestead such as learning how to cook, coping with homesickness, being chased by a bear, and a difficult childbirth that nearly kills her. With the support of both her loving husband Marty, and her dear friends, Ingrid and Gina, Ginny perseveres.

As you trace Ginny's life, from a time when she was a rich girl adjusting to the rigours of the homestead, to a time when she is offering wise counsel to her grandchildren of the baby boomer era - you will come to appreciate that this work is a triumphant story of love and friendship.

For additional copies of

Anna – Her odyssey to Freedom

Ginny - A Canadian Story of Love and Friend-ship

Ingrid – An Immigrant's Tale

Write to
Magnolia Press
Box 499
Entwistle, Alberta
T0E 0S0

Or

E-Mail mag_press@hotmail.com